Emma

By
Jane Austen

Volume 1 of 2

EasyRead Super Large

TABLE OF CONTENTS

VOLUME I

CHAPTER I

Emma Woodhouse, handsome, clever, and rich, with a comfortable home and happy disposition, seemed to unite some of the best blessings of existence; and had lived nearly twenty-one years in the world with very little to distress or vex her.

She was the youngest of the two daughters of a most affectionate, indulgent father; and had, in consequence of her sister's marriage, been mistress of his house from a very early period. Her mother had died too long ago for her to have more than an indistinct remembrance of her caresses; and her place had been supplied by an excellent woman as governess, who had fallen little short of a mother in affection.

Sixteen years had Miss Taylor been in Mr. Woodhouse's family, less as a governess than a friend, very fond of both daughters, but particularly of Emma. Between *them* it was more the intimacy of sisters. Even before Miss Taylor had ceased to hold the nominal office of governess, the mildness of her temper had hardly allowed her to impose any restraint; and the shadow of authority being now long passed away, they had been living together as friend and friend very mutually attached, and Emma doing just what she liked; highly esteeming Miss Taylor's judgment, but directed chiefly by her own.

The real evils, indeed, of Emma's situation were the power of having rather too much her own way, and a disposition to think a little too well of herself; these were the disadvantages which threatened alloy to her many enjoyments. The danger, however, was at present so unperceived, that they did not by any means rank as misfortunes with her.

Sorrow came – a gentle sorrow – but not at all in the shape of any disagreeable consciousness. – Miss Taylor married. It was Miss Taylor's loss which first brought grief. It was on the wedding-day of this beloved friend that Emma first sat in mournful thought of any continuance. The wedding over, and the bride-people gone, her father and herself were left to dine together, with no prospect of a third to cheer a long evening. Her father composed himself to sleep after dinner, as usual, and she had then only to sit and think of what she had lost.

The event had every promise of happiness for her friend. Mr. Weston was a man of unexceptionable character, easy fortune, suitable age, and pleasant manners; and there was some satisfaction in considering with what self-denying, generous friendship she had always wished and promoted the match; but it was a black morning's work for her. The want of Miss Taylor would be felt every hour of every day. She recalled her past kindness – the kindness, the affection of sixteen years – how she had taught and how she had played with her from five years old – how she had devoted all her powers to attach and amuse her in health – and how nursed her through the various illnesses of childhood. A large debt of gratitude was owing here; but the intercourse of the last seven years, the equal footing and perfect unreserve which had soon followed Isabella's marriage, on their being left to each other, was yet a dearer, tenderer recollection. She had been a friend and companion such as few possessed: intelligent, well-informed, useful, gentle, knowing all the ways of the family, interested in all its concerns, and peculiarly interested in herself, in every pleasure, every scheme of hers – one to whom she could speak every thought as it arose, and who had such an affection for her as could never find fault.

How was she to bear the change? – It was true that her friend was going only half a mile from them; but Emma was aware that great must be the difference between a Mrs. Weston, only half a mile from them, and a Miss Taylor in the house; and with all her advantages, natural and domestic, she was now in great danger of suffering from intellectual solitude. She dearly loved her father, but he was no companion for her. He could not meet her in conversation, rational or playful.

The evil of the actual disparity in their ages (and Mr. Woodhouse had not married early) was much increased by his constitution and habits; for having been a valetudinarian all his life, without activity of mind or body, he was a much older man in ways than in years; and though everywhere beloved for the friendliness of his heart and his amiable temper, his talents could not have recommended him at any time.

Her sister, though comparatively but little removed by matrimony, being settled in London, only sixteen miles off, was much beyond her daily reach; and many a long October and November evening must be struggled through at Hartfield, before Christmas brought the next visit from Isabella and her husband, and their little children, to fill the house, and give her pleasant society again.

Highbury, the large and populous village, almost amounting to a town, to which Hartfield, in spite of its separate lawn, and shrubberies, and name, did really belong, afforded her no equals. The Woodhouses were first in consequence there. All looked up to them. She had many acquaintance in the place, for her father was universally civil, but not one among them who could be accepted in lieu of Miss Taylor for even half a day. It was a melancholy change; and Emma could not but sigh over it, and wish for impossible things, till her father awoke, and made it necessary to be cheerful. His spirits required support. He was a nervous man, easily depressed; fond of every body that he was used to, and hating to part with them; hating change of every kind. Matrimony, as the origin of change, was always disagreeable;

and he was by no means yet reconciled to his own daughter's marrying, nor could ever speak of her but with compassion, though it had been entirely a match of affection, when he was now obliged to part with Miss Taylor too; and from his habits of gentle selfishness, and of being never able to suppose that other people could feel differently from himself, he was very much disposed to think Miss Taylor had done as sad a thing for herself as for them, and would have been a great deal happier if she had spent all the rest of her life at Hartfield. Emma smiled and chatted as cheerfully as she could, to keep him from such thoughts; but when tea came, it was impossible for him not to say exactly as he had said at dinner,

"Poor Miss Taylor! – I wish she were here again. What a pity it is that Mr. Weston ever thought of her!"

"I cannot agree with you, papa; you know I cannot. Mr. Weston is such a good-humoured, pleasant, excellent man, that he thoroughly deserves a good wife; – and you would not have had Miss Taylor live with us for ever, and bear all my odd humours, when she might have a house of her own?"

"A house of her own! – But where is the advantage of a house of her own? This is three times as large. – And you have never any odd humours, my dear."

"How often we shall be going to see them, and they coming to see us! – We shall be always meeting! We must begin; we must go and pay wedding visit very soon."

"My dear, how am I to get so far? Randalls is such a distance. I could not walk half so far."

"No, papa, nobody thought of your walking. We must go in the carriage, to be sure."

"The carriage! But James will not like to put the horses to for such a little way; – and where are the poor horses to be while we are paying our visit?"

"They are to be put into Mr. Weston's stable, papa. You know we have settled all that already. We talked it all over with Mr. Weston last night. And as for James, you may be very sure he will always like going to Randalls, because of his daughter's being housemaid there. I only doubt whether he will ever take us anywhere else. That was your doing, papa. You got Hannah that good place. Nobody thought of Hannah till you mentioned her – James is so obliged to you!"

"I am very glad I did think of her. It was very lucky, for I would not have had poor James think himself slighted upon any account; and I am sure she will make a very good servant: she is a civil, pretty-spoken girl; I have a great opinion of her. Whenever I see her, she always curtseys and asks me how I do, in a very pretty manner; and when you have had her here to do needlework, I observe she always turns the lock of the door the right way and never bangs it. I am sure she will be an excellent servant; and it will be a great comfort to poor Miss Taylor to have somebody about her that she is used to see. Whenever James goes over to see his daughter, you know, she will be hearing of us. He will be able to tell her how we all are."

Emma spared no exertions to maintain this happier flow of ideas, and hoped, by the help of backgammon, to get her father tolerably through the evening, and be attacked by no regrets but her own. The backgammon-table was placed; but a visitor immediately afterwards walked in and made it unnecessary.

Mr. Knightley, a sensible man about seven or eight-and-thirty, was not only a very old and intimate friend of the family, but particularly connected with it, as the elder brother of Isabella's husband. He lived about a mile from Highbury, was a frequent visitor, and always welcome, and at this time more welcome than usual, as coming directly from their mutual connexions in London. He had returned to a late dinner, after some days' absence, and now walked up to Hartfield to say that all were well in Brunswick Square. It was a happy circumstance, and animated Mr. Woodhouse for some time. Mr. Knightley had a cheerful manner, which always did him good; and his many inquiries after "poor Isabella" and her children were answered most satisfactorily. When this was over, Mr. Woodhouse gratefully observed, "It is very kind of you, Mr. Knightley, to come out at this late hour to call upon us. I am afraid you must have had a shocking walk."

"Not at all, sir. It is a beautiful moonlight night; and so mild that I must draw back from your great fire."

"But you must have found it very damp and dirty. I wish you may not catch cold."

"Dirty, sir! Look at my shoes. Not a speck on them."

"Well! that is quite surprising, for we have had a vast deal of rain here. It rained dreadfully hard for half an hour while we were at breakfast. I wanted them to put off the wedding."

"By the bye – I have not wished you joy. Being pretty well aware of what sort of joy you must both be feeling, I have been in no hurry with my congratulations; but I hope it all went off tolerably well. How did you all behave? Who cried most?"

"Ah! poor Miss Taylor! 'Tis a sad business."

"Poor Mr. and Miss Woodhouse, if you please; but I cannot possibly say 'poor Miss Taylor.' I have a great regard for you and Emma; but when it comes to the question of dependence or independence! – At any rate, it must be better to have only one to please than two."

"Especially when *one* of those two is such a fanciful, troublesome creature!" said Emma playfully. "That is what you have in your head, I know – and what you would certainly say if my father were not by."

"I believe it is very true, my dear, indeed," said Mr. Woodhouse, with a sigh. "I am afraid I am sometimes very fanciful and troublesome."

"My dearest papa! You do not think I could mean you, or suppose Mr. Knightley to mean *you*. What a horrible idea! Oh no! I meant only myself. Mr. Knightley loves to find fault with me, you know – in a joke – it is all a joke. We always say what we like to one another."

Mr. Knightley, in fact, was one of the few people who could see faults in Emma Woodhouse, and the only one who ever told her of them: and though this was not particularly agreeable to Emma herself, she knew it would be so much less so to her father, that she would not have him really suspect such a circumstance as her not being thought perfect by every body.

"Emma knows I never flatter her," said Mr. Knightley, "but I meant no reflection on any body. Miss Taylor has been used to have two persons to please; she will now have but one. The chances are that she must be a gainer."

"Well," said Emma, willing to let it pass – "you want to hear about the wedding; and I shall be happy to tell you, for we all behaved charmingly. Every body was punctual, every body in their best looks: not a tear, and hardly a long face to be seen. Oh no; we all felt that we were going to be only half a mile apart, and were sure of meeting every day."

"Dear Emma bears every thing so well," said her father. "But, Mr. Knightley, she is really very sorry to lose poor Miss Taylor, and I am sure she *will* miss her more than she thinks for."

Emma turned away her head, divided between tears and smiles. "It is impossible that Emma should not miss such a companion," said Mr. Knightley. "We should not like her so well as we do, sir, if we could suppose it; but she knows how much the marriage is to Miss Taylor's advantage; she knows how very acceptable it must be, at Miss Taylor's time of life, to be settled in a home of her own, and how important to her to be secure of a comfortable provision, and therefore cannot allow herself to feel so much pain as pleasure. Every friend of Miss Taylor must be glad to have her so happily married."

"And you have forgotten one matter of joy to me," said Emma, "and a very considerable one – that I made the match myself. I made the match, you know, four years ago; and to have it take place, and be proved in the right, when so many people said Mr. Weston would never marry again, may comfort me for any thing."

Mr. Knightley shook his head at her. Her father fondly replied, "Ah! my dear, I wish you would not make matches and foretell things, for whatever you say always comes to pass. Pray do not make any more matches."

"I promise you to make none for myself, papa; but I must, indeed, for other people. It is the greatest amusement in the world! And after such success, you know! – Every body said that Mr. Weston would never marry again. Oh dear, no! Mr. Weston, who had been a widower so long, and who seemed so perfectly comfortable without a wife, so constantly occupied either in his business in town or among his friends here, always acceptable wherever he went, always cheerful – Mr. Weston need not spend a single evening in the year alone if he did not like it. Oh no! Mr. Weston certainly would never marry again. Some people even talked of a promise to his wife on her deathbed, and others of the son and the uncle not letting him. All manner of solemn nonsense was talked on the subject, but I believed none of it.

"Ever since the day – about four years ago – that Miss Taylor and I met with him in Broadway Lane, when, because it began to drizzle, he darted away with so much gallantry, and borrowed two umbrellas for us from Farmer Mitchell's, I made up my mind on the subject. I planned the match from that hour; and when such success has blessed me in this instance, dear papa, you cannot think that I shall leave off match-making."

"I do not understand what you mean by 'success,'" said Mr. Knightley. "Success supposes endeavour. Your time has been properly and delicately spent, if you have been endeavouring for the last four years to bring about this marriage. A worthy employment for a young lady's mind! But if, which I rather imagine, your making the match, as you call it, means only your planning it, your saying to yourself one idle day, 'I think it would be a very good thing for Miss Taylor if Mr. Weston were to marry her,' and saying it again to yourself every now and then afterwards, why do you talk of success? Where is your merit? What are you proud of? You made a lucky guess; and *that* is all that can be said."

"And have you never known the pleasure and triumph of a lucky guess? – I pity you. – I thought you cleverer – for, depend upon it a lucky guess is never merely luck. There is always some talent in it. And as to my poor word 'success,' which you quarrel with, I do not know that I am so entirely without any claim to it. You have drawn two pretty pictures; but I think there may be a third – a something between the do-nothing and the do-all. If I had not promoted Mr. Weston's visits here, and given many little encouragements, and smoothed many little matters, it might not have come to any thing after all. I think you must know Hartfield enough to comprehend that."

"A straightforward, open-hearted man like Weston, and a rational, unaffected woman like Miss Taylor, may be safely left to manage their own concerns. You are more likely to have done harm to yourself, than good to them, by interference."

"Emma never thinks of herself, if she can do good to others," rejoined Mr. Woodhouse, understanding but in part. "But, my dear, pray do not make any more matches; they are silly things, and break up one's family circle grievously."

"Only one more, papa; only for Mr. Elton. Poor Mr. Elton! You like Mr. Elton, papa, – I must look about for a wife for him. There is nobody in Highbury who deserves him – and he has been here a whole year, and has fitted up his house so comfortably, that it would be a shame to have him single any longer – and I thought when he was joining their hands to-day, he looked so very much as if he would like to have the same kind office done for him! I think very well of Mr. Elton, and this is the only way I have of doing him a service."

"Mr. Elton is a very pretty young man, to be sure, and a very good young man, and I have a great regard for him. But if you want to shew him any attention, my dear, ask him to come and dine with us some day. That will be a much better thing. I dare say Mr. Knightley will be so kind as to meet him."

"With a great deal of pleasure, sir, at any time," said Mr. Knightley, laughing, "and I agree with you entirely, that it will be a much better thing. Invite him to dinner, Emma, and help him to the best of the fish and the chicken, but leave him to chuse his own wife. Depend upon it, a man of six or seven-and-twenty can take care of himself."

CHAPTER II

Mr. Weston was a native of Highbury, and born of a respectable family, which for the last two or three generations had been rising into gentility and property. He had received a good education, but, on succeeding early in life to a small independence, had become indisposed for any of the more homely pursuits in which his brothers were engaged, and had satisfied an active, cheerful mind and social temper by entering into the militia of his county, then embodied.

Captain Weston was a general favourite; and when the chances of his military life had introduced him to Miss Churchill, of a great Yorkshire family, and Miss Churchill fell in love with him, nobody was surprized, except her brother and his wife, who had never seen him, and who were full of pride and importance, which the connexion would offend.

Miss Churchill, however, being of age, and with the full command of her fortune – though her fortune bore no proportion to the family-estate – was not to be dissuaded from the marriage, and it took place, to the infinite mortification of Mr.

and Mrs. Churchill, who threw her off with due decorum. It was an unsuitable connexion, and did not produce much happiness. Mrs. Weston ought to have found more in it, for she had a husband whose warm heart and sweet temper made him think every thing due to her in return for the great goodness of being in love with him; but though she had one sort of spirit, she had not the best. She had resolution enough to pursue her own will in spite of her brother, but not enough to refrain from unreasonable regrets at that brother's unreasonable anger, nor from missing the luxuries of her former home. They lived beyond their income, but still it was nothing in comparison of Enscombe: she did not cease to love her husband, but she wanted at once to be the wife of Captain Weston, and Miss Churchill of Enscombe.

Captain Weston, who had been considered, especially by the Churchills, as making such an amazing match, was proved to have much the worst of the bargain; for when his wife died, after a three years' marriage, he was rather a poorer man than at first, and with a child to maintain. From the expense of the child, however, he was soon relieved. The boy had, with the additional softening claim of a lingering illness of his mother's, been the means of a sort of reconciliation; and Mr. and Mrs. Churchill, having no children of their own, nor any other young creature of equal kindred to care for, offered to take the whole charge of the little Frank soon after her decease. Some scruples and some reluctance the widower-father may be supposed to have felt; but as they were overcome by other considerations, the child was given up to the care and the wealth of the Churchills, and he had only his own comfort to seek, and his own situation to improve as he could.

A complete change of life became desirable. He quitted the militia and engaged in trade, having brothers already established in a good way in London, which afforded him a favourable opening. It was a concern which brought just employment enough. He had still a small house in Highbury, where most of his leisure days were spent; and between useful occupation and the pleasures of society, the next eighteen or twenty years of his life passed cheerfully away. He had, by that time, realised an easy competence – enough to secure the purchase of a little estate adjoining Highbury, which he had always longed for – enough to marry a woman as portionless even as Miss

Taylor, and to live according to the wishes of his own friendly and social disposition.

It was now some time since Miss Taylor had begun to influence his schemes; but as it was not the tyrannic influence of youth on youth, it had not shaken his determination of never settling till he could purchase Randalls, and the sale of Randalls was long looked forward to; but he had gone steadily on, with these objects in view, till they were accomplished. He had made his fortune, bought his house, and obtained his wife; and was beginning a new period of existence, with every probability of greater happiness than in any yet passed through. He had never been an unhappy man; his own temper had secured him from that, even in his first marriage; but his second must shew him how delightful a well-judging and truly amiable woman could be, and must give him the pleasantest proof of its being a great deal better to choose than to be chosen, to excite gratitude than to feel it.

He had only himself to please in his choice: his fortune was his own; for as to Frank, it was more than being tacitly brought up as his uncle's heir, it had become so avowed an adoption as to have him assume the name of Churchill on coming of age. It was most unlikely, therefore, that he should ever want his father's assistance. His father had no apprehension of it. The aunt was a capricious woman, and governed her husband entirely; but it was not in Mr. Weston's nature to imagine that any caprice could be strong enough to affect one so dear, and, as he believed, so deservedly dear. He saw his son every year in London, and was proud of him; and his fond report of him as a very fine young man had made Highbury feel a sort of pride in him too. He was looked on as sufficiently belonging to the place to make his merits and prospects a kind of common concern.

Mr. Frank Churchill was one of the boasts of Highbury, and a lively curiosity to see him prevailed, though the compliment was so little returned that he had never been there in his life. His coming to visit his father had been often talked of but never achieved.

Now, upon his father's marriage, it was very generally proposed, as a most proper attention, that the visit should take place. There was not a dissentient voice on the subject, either when Mrs.

Perry drank tea with Mrs. and Miss Bates, or when Mrs. and Miss Bates returned the visit. Now was the time for Mr. Frank Churchill to come among them; and the hope strengthened when it was understood that he had written to his new mother on the occasion. For a few days, every morning visit in Highbury included some mention of the handsome letter Mrs. Weston had received. "I suppose you have heard of the handsome letter Mr. Frank Churchill has written to Mrs. Weston? I understand it was a very handsome letter, indeed. Mr. Woodhouse told me of it. Mr. Woodhouse saw the letter, and he says he never saw such a handsome letter in his life."

It was, indeed, a highly prized letter. Mrs. Weston had, of course, formed a very favourable idea of the young man; and such a pleasing attention was an irresistible proof of his great good sense, and a most welcome addition to every source and every expression of congratulation which her marriage had already secured. She felt herself a most fortunate woman; and she had lived long enough to know how fortunate she might well be thought, where the only regret was for a partial separation from friends whose friendship for her had never cooled, and who could ill bear to part with her.

She knew that at times she must be missed; and could not think, without pain, of Emma's losing a single pleasure, or suffering an hour's ennui, from the want of her companionableness: but dear Emma was of no feeble character; she was more equal to her situation than most girls would have been, and had sense, and energy, and spirits that might be hoped would bear her well and happily through its little difficulties and privations. And then there was such comfort in the very easy distance of Randalls from Hartfield, so convenient for even solitary female walking, and in Mr. Weston's disposition and circumstances, which would make the approaching season no hindrance to their spending half the evenings in the week together.

Her situation was altogether the subject of hours of gratitude to Mrs. Weston, and of moments only of regret; and her satisfaction – her more than satisfaction – her cheerful enjoyment, was so just and so apparent, that Emma, well as she knew her father, was sometimes taken by surprize at his being still able to pity 'poor Miss Taylor,' when they left her at Randalls in the centre of every domestic comfort, or saw her go away in the evening attended by her pleasant husband to a carriage of her own. But never did she go without

Mr. Woodhouse's giving a gentle sigh, and saying, "Ah, poor Miss Taylor! She would be very glad to stay."

There was no recovering Miss Taylor – nor much likelihood of ceasing to pity her; but a few weeks brought some alleviation to Mr. Woodhouse. The compliments of his neighbours were over; he was no longer teased by being wished joy of so sorrowful an event; and the wedding-cake, which had been a great distress to him, was all eat up. His own stomach could bear nothing rich, and he could never believe other people to be different from himself. What was unwholesome to him he regarded as unfit for any body; and he had, therefore, earnestly tried to dissuade them from having any wedding-cake at all, and when that proved vain, as earnestly tried to prevent any body's eating it. He had been at the pains of consulting Mr. Perry, the apothecary, on the subject. Mr. Perry was an intelligent, gentlemanlike man, whose frequent visits were one of the comforts of Mr. Woodhouse's life; and upon being applied to, he could not but acknowledge (though it seemed rather against the bias of inclination) that wedding-cake might certainly disagree with many – perhaps with most people, unless taken moderately. With such an opinion, in confirmation of his own, Mr. Woodhouse hoped to influence every visitor of the newly married pair; but still the cake was eaten; and there was no rest for his benevolent nerves till it was all gone.

There was a strange rumour in Highbury of all the little Perrys being seen with a slice of Mrs. Weston's wedding-cake in their hands: but Mr. Woodhouse would never believe it.

CHAPTER III

Mr. Woodhouse was fond of society in his own way. He liked very much to have his friends come and see him; and from various united causes, from his long residence at Hartfield, and his good nature, from his fortune, his house, and his daughter, he could command the visits of his own little circle, in a great measure, as he liked. He had not much intercourse with any families beyond that circle; his horror of late hours, and large dinner-parties, made him unfit for any acquaintance but such as would visit him on his own terms. Fortunately for him, Highbury, including Randalls in the same parish, and Donwell Abbey in the parish adjoining, the seat of Mr. Knightley, comprehended many such. Not unfrequently, through Emma's persuasion, he had some of the chosen and the best to dine with him: but evening parties were what he preferred; and, unless he fancied himself at any time unequal to company, there was scarcely an evening in the week in which Emma could not make up a card-table for him.

Real, long-standing regard brought the Westons and Mr. Knightley; and by Mr. Elton, a young man living alone without liking it, the privilege of exchanging any vacant evening of his own blank solitude for the elegancies and society of Mr. Woodhouse's drawing-room, and the smiles of his lovely daughter, was in no danger of being thrown away.

After these came a second set; among the most come-at-able of whom were Mrs. and Miss Bates, and Mrs. Goddard, three ladies almost always at the service of an invitation from Hartfield, and who were fetched and carried home so often, that Mr. Woodhouse thought it no hardship for either James or the horses. Had it taken place only once a year, it would have been a grievance.

Mrs. Bates, the widow of a former vicar of High-bury, was a very old lady, almost past every thing but tea and quadrille. She lived with her single daughter in a very small way, and was considered with all the regard and respect which a harmless old lady, under such untoward circumstances, can excite. Her daughter enjoyed a most uncommon degree of popularity for a woman neither young, handsome, rich, nor married. Miss Bates stood in the very worst predicament in the world for having much of the public favour; and she had no intellectual superiority to make atonement to herself, or frighten those who might hate her into outward respect. She had never boasted either beauty or cleverness. Her youth had passed without distinction, and her middle of life was devoted to the care of a failing mother, and the endeavour to make a small income go as far as possible. And yet she was a happy woman, and a woman whom no one named without good-will. It was her own universal good-will and contented temper which worked such wonders. She loved every body, was interested in every body's happiness, quick-sighted to every body's merits; thought herself a most fortunate creature, and surrounded with blessings in such an excellent mother, and so many good neighbours and friends, and a home that wanted for nothing. The simplicity and cheerfulness of her nature, her contented and grateful spirit, were a recommendation to every body, and a mine of felicity to herself. She was a great talker upon little matters, which exactly suited Mr. Woodhouse, full of trivial communications and harmless gossip.

Mrs. Goddard was the mistress of a School – not of a seminary, or an establishment, or any thing which professed, in long sentences of refined nonsense, to combine liberal acquirements with elegant morality, upon new principles and new systems – and where young ladies for enormous pay might be screwed out of health and into vanity – but a real, honest, old-fashioned Boarding-school, where a reasonable quantity of accomplishments were sold at a reasonable price, and where girls might be sent to be out of the way, and scramble themselves into a little education, without any danger of coming back prodigies. Mrs. Goddard's school was in high repute – and very deservedly; for Highbury was reckoned a particularly healthy spot: she had an ample house and garden, gave the children plenty of wholesome food, let them run about a great deal in the summer, and in winter dressed their chilblains with her own hands. It was no wonder that a train of twenty young couple now walked after her to church. She was a plain, motherly kind of woman, who had worked hard in her youth, and now thought herself entitled to the occasional holiday of a tea-visit; and having formerly owed much to Mr. Woodhouse's kindness, felt his particular claim on her to leave her neat parlour, hung round with fancy-work, whenever she could, and win or lose a few sixpences by his fireside.

These were the ladies whom Emma found herself very frequently able to collect; and happy was she, for her father's sake, in the power; though, as far as she was herself concerned, it was no remedy for the absence of Mrs. Weston. She was delighted to see her father look comfortable, and very much pleased with herself for contriving things so well; but the quiet prosings of three such women made her feel that every evening so spent was indeed one of the long evenings she had fearfully anticipated.

As she sat one morning, looking forward to exactly such a close of the present day, a note was brought from Mrs. Goddard, requesting, in most respectful terms, to be allowed to bring Miss Smith with her; a most welcome request: for Miss Smith was a girl of seventeen, whom Emma knew very well by sight, and had long felt an interest in, on account of her beauty. A very gracious invitation was returned, and the evening no longer dreaded by the fair mistress of the mansion.

Harriet Smith was the natural daughter of somebody. Somebody had placed her, several years back, at Mrs. Goddard's school, and somebody had lately raised her from the condition of scholar to that of parlour-boarder. This was all that was generally known of her history. She had no visible friends but what had been acquired at Highbury, and was now just returned from a long visit in the country to some young ladies who had been at school there with her.

She was a very pretty girl, and her beauty happened to be of a sort which Emma particularly admired. She was short, plump, and fair, with a fine bloom, blue eyes, light hair, regular features, and a look of great sweetness, and, before the end of the evening, Emma was as much pleased with her manners as her person, and quite determined to continue the acquaintance.

She was not struck by any thing remarkably clever in Miss Smith's conversation, but she found her altogether very engaging – not inconveniently shy, not unwilling to talk – and yet so far from pushing, shewing so proper and becoming a deference, seeming so pleasantly grateful for being admitted to Hartfield, and so artlessly impressed by the appearance of every thing in so superior a style to what she had been used to, that she must have good sense, and deserve encouragement. Encouragement should be given. Those soft blue eyes, and all those natural graces, should not be wasted on the inferior society of Highbury and its connexions. The acquaintance she had already formed were unworthy of her. The friends from whom she had just parted, though very good sort of people, must be doing her harm. They were a family of the name of Martin, whom Emma well knew by character, as renting a large farm of Mr. Knightley, and residing in the parish of Donwell – very creditably, she believed – she knew Mr. Knightley thought highly of them – but they must be coarse and unpolished, and very unfit to be the intimates of a girl who wanted only a little more knowledge and elegance to be quite perfect. She would notice her; she would improve her; she would detach her from her bad acquaintance, and introduce her into good society; she would form her opinions and her manners. It would be an interesting, and certainly a very kind undertaking; highly becoming her own situation in life, her leisure, and powers.

She was so busy in admiring those soft blue eyes, in talking and listening, and forming all these schemes in the in-betweens, that the evening flew away at a very unusual rate; and the supper-table, which always closed such parties, and for which she had been used to sit and watch the due time, was all set out and ready, and moved forwards to the fire, before she was aware. With an alacrity beyond the common impulse of a spirit which yet was never indifferent to the credit of doing every thing well and attentively, with the real good-will of a mind delighted with its own ideas, did she then do all the honours of the meal, and help and recommend the minced chicken and scalloped oysters, with an urgency which she knew would be acceptable to the early hours and civil scruples of their guests.

Upon such occasions poor Mr. Woodhouses feelings were in sad warfare. He loved to have the cloth laid, because it had been the fashion of his youth, but his conviction of suppers being very unwholesome made him rather sorry to see any thing put on it; and while his hospitality would have welcomed his visitors to every thing, his care for their health made him grieve that they would eat.

Such another small basin of thin gruel as his own was all that he could, with thorough self-approbation, recommend; though he might constrain himself, while the ladies were comfortably clearing the nicer things, to say:

"Mrs. Bates, let me propose your venturing on one of these eggs. An egg boiled very soft is not unwholesome. Serle understands boiling an egg better than any body. I would not recommend an egg boiled by any body else; but you need not be afraid, they are very small, you see – one of our small eggs will not hurt you. Miss Bates, let Emma help you to a *little* bit of tart – a *very* little bit. Ours are all apple-tarts. You need not be afraid of unwholesome preserves here. I do not advise the custard. Mrs. Goddard, what say you to *half* a glass of wine? A *small* half-glass, put into a tumbler of water? I do not think it could disagree with you."

Emma allowed her father to talk – but supplied her visitors in a much more satisfactory style, and on the present evening had particular pleasure in sending them away happy. The happiness of Miss Smith was quite equal to her intentions. Miss Woodhouse was so great a personage in Highbury, that the prospect of the introduction had given as much panic as pleasure; but the humble, grateful little girl went off with highly gratified feelings, delighted with the affability with which Miss Woodhouse had treated her all the evening, and actually shaken hands with her at last!

CHAPTER IV

Harriet Smith's intimacy at Hartfield was soon a settled thing. Quick and decided in her ways, Emma lost no time in inviting, encouraging, and telling her to come very often; and as their acquaintance increased, so did their satisfaction in each other. As a walking companion, Emma had very early foreseen how useful she might find her. In that respect Mrs. Weston's loss had been important. Her father never went beyond the shrubbery, where two divisions of the ground sufficed him for his long walk, or his short, as the year varied; and since Mrs. Weston's marriage her exercise had been too much confined. She had ventured once alone to Randalls, but it was not pleasant; and a Harriet Smith, therefore, one whom she could summon at any time to a walk, would be a valuable addition to her privileges. But in every respect, as she saw more of her, she approved her, and was confirmed in all her kind designs.

Harriet certainly was not clever, but she had a sweet, docile, grateful disposition, was totally free from conceit, and only desiring to be guided by any one she looked up to. Her early attachment to herself was very amiable; and her inclination for good company, and power of appreciating what was elegant and clever, shewed that there was no want of taste, though strength of understanding must not be expected. Altogether she was quite convinced of Harriet Smith's being exactly the young friend she wanted – exactly the something which her home required. Such a friend as Mrs. Weston was out of the question. Two such could never be granted. Two such she did not want. It was quite a different sort of thing, a sentiment distinct and independent. Mrs. Weston was the object of a regard which had its basis in gratitude and esteem. Harriet would be loved as one to whom she could be useful. For Mrs. Weston there was nothing to be done; for Harriet every thing.

Her first attempts at usefulness were in an endeavour to find out who were the parents, but Harriet could not tell. She was ready to tell every thing in her power, but on this subject questions were vain. Emma was obliged to fancy what she liked – but she could never believe that in the same situation *she* should not have discovered the truth. Harriet had no penetration. She had been satisfied to hear and believe just what Mrs. Goddard chose to tell her; and looked no farther.

Mrs. Goddard, and the teachers, and the girls and the affairs of the school in general, formed naturally a great part of the conversation – and but for her acquaintance with the Martins of Abbey-Mill Farm, it must have been the whole. But the Martins occupied her thoughts a good deal; she had spent two very happy months with them, and now loved to talk of the pleasures of her visit, and describe the many comforts and wonders of the place. Emma encouraged her talkativeness – amused by such a picture of another set of beings, and enjoying the youthful simplicity which could speak with so much exultation of Mrs. Martin's having "two parlours, two very good parlours, indeed; one of them quite as large as Mrs. Goddard's drawing-room; and of her having an upper maid who had lived five-and-twenty years with her; and of their having eight cows, two of them Alderneys, and one a little Welch cow, a very pretty little Welch cow indeed; and of Mrs. Martin's saying as she was so fond of it, it should be called her cow; and of their having a very handsome summer-house in their garden, where some day next year they were all to drink tea:– a very handsome summer-house, large enough to hold a dozen people."

For some time she was amused, without thinking beyond the immediate cause; but as she came to understand the family better, other feelings arose. She had taken up a wrong idea, fancying it was a mother and daughter, a son and son's wife, who all lived together; but when it appeared that the Mr. Martin, who bore a part in the narrative, and was always mentioned with approbation for his great good-nature in doing something or other, was a single man; that there was no young Mrs. Martin, no wife in the case; she did suspect danger to her poor little friend from all this hospitality and kindness, and that, if she were not taken care of, she might be required to sink herself forever.

With this inspiriting notion, her questions increased in number and meaning; and she particularly led Harriet to talk more of Mr. Martin, and there was evidently no dislike to it. Harriet was very ready to speak of the share he had had in their moonlight walks and merry evening games; and dwelt a good deal upon his being so very good-humoured and obliging. He had gone three miles round one day in order to bring her some walnuts, because she had said how fond she was of them, and in every thing else he was so very obliging. He had his shepherd's son into the parlour one night on purpose to sing to her. She was very fond of singing. He could sing a little himself. She believed he was very clever, and understood every thing. He had a very fine flock, and, while she was with them, he had been bid more for his wool than any body in the country. She believed every body spoke well of him. His mother and sisters were very fond of him. Mrs. Martin had told her one day (and there was a blush as she said it,) that it was impossible for any body to be a better son, and therefore she was sure, whenever he married, he would make a good husband. Not that she *wanted* him to marry. She was in no hurry at all.

"Well done, Mrs. Martin!" thought Emma. "You know what you are about."

"And when she had come away, Mrs. Martin was so very kind as to send Mrs. Goddard a beautiful goose – the finest goose Mrs. Goddard had ever seen. Mrs. Goddard had dressed it on a Sunday, and asked all the three teachers, Miss Nash, and Miss Prince, and Miss Richardson, to sup with her."

"Mr. Martin, I suppose, is not a man of information beyond the line of his own business? He does not read?"

"Oh yes! – that is, no – I do not know – but I believe he has read a good deal – but not what you would think any thing of. He reads the Agricultural Reports, and some other books that lay in one of the window seats – but he reads all *them* to himself. But sometimes of an evening, before we went to cards, he would read something aloud out of the Elegant Extracts, very entertaining. And I know he has read the Vicar of Wakefield. He never read the Romance of the Forest, nor The Children of the Abbey. He had never heard of such books before I mentioned them, but he is determined to get them now as soon as ever he can."

The next question was–

"What sort of looking man is Mr. Martin?"

"Oh! not handsome – not at all handsome. I thought him very plain at first, but I do not think him so plain now. One does not, you know, after a time. But did you never see him? He is in Highbury every now and then, and he is sure to ride through every week in his way to Kingston. He has passed you very often."

"That may be, and I may have seen him fifty times, but without having any idea of his name. A young farmer, whether on horseback or on foot, is the very last sort of person to raise my curiosity. The yeomanry are precisely the order of people with whom I feel I can have nothing to do. A degree or two lower, and a creditable appearance might interest me; I might hope to be useful to their families in some way or other. But a farmer can need none of my help, and is, therefore, in one sense, as much above my notice as in every other he is below it."

"To be sure. Oh yes! It is not likely you should ever have observed him; but he knows you very well indeed – I mean by sight."

"I have no doubt of his being a very re-spectable young man. I know, indeed, that he is so, and, as such, wish him well. What do you imagine his age to be?"

"He was four-and-twenty the 8th of last June, and my birthday is the 23rd just a fortnight and a day's difference – which is very odd."

"Only four-and-twenty. That is too young to settle. His mother is perfectly right not to be in a hurry. They seem very comfortable as they are, and if she were to take any pains to marry him, she would probably repent it. Six years hence, if he could meet with a good sort of young woman in the same rank as his own, with a little money, it might be very desirable."

"Six years hence! Dear Miss Woodhouse, he would be thirty years old!"

"Well, and that is as early as most men can afford to marry, who are not born to an independence. Mr. Martin, I imagine, has his fortune entirely to make – cannot be at all beforehand with the world. Whatever money he might come into when his father died, whatever his share of the family property, it is, I dare say, all afloat, all employed in his stock, and so forth; and though, with diligence and good luck, he may be rich in time, it is next to impossible that he should have realised any thing yet."

"To be sure, so it is. But they live very comfortably. They have no indoors man, else they do not want for any thing; and Mrs. Martin talks of taking a boy another year."

"I wish you may not get into a scrape, Harriet, whenever he does marry; – I mean, as to being acquainted with his wife – for though his sisters, from a superior education, are not to be altogether objected to, it does not follow that he might marry any body at all fit for you to notice. The misfortune of your birth ought to make you particularly careful as to your associates. There can be no doubt of your being a gentleman's daughter, and you must support your claim to that station by every thing within your own power, or there will be plenty of people who would take pleasure in degrading you."

"Yes, to be sure, I suppose there are. But while I visit at Hartfield, and you are so kind to me, Miss Woodhouse, I am not afraid of what any body can do."

"You understand the force of influence pretty well, Harriet; but I would have you so firmly established in good society, as to be independent even of Hartfield and Miss Woodhouse. I want to see you permanently well connected, and to that end it will be advisable to have as few odd acquaintance as may be; and, therefore, I say that if you should still be in this country when Mr. Martin marries, I wish you may not be drawn in by your intimacy with the sisters, to be acquainted with the wife, who will probably be some mere farmer's daughter, without education."

"To be sure. Yes. Not that I think Mr. Martin would ever marry any body but what had had some education – and been very well brought up. However, I do not mean to set up my opinion against your's – and I am sure I shall not wish for the acquaintance of his wife. I shall always have a great regard for the Miss Martins, especially Elizabeth, and should be very sorry to give them up, for they are quite as well educated as me. But if he marries a very ignorant, vulgar woman, certainly I had better not visit her, if I can help it."

Emma watched her through the fluctuations of this speech, and saw no alarming symptoms of love. The young man had been the first admirer, but she trusted there was no other hold, and that there would be no serious difficulty, on Harriet's side, to oppose any friendly arrangement of her own.

They met Mr. Martin the very next day, as they were walking on the Donwell road. He was on foot, and after looking very respectfully at her, looked with most unfeigned satisfaction at her companion. Emma was not sorry to have such an opportunity of survey; and walking a few yards forward, while they talked together, soon made her quick eye sufficiently acquainted with Mr. Robert Martin. His appearance was very neat, and he looked like a sensible young man, but his person had no other advantage; and when he came to be contrasted with gentlemen, she thought he must lose all the ground he had gained in Harriet's inclination. Harriet was not insensible of manner; she had voluntarily noticed her father's gentleness with admiration as well as wonder. Mr. Martin looked as if he did not know what manner was.

They remained but a few minutes together, as Miss Woodhouse must not be kept waiting; and Harriet then came running to her with a smiling face, and in a flutter of spirits, which Miss Woodhouse hoped very soon to compose.

"Only think of our happening to meet him! – How very odd! It was quite a chance, he said, that he had not gone round by Randalls. He did not think we ever walked this road. He thought we walked towards Randalls most days. He has not been able to get the Romance of the Forest yet. He was so busy the last time he was at Kingston that he quite forgot it, but he goes again to-morrow. So very odd we should happen to meet! Well, Miss Woodhouse, is he like what you expected? What do you think of him? Do you think him so very plain?"

"He is very plain, undoubtedly – remarkably plain:– but that is nothing compared with his entire want of gentility. I had no right to expect much, and I did not expect much; but I had no idea that he could be so very clownish, so totally without air. I had imagined him, I confess, a degree or two nearer gentility."

"To be sure," said Harriet, in a mortified voice, "he is not so genteel as real gentlemen."

"I think, Harriet, since your acquaintance with us, you have been repeatedly in the company of some such very real gentlemen, that you must yourself be struck with the difference in Mr. Martin. At Hartfield, you have had very good specimens of well educated, well bred men. I should be surprized if, after seeing them, you could be in company with Mr. Martin again without perceiving him to be a very inferior creature – and rather wondering at yourself for having ever thought him at all agreeable before. Do not you begin to feel that now? Were not you struck? I am sure you must have been struck by his awkward look and abrupt manner, and the uncouthness of a voice which I heard to be wholly unmodulated as I stood here."

"Certainly, he is not like Mr. Knightley. He has not such a fine air and way of walking as Mr. Knightley. I see the difference plain enough. But Mr. Knightley is so very fine a man!"

"Mr. Knightley's air is so remarkably good that it is not fair to compare Mr. Martin with *him*. You might not see one in a hundred with *gentleman* so plainly written as in Mr. Knightley. But he is not the only gentleman you have been lately used to. What say you to Mr. Weston and Mr. Elton? Compare Mr. Martin with either of *them*. Compare their manner of carrying themselves; of walking; of speaking; of being silent. You must see the difference."

"Oh yes! – there is a great difference. But Mr. Weston is almost an old man. Mr. Weston must be between forty and fifty."

"Which makes his good manners the more valuable. The older a person grows, Harriet, the more important it is that their manners should not be bad; the more glaring and disgusting any loudness, or coarseness, or awkwardness becomes. What is passable in youth is detestable in later age. Mr. Martin is now awkward and abrupt; what will he be at Mr. Weston's time of life?"

"There is no saying, indeed," replied Harriet rather solemnly.

"But there may be pretty good guessing. He will be a completely gross, vulgar farmer, totally inattentive to appearances, and thinking of nothing but profit and loss."

"Will he, indeed? That will be very bad."

"How much his business engrosses him already is very plain from the circumstance of his forgetting to inquire for the book you recommended. He was a great deal too full of the market to think of any thing else – which is just as it should be, for a thriving man. What has he to do with books? And I have no doubt that he *will* thrive, and be a very rich man in time – and his being illiterate and coarse need not disturb *us*."

"I wonder he did not remember the book" – was all Harriet's answer, and spoken with a degree of grave displeasure which Emma thought might be safely left to itself. She, therefore, said no more for some time. Her next beginning was,

"In one respect, perhaps, Mr. Elton's manners are superior to Mr. Knightley's or Mr. Weston's. They have more gentleness. They might be more safely held up as a pattern. There is an openness, a quickness, almost a bluntness in Mr. Weston, which every body likes in *him*, because there is so much good-humour with it – but that would not do to be copied. Neither would Mr. Knightley's downright, decided, commanding sort of manner, though it suits *him* very well; his figure, and look, and situation in life seem to allow it; but if any young man were to set about copying him, he would not be sufferable. On the contrary, I think a young man might be very safely recommended to take Mr. Elton as a model. Mr. Elton is good-humoured, cheerful, obliging, and gentle. He seems to me to be grown particularly gentle of late. I do not know whether he has any design of ingratiating himself with either of us, Harriet, by additional softness, but it strikes me that his manners are softer than they used to be. If he means any thing, it must be to please you. Did not I tell you what he said of you the other day?"

She then repeated some warm personal praise which she had drawn from Mr. Elton, and now did full justice to; and Harriet blushed and smiled, and said she had always thought Mr. Elton very agreeable.

Mr. Elton was the very person fixed on by Emma for driving the young farmer out of Harriet's head. She thought it would be an excellent match; and only too palpably desirable, natural, and probable, for her to have much merit in planning it. She feared it was what every body else must think of and predict. It was not likely, however, that any body should have equalled her in the date of the plan, as it had entered her brain during the very first evening of Harriet's coming to Hartfield. The longer she considered it, the greater was her sense of its expediency. Mr. Elton's situation was most suitable, quite the gentleman himself, and without low connexions; at the same time, not of any family that could fairly object to the doubtful birth of Harriet. He had a comfortable home for her, and Emma imagined a very sufficient income; for though the vicarage of Highbury was not large, he was known to have some independent property; and she thought very highly of him as a good-humoured, well-meaning, respectable young man, without any deficiency of useful understanding or knowledge of the world.

She had already satisfied herself that he thought Harriet a beautiful girl, which she trusted, with such frequent meetings at Hartfield, was foundation enough on his side; and on Harriet's there could be little doubt that the idea of being preferred by him would have all the usual weight and efficacy. And he was really a very pleasing young man, a young man whom any woman not fastidious might like. He was reckoned very handsome; his person much admired in general, though not by her, there being a want of elegance of feature which she could not dispense with:– but the girl who could be gratified by a Robert Martin's riding about the country to get walnuts for her might very well be conquered by Mr. Elton's admiration.

CHAPTER V

"I do not know what your opinion may be, Mrs. Weston," said Mr. Knightley, "of this great intimacy between Emma and Harriet Smith, but I think it a bad thing."

"A bad thing! Do you really think it a bad thing? – why so?"

"I think they will neither of them do the other any good."

"You surprize me! Emma must do Harriet good: and by supplying her with a new object of interest, Harriet may be said to do Emma good. I have been seeing their intimacy with the greatest pleasure. How very differently we feel! – Not think they will do each other any good! This will certainly be the beginning of one of our quarrels about Emma, Mr. Knightley."

"Perhaps you think I am come on purpose to quarrel with you, knowing Weston to be out, and that you must still fight your own battle."

"Mr. Weston would undoubtedly support me, if he were here, for he thinks exactly as I do on the subject. We were speaking of it only yesterday, and agreeing how fortunate it was for Emma, that there should be such a girl in Highbury for her to associate with. Mr. Knightley, I shall not allow you to be a fair judge in this case. You are so much used to live alone, that you do not know the value of a companion; and, perhaps no man can be a good judge of the comfort a woman feels in the society of one of her own sex, after being used to it all her life. I can imagine your objection to Harriet Smith. She is not the superior young woman which Emma's friend ought to be. But on the other hand, as Emma wants to see her better informed, it will be an inducement to her to read more herself. They will read together. She means it, I know."

"Emma has been meaning to read more ever since she was twelve years old. I have seen a great many lists of her drawing-up at various times of books that she meant to read regularly through – and very good lists they were – very well chosen, and very neatly arranged – sometimes alphabetically, and sometimes by some other rule. The list she drew up when only fourteen – I remember thinking it did her judgment so much credit, that I preserved it some time; and I dare say she may have made out a very good list now. But I have done with expecting any course of steady reading from Emma. She will never submit to any thing requiring industry and patience, and a subjection of the fancy to the understanding. Where Miss Taylor failed to stimulate, I may safely affirm that Harriet Smith will do nothing. – You never could persuade her to read half so much as you wished. – You know you could not."

"I dare say," replied Mrs. Weston, smiling, "that I thought so then but since we have parted, I can never remember Emma's omitting to do any thing I wished."

"There is hardly any desiring to refresh such a memory as *that*," – said Mr. Knightley, feelingly; and for a moment or two he had done. "But I," he soon added, "who have had no such charm thrown over my senses, must still see, hear, and remember. Emma is spoiled by being the cleverest of her family. At ten years old, she had the misfortune of being able to answer questions which puzzled her sister at seventeen. She was always quick and assured: Isabella slow and diffident. And ever since she was twelve, Emma has been mistress of the house and of you all. In her mother she lost the only person able to cope with her. She inherits her mother's talents, and must have been under subjection to her."

"I should have been sorry, Mr. Knightley, to be dependent on *your* recommendation, had I quitted Mr. Woodhouse's family and wanted another situation; I do not think you would have spoken a good word for me to any body. I am sure you always thought me unfit for the office I held."

"Yes," said he, smiling. "You are better placed *here*; very fit for a wife, but not at all for a governess. But you were preparing yourself to be an excellent wife all the time you were at Hartfield. You might not give Emma such a complete education as your powers would seem to promise; but you were receiving a very good education from *her*, on the very material matrimonial point of submitting your own will, and doing as you were bid; and if Weston had asked me to recommend him a wife, I should certainly have named Miss Taylor."

"Thank you. There will be very little merit in making a good wife to such a man as Mr. Weston."

"Why, to own the truth, I am afraid you are rather thrown away, and that with every disposition to bear, there will be nothing to be borne. We will not despair, however. Weston may grow cross from the wantonness of comfort, or his son may plague him."

"I hope not *that*. It is not likely. No, Mr. Knightley, do not foretell vexation from that quarter."

"Not I, indeed. I only name possibilities. I do not pretend to Emma's genius for foretelling and guessing. I hope, with all my heart, the young man may be a Weston in merit, and a Churchill in fortune. – But Harriet Smith – I have not half done about Harriet Smith. I think her the very worst sort of companion that Emma could possibly have. She knows nothing herself, and looks upon Emma as knowing every thing. She is a flatterer in all her ways; and so much the worse, because undesigned. Her ignorance is hourly flattery. How can Emma imagine she has any thing to learn herself, while Harriet is presenting such a delightful inferiority? And as for Harriet, I will venture to say that *she* cannot gain by the acquaintance. Hartfield will only put her out of conceit with all the other places she belongs to. She will grow just refined enough to be uncomfortable with those among whom birth and circumstances have placed her home. I am much mistaken if Emma's doctrines give any strength of mind, or tend at all to make a girl adapt herself rationally to the varieties of her situation in life. – They only give a little polish."

"I either depend more upon Emma's good sense than you do, or am more anxious for her present comfort; for I cannot lament the acquaintance. How well she looked last night!"

"Oh! you would rather talk of her person than her mind, would you? Very well; I shall not attempt to deny Emma's being pretty."

"Pretty! say beautiful rather. Can you imagine any thing nearer perfect beauty than Emma alto-gether – face and figure?"

"I do not know what I could imagine, but I confess that I have seldom seen a face or figure more pleasing to me than hers. But I am a partial old friend."

"Such an eye! – the true hazle eye – and so brilliant! regular features, open countenance, with a complexion! oh! what a bloom of full health, and such a pretty height and size; such a firm and upright figure! There is health, not merely in her bloom, but in her air, her head, her glance. One hears sometimes of a child being 'the picture of health;' now, Emma always gives me the idea of being the complete picture of grown-up health. She is loveliness itself. Mr. Knightley, is not she?"

"I have not a fault to find with her person," he replied. "I think her all you describe. I love to look at her; and I will add this praise, that I do not think her personally vain. Considering how very handsome she is, she appears to be little occupied with it; her vanity lies another way. Mrs. Weston, I am not to be talked out of my dislike of Harriet Smith, or my dread of its doing them both harm."

"And I, Mr. Knightley, am equally stout in my confidence of its not doing them any harm. With all dear Emma's little faults, she is an excellent creature. Where shall we see a better daughter, or a kinder sister, or a truer friend? No, no; she has qualities which may be trusted; she will never lead any one really wrong; she will make no lasting blunder; where Emma errs once, she is in the right a hundred times."

"Very well; I will not plague you any more. Emma shall be an angel, and I will keep my spleen to myself till Christmas brings John and Isabella. John loves Emma with a reasonable and therefore not a blind affection, and Isabella always thinks as he does; except when he is not quite frightened enough about the children. I am sure of having their opinions with me."

"I know that you all love her really too well to be unjust or unkind; but excuse me, Mr. Knightley, if I take the liberty (I consider myself, you know, as having somewhat of the privilege of speech that Emma's mother might have had) the liberty of hinting that I do not think any possible good can arise from Harriet Smith's intimacy being made a matter of much discussion among you. Pray excuse me; but supposing any little inconvenience may be apprehended from the intimacy, it cannot be expected that Emma, accountable to nobody but her father, who perfectly approves the acquaintance, should put an end to it, so long as it is a source of pleasure to herself. It has been so many years my province to give advice, that you cannot be surprized, Mr. Knightley, at this little remains of office."

"Not at all," cried he; "I am much obliged to you for it. It is very good advice, and it shall have a better fate than your advice has often found; for it shall be attended to."

"Mrs. John Knightley is easily alarmed, and might be made unhappy about her sister."

"Be satisfied," said he, "I will not raise any outcry. I will keep my ill-humour to myself. I have a very sincere interest in Emma. Isabella does not seem more my sister; has never excited a greater inter-est; perhaps hardly so great. There is an anxiety, a curiosity in what one feels for Emma. I wonder what will become of her!"

"So do I," said Mrs. Weston gently, "very much."

"She always declares she will never marry, which, of course, means just nothing at all. But I have no idea that she has yet ever seen a man she cared for. It would not be a bad thing for her to be very much in love with a proper object. I should like to see Emma in love, and in some doubt of a return; it would do her good. But there is nobody hereabouts to attach her; and she goes so seldom from home."

"There does, indeed, seem as little to tempt her to break her resolution at present," said Mrs. Weston, "as can well be; and while she is so happy at Hartfield, I cannot wish her to be forming any attachment which would be creating such difficulties on poor Mr. Woodhouse's account. I do not recommend matrimony at present to Emma, though I mean no slight to the state, I assure you."

Part of her meaning was to conceal some favourite thoughts of her own and Mr. Weston's on the subject, as much as possible. There were wishes at Randalls respecting Emma's destiny, but it was not desirable to have them suspected; and the quiet transition which Mr. Knightley soon afterwards made to "What does Weston think of the weather; shall we have rain?" convinced her that he had nothing more to say or surmise about Hartfield.

CHAPTER VI

Emma could not feel a doubt of having given Harriet's fancy a proper direction and raised the gratitude of her young vanity to a very good purpose, for she found her decidedly more sensible than before of Mr. Elton's being a remarkably handsome man, with most agreeable manners; and as she had no hesitation in following up the assurance of his admiration by agreeable hints, she was soon pretty confident of creating as much liking on Harriet's side, as there could be any occasion for. She was quite convinced of Mr. Elton's being in the fairest way of falling in love, if not in love already. She had no scruple with regard to him. He talked of Harriet, and praised her so warmly, that she could not suppose any thing wanting which a little time would not add. His perception of the striking improvement of Harriet's manner, since her introduction at Hartfield, was not one of the least agreeable proofs of his growing attachment.

"You have given Miss Smith all that she required," said he; "you have made her graceful and easy. She was a beautiful creature when she came to you, but, in my opinion, the attractions you have added are infinitely superior to what she received from nature."

"I am glad you think I have been useful to her; but Harriet only wanted drawing out, and receiving a few, very few hints. She had all the natural grace of sweetness of temper and artlessness in herself. I have done very little."

"If it were admissible to contradict a lady," said the gallant Mr. Elton—

"I have perhaps given her a little more decision of character, have taught her to think on points which had not fallen in her way before."

"Exactly so; that is what principally strikes me. So much superadded decision of character! Skilful has been the hand!"

"Great has been the pleasure, I am sure. I never met with a disposition more truly amiable."

"I have no doubt of it." And it was spoken with a sort of sighing animation, which had a vast deal of the lover. She was not less pleased another day with the manner in which he seconded a sudden wish of hers, to have Harriet's picture.

"Did you ever have your likeness taken, Harriet?" said she: "did you ever sit for your picture?"

Harriet was on the point of leaving the room, and only stopt to say, with a very interesting naivete,

"Oh! dear, no, never."

No sooner was she out of sight, than Emma exclaimed,

"What an exquisite possession a good picture of her would be! I would give any money for it. I almost long to attempt her likeness myself. You do not know it I dare say, but two or three years ago I had a great passion for taking likenesses, and attempted several of my friends, and was thought to have a tolerable eye in general. But from one cause or another, I gave it up in disgust. But really, I could almost venture, if Harriet would sit to me. It would be such a delight to have her picture!"

"Let me entreat you," cried Mr. Elton; "it would indeed be a delight! Let me entreat you, Miss Woodhouse, to exercise so charming a talent in favour of your friend. I know what your drawings are. How could you suppose me ignorant? Is not this room rich in specimens of your landscapes and flowers; and has not Mrs. Weston some inimitable figure-pieces in her drawing-room, at Randalls?"

Yes, good man! – thought Emma – but what has all that to do with taking likenesses? You know nothing of drawing. Don't pretend to be in raptures about mine. Keep your raptures for Harriet's face. "Well, if you give me such kind encouragement, Mr. Elton, I believe I shall try what I can do. Harriet's features are very delicate, which makes a likeness difficult; and yet there is a peculiarity in the shape of the eye and the lines about the mouth which one ought to catch."

"Exactly so – The shape of the eye and the lines about the mouth – I have not a doubt of your success. Pray, pray attempt it. As you will do it, it will indeed, to use your own words, be an exquisite possession."

"But I am afraid, Mr. Elton, Harriet will not like to sit. She thinks so little of her own beauty. Did not you observe her manner of answering me? How completely it meant, 'why should my picture be drawn?'"

"Oh! yes, I observed it, I assure you. It was not lost on me. But still I cannot imagine she would not be persuaded."

Harriet was soon back again, and the proposal almost immediately made; and she had no scruples which could stand many minutes against the earnest pressing of both the others. Emma wished to go to work directly, and therefore produced the portfolio containing her various attempts at portraits, for not one of them had ever been finished, that they might decide together on the best size for Harriet. Her many beginnings were displayed. Miniatures, half-lengths, whole-lengths, pencil, crayon, and water-colours had been all tried in turn. She had always wanted to do every thing, and had made more progress both in drawing and music than many might have done with so little labour as she would ever submit to. She played and sang; – and drew in almost every style; but steadiness had always been wanting; and in nothing had she approached the degree of excellence which she would have been glad to command, and ought not to have failed of. She was not much deceived as to her own skill either as an artist or a musician, but she was not unwilling to have others deceived, or sorry to know her reputation for accomplishment often higher than it deserved.

There was merit in every drawing – in the least finished, perhaps the most; her style was spirited; but had there been much less, or had there been ten times more, the delight and admiration of her two companions would have been the same. They were both in ecstasies. A likeness pleases every body; and Miss Woodhouse's performances must be capital.

"No great variety of faces for you," said Emma. "I had only my own family to study from. There is my father – another of my father – but the idea of sitting for his picture made him so nervous, that I could only take him by stealth; neither of them very like therefore. Mrs. Weston again, and again, and again, you see. Dear Mrs. Weston! always my kindest friend on every occasion. She would sit whenever I asked her. There is my sister; and really quite her own little elegant figure! –

and the face not unlike. I should have made a good likeness of her, if she would have sat longer, but she was in such a hurry to have me draw her four children that she would not be quiet. Then, here come all my attempts at three of those four children; – there they are, Henry and John and Bella, from one end of the sheet to the other, and any one of them might do for any one of the rest. She was so eager to have them drawn that I could not refuse; but there is no making children of three or four years old stand still you know; nor can it be very easy to take any likeness of them, beyond the air and complexion, unless they are coarser featured than any of mama's children ever were. Here is my sketch of the fourth, who was a baby. I took him as he was sleeping on the sofa, and it is as strong a likeness of his cockade as you would wish to see. He had nestled down his head most conveniently. That's very like. I am rather proud of little George. The corner of the sofa is very good. Then here is my last," – unclosing a pretty sketch of a gentleman in small size, whole-length – "my last and my best – my brother, Mr. John Knightley. – This did not want much of be-ing finished, when I put it away in a pet, and vowed I would never take another likeness. I could not help being provoked; for after all my pains, and when I had really made a very good likeness of it – (Mrs. Weston and I were quite agreed in thinking it very like) – only too hand-some – too flattering – but that was a fault on the right side – after all this, came poor dear Isabella's cold approbation of – 'Yes, it was a little like – but to be sure it did not do him jus-tice.' We had had a great deal of trouble in per-suading him to sit at all. It was made a great favour of; and altogether it was more than I could bear; and so I never would finish it, to have it apologised over as an unfavourable like-ness, to every morning visitor in Brunswick Square; – and, as I said, I did then forswear ever drawing any body again. But for Harriet's sake, or rather for my own, and as there are no hus-bands and wives in the case at present, I will break my resolution now.”

Mr. Elton seemed very properly struck and de-lighted by the idea, and was repeating, “No husbands and wives in the case at present in-deed, as you observe. Exactly so. No husbands and wives,” with so interesting a consciousness, that Emma began to consider whether she had not better leave them together at once. But as she wanted to be drawing, the declaration must wait a little longer.

She had soon fixed on the size and sort of portrait. It was to be a whole-length in water-colours, like Mr. John Knightley's, and was destined, if she could please herself, to hold a very honourable station over the mantelpiece.

The sitting began; and Harriet, smiling and blushing, and afraid of not keeping her attitude and countenance, presented a very sweet mixture of youthful expression to the steady eyes of the artist. But there was no doing any thing, with Mr. Elton fidgeting behind her and watching every touch. She gave him credit for stationing himself where he might gaze and gaze again without offence; but was really obliged to put an end to it, and request him to place himself elsewhere. It then occurred to her to employ him in reading.

"If he would be so good as to read to them, it would be a kindness indeed! It would amuse away the difficulties of her part, and lessen the irksomeness of Miss Smith's."

Mr. Elton was only too happy. Harriet listened, and Emma drew in peace. She must allow him to be still frequently coming to look; any thing less would certainly have been too little in a lover; and he was ready at the smallest intermission of the pencil, to jump up and see the progress, and be charmed. – There was no being displeased with such an encourager, for his admiration made him discern a likeness almost before it was possible. She could not respect his eye, but his love and his complaisance were unexceptionable.

The sitting was altogether very satisfactory; she was quite enough pleased with the first day's sketch to wish to go on. There was no want of likeness, she had been fortunate in the attitude, and as she meant to throw in a little improvement to the figure, to give a little more height, and considerably more elegance, she had great confidence of its being in every way a pretty drawing at last, and of its filling its destined place with credit to them both – a standing memorial of the beauty of one, the skill of the other, and the friendship of both; with as many other agreeable associations as Mr. Elton's very promising attachment was likely to add.

Harriet was to sit again the next day; and Mr. Elton, just as he ought, entreated for the permission of attending and reading to them again.

"By all means. We shall be most happy to consider you as one of the party."

The same civilities and courtesies, the same success and satisfaction, took place on the morrow, and accompanied the whole progress of the picture, which was rapid and happy. Every body who saw it was pleased, but Mr. Elton was in continual raptures, and defended it through every criticism.

"Miss Woodhouse has given her friend the only beauty she wanted," – observed Mrs. Weston to him – not in the least suspecting that she was addressing a lover. – "The expression of the eye is most correct, but Miss Smith has not those eyebrows and eyelashes. It is the fault of her face that she has them not."

"Do you think so?" replied he. "I cannot agree with you. It appears to me a most perfect resemblance in every feature. I never saw such a likeness in my life. We must allow for the effect of shade, you know."

"You have made her too tall, Emma," said Mr. Knightley.

Emma knew that she had, but would not own it; and Mr. Elton warmly added,

"Oh no! certainly not too tall; not in the least too tall. Consider, she is sitting down – which naturally presents a different – which in short gives exactly the idea – and the proportions must be preserved, you know. Proportions, fore-shortening. – Oh no! it gives one exactly the idea of such a height as Miss Smith's. Exactly so indeed!"

"It is very pretty," said Mr. Woodhouse. "So prettily done! Just as your drawings always are, my dear. I do not know any body who draws so well as you do. The only thing I do not thoroughly like is, that she seems to be sitting out of doors, with only a little shawl over her shoulders – and it makes one think she must catch cold."

"But, my dear papa, it is supposed to be summer; a warm day in summer. Look at the tree."

"But it is never safe to sit out of doors, my dear."

"You, sir, may say any thing," cried Mr. Elton, "but I must confess that I regard it as a most happy thought, the placing of Miss Smith out of doors; and the tree is touched with such inimitable spirit! Any other situation would have been much less in character. The naivete of Miss Smith's manners – and altogether – Oh, it is most admirable! I cannot keep my eyes from it. I never saw such a likeness."

The next thing wanted was to get the picture framed; and here were a few difficulties. It must be done directly; it must be done in London; the order must go through the hands of some intelligent person whose taste could be depended on; and Isabella, the usual doer of all commissions, must not be applied to, because it was December, and Mr. Woodhouse could not bear the idea of her stirring out of her house in the fogs of December. But no sooner was the distress known to Mr. Elton, than it was removed. His gallantry was always on the alert. "Might he be trusted with the commission, what infinite pleasure should he have in executing it! he could ride to London at any time. It was impossible to say how much he should be gratified by being employed on such an errand."

"He was too good! – she could not endure the thought! – she would not give him such a troublesome office for the world," – brought on the desired repetition of entreaties and assurances, – and a very few minutes settled the business.

Mr. Elton was to take the drawing to London, chuse the frame, and give the directions; and Emma thought she could so pack it as to ensure its safety without much incommoding him, while he seemed mostly fearful of not being incommoded enough.

"What a precious deposit!" said he with a tender sigh, as he received it.

"This man is almost too gallant to be in love," thought Emma. "I should say so, but that I suppose there may be a hundred different ways of being in love. He is an excellent young man, and will suit Harriet exactly; it will be an 'Exactly so,' as he says himself; but he does sigh and languish, and study for compliments rather more than I could endure as a principal. I come in for a pretty good share as a second. But it is his gratitude on Harriet's account."

CHAPTER VII

The very day of Mr. Elton's going to London produced a fresh occasion for Emma's services towards her friend. Harriet had been at Hartfield, as usual, soon after breakfast; and, after a time, had gone home to return again to dinner: she returned, and sooner than had been talked of, and with an agitated, hurried look, announcing something extraordinary to have happened which she was longing to tell. Half a minute brought it all out. She had heard, as soon as she got back to Mrs. Goddard's, that Mr. Martin had been there an hour before, and finding she was not at home, nor particularly expected, had left a little parcel for her from one of his sisters, and gone away; and on opening this parcel, she had actually found, besides the two songs which she had lent Elizabeth to copy, a letter to herself; and this letter was from him, from Mr. Martin, and contained a direct proposal of marriage. "Who could have thought it? She was so surprized she did not know what to do. Yes, quite a proposal of marriage; and a very good letter, at least she thought so. And he wrote as if he really loved her very much – but she did not know – and so, she was come as fast as she could to ask Miss Woodhouse what she should do. –" Emma was half-ashamed of her friend for seeming so pleased and so doubtful.

"Upon my word," she cried, "the young man is determined not to lose any thing for want of asking. He will connect himself well if he can."

"Will you read the letter?" cried Harriet. "Pray do. I'd rather you would."

Emma was not sorry to be pressed. She read, and was surprized. The style of the letter was much above her expectation. There were not merely no grammatical errors, but as a composition it would not have disgraced a gentleman; the language, though plain, was strong and unaffected, and the sentiments it conveyed very much to the credit of the writer. It was short, but expressed good sense, warm attachment, liberality, propriety, even deli-cacy of feeling. She paused over it, while Harriet stood anxiously watching for her opinion, with a "Well, well," and was at last forced to add, "Is it a good letter? or is it too short?"

"Yes, indeed, a very good letter," replied Emma rather slowly – "so good a letter, Harriet, that every thing considered, I think one of his sisters must have helped him. I can hardly imagine the young man whom I saw talking with you the other day could express himself so well, if left quite to his own powers, and yet it is not the style of a woman; no, certainly, it is too strong and concise; not diffuse enough for a woman. No doubt he is a sensible man, and I suppose may have a natural talent for – thinks strongly and clearly – and when he takes a pen in hand, his thoughts naturally find proper words. It is so with some men. Yes, I understand the sort of mind. Vigorous, decided, with sentiments to a certain point, not coarse. A better written letter, Harriet (returning it,) than I had expected."

"Well," said the still waiting Harriet; – "well – and – and what shall I do?"

"What shall you do! In what respect? Do you mean with regard to this letter?"

"Yes."

"But what are you in doubt of? You must answer it of course – and speedily."

"Yes. But what shall I say? Dear Miss Woodhouse, do advise me."

"Oh no, no! the letter had much better be all your own. You will express yourself very properly, I am sure. There is no danger of your not being intelligible, which is the first thing. Your meaning must be unequivocal; no doubts or demurs: and such expressions of gratitude and concern for the pain you are inflicting as propriety requires, will present themselves unbidden to *your* mind, I am persuaded. *You* need not be prompted to write with the appearance of sorrow for his disappointment."

"You think I ought to refuse him then," said Harriet, looking down.

"Ought to refuse him! My dear Harriet, what do you mean? Are you in any doubt as to that? I thought – but I beg your pardon, perhaps I have been under a mistake. I certainly have been misunderstanding you, if you feel in doubt as to the purport of your answer. I had imagined you were consulting me only as to the wording of it."

Harriet was silent. With a little reserve of manner, Emma continued:

"You mean to return a favourable answer, I collect."

"No, I do not; that is, I do not mean – What shall I do? What would you advise me to do? Pray, dear Miss Woodhouse, tell me what I ought to do."

"I shall not give you any advice, Harriet. I will have nothing to do with it. This is a point which you must settle with your feelings."

"I had no notion that he liked me so very much," said Harriet, contemplating the letter. For a little while Emma persevered in her silence; but beginning to apprehend the bewitching flattery of that letter might be too powerful, she thought it best to say,

"I lay it down as a general rule, Harriet, that if a woman *doubts* as to whether she should accept a man or not, she certainly ought to refuse him. If she can hesitate as to 'Yes,' she ought to say 'No' directly. It is not a state to be safely entered into with doubtful feelings, with half a heart. I thought it my duty as a friend, and older than yourself, to say thus much to you. But do not imagine that I want to influence you."

"Oh! no, I am sure you are a great deal too kind to – but if you would just advise me what I had best do – No, no, I do not mean that – As you say, one's mind ought to be quite made up – One should not be hesitating – It is a very serious thing. – It will be safer to say 'No,' perhaps. – Do you think I had better say 'No?'"

"Not for the world," said Emma, smiling graciously, "would I advise you either way. You must be the best judge of your own happiness. If you prefer Mr. Martin to every other person; if you think him the most agreeable man you have ever been in company with, why should you hesitate? You blush, Harriet. – Does any body else occur to you at this moment under such a definition? Harriet, Harriet, do not deceive yourself; do not be run away with by gratitude and compassion. At this moment whom are you thinking of?"

The symptoms were favourable. – Instead of answering, Harriet turned away confused, and stood thoughtfully by the fire; and though the letter was still in her hand, it was now mechanically twisted about without regard. Emma waited the result with impatience, but not without strong hopes. At last, with some hesitation, Harriet said—

"Miss Woodhouse, as you will not give me your opinion, I must do as well as I can by myself; and I have now quite determined, and really almost made up my mind – to refuse Mr. Martin. Do you think I am right?"

"Perfectly, perfectly right, my dearest Harriet; you are doing just what you ought. While you were at all in suspense I kept my feelings to myself, but now that you are so completely decided I have no hesitation in approving. Dear Harriet, I give myself joy of this. It would have grieved me to lose your acquaintance, which must have been the consequence of your marrying Mr. Martin. While you were in the smallest degree wavering, I said nothing about it, because I would not influence; but it would have been the loss of a friend to me. I could not have visited Mrs. Robert Martin, of Abbey-Mill Farm. Now I am secure of you for ever."

Harriet had not surmised her own danger, but the idea of it struck her forcibly.

"You could not have visited me!" she cried, looking aghast. "No, to be sure you could not; but I never thought of that before. That would have been too dreadful! – What an escape! – Dear Miss Wood-house, I would not give up the pleasure and honour of being intimate with you for any thing in the world."

"Indeed, Harriet, it would have been a severe pang to lose you; but it must have been. You would have thrown yourself out of all good society. I must have given you up."

"Dear me! – How should I ever have borne it! It would have killed me never to come to Hartfield any more!"

"Dear affectionate creature! – *You* banished to Abbey-Mill Farm! – *You* confined to the society of the illiterate and vulgar all your life! I wonder how the young man could have the assurance to ask it. He must have a pretty good opinion of himself."

"I do not think he is conceited either, in general," said Harriet, her conscience opposing such censure; "at least, he is very good natured, and I shall always feel much obliged to him, and have a great regard for – but that is quite a different thing from – and you know, though he may like me, it does not follow that I should – and certainly I must confess that since my visiting here I have seen people – and if one comes to compare them, person and manners, there is no comparison at all, *one* is so very handsome and agreeable. However, I do really think Mr. Martin a very amiable young man, and have a great opinion of him; and his being so much attached to me – and his writing such a letter – but as to leaving you, it is what I would not do upon any consideration."

"Thank you, thank you, my own sweet little friend. We will not be parted. A woman is not to marry a man merely because she is asked, or because he is attached to her, and can write a tolerable letter."

"Oh no; – and it is but a short letter too."

Emma felt the bad taste of her friend, but let it pass with a "very true; and it would be a small consolation to her, for the clownish manner which might be offending her every hour of the day, to know that her husband could write a good letter."

"Oh! yes, very. Nobody cares for a letter; the thing is, to be always happy with pleasant companions. I am quite determined to refuse him. But how shall I do? What shall I say?"

Emma assured her there would be no difficulty in the answer, and advised its being written directly, which was agreed to, in the hope of her assistance; and though Emma continued to protest against any assistance being wanted, it was in fact given in the formation of every sentence. The looking over his letter again, in replying to it, had such a softening tendency, that it was particularly necessary to brace her up with a few decisive expressions; and she was so very much concerned at the idea of making him unhappy, and thought so much of what his mother and sisters would think and say, and was so anxious that they should not fancy her ungrateful, that Emma believed if the young man had come in her way at that moment, he would have been accepted after all.

This letter, however, was written, and sealed, and sent. The business was finished, and Harriet safe. She was rather low all the evening, but Emma could allow for her amiable regrets, and sometimes relieved them by speaking of her own affection, sometimes by bringing forward the idea of Mr. Elton.

"I shall never be invited to Abbey-Mill again," was said in rather a sorrowful tone.

"Nor, if you were, could I ever bear to part with you, my Harriet. You are a great deal too necessary at Hartfield to be spared to Abbey-Mill."

"And I am sure I should never want to go there; for I am never happy but at Hartfield."

Some time afterwards it was, "I think Mrs. Goddard would be very much surprized if she knew what had happened. I am sure Miss Nash would – for Miss Nash thinks her own sister very well married, and it is only a linen-draper."

"One should be sorry to see greater pride or refinement in the teacher of a school, Harriet. I dare say Miss Nash would envy you such an opportunity as this of being married. Even this conquest would appear valuable in her eyes. As to any thing superior for you, I suppose she is quite in the dark. The attentions of a certain person can hardly be among the tittle-tattle of Highbury yet. Hitherto I fancy you and I are the only people to whom his looks and manners have explained themselves."

Harriet blushed and smiled, and said something about wondering that people should like her so much. The idea of Mr. Elton was certainly cheering; but still, after a time, she was tender-hearted again towards the rejected Mr. Martin.

"Now he has got my letter," said she softly. "I wonder what they are all doing – whether his sisters know – if he is unhappy, they will be unhappy too. I hope he will not mind it so very much."

"Let us think of those among our absent friends who are more cheerfully employed," cried Emma. "At this moment, perhaps, Mr. Elton is shewing your picture to his mother and sisters, telling how much more beautiful is the original, and after being asked for it five or six times, allowing them to hear your name, your own dear name."

"My picture! – But he has left my picture in Bond-street."

"Has he so! – Then I know nothing of Mr. Elton. No, my dear little modest Harriet, depend upon it the picture will not be in Bond-street till just before he mounts his horse to-morrow. It is his companion all this evening, his solace, his delight. It opens his designs to his family, it introduces you among them, it diffuses through the party those pleasantest feelings of our nature, eager curiosity and warm prepossession. How cheerful, how animated, how suspicious, how busy their imaginations all are!"

Harriet smiled again, and her smiles grew stronger.

CHAPTER VIII

Harriet slept at Hartfield that night. For some weeks past she had been spending more than half her time there, and gradually getting to have a bed-room appropriated to herself; and Emma judged it best in every respect, safest and kindest, to keep her with them as much as possible just at present. She was obliged to go the next morning for an hour or two to Mrs. Goddard's, but it was then to be settled that she should return to Hartfield, to make a regular visit of some days.

While she was gone, Mr. Knightley called, and sat some time with Mr. Woodhouse and Emma, till Mr. Woodhouse, who had previously made up his mind to walk out, was persuaded by his daughter not to defer it, and was induced by the entreaties of both, though against the scruples of his own civility, to leave Mr. Knightley for that purpose. Mr. Knightley, who had nothing of ceremony about him, was offering by his short, decided answers, an amusing contrast to the protracted apologies and civil hesitations of the other.

"Well, I believe, if you will excuse me, Mr. Knightley, if you will not consider me as doing a very rude thing, I shall take Emma's advice and go out for a quarter of an hour. As the sun is out, I believe I had better take my three turns while I can. I treat you without ceremony, Mr. Knightley. We invalids think we are privileged people."

"My dear sir, do not make a stranger of me."

"I leave an excellent substitute in my daughter. Emma will be happy to entertain you. And therefore I think I will beg your excuse and take my three turns – my winter walk."

"You cannot do better, sir."

"I would ask for the pleasure of your company, Mr. Knightley, but I am a very slow walker, and my pace would be tedious to you; and, besides, you have another long walk before you, to Donwell Abbey."

"Thank you, sir, thank you; I am going this moment myself; and I think the sooner you go the better. I will fetch your greatcoat and open the garden door for you.”

Mr. Woodhouse at last was off; but Mr. Knightley, instead of being immediately off likewise, sat down again, seemingly inclined for more chat. He began speaking of Harriet, and speaking of her with more voluntary praise than Emma had ever heard before.

“I cannot rate her beauty as you do,” said he; “but she is a pretty little creature, and I am inclined to think very well of her disposition. Her character depends upon those she is with; but in good hands she will turn out a valuable woman.”

“I am glad you think so; and the good hands, I hope, may not be wanting.”

“Come,” said he, “you are anxious for a compliment, so I will tell you that you have improved her. You have cured her of her school-girl's giggle; she really does you credit.”

“Thank you. I should be mortified indeed if I did not believe I had been of some use; but it is not every body who will bestow praise where they may. *You* do not often overpower me with it."

"You are expecting her again, you say, this morning?"

"Almost every moment. She has been gone longer already than she intended."

"Something has happened to delay her; some visitors perhaps."

"Highbury gossips! – Tiresome wretches!"

"Harriet may not consider every body tiresome that you would."

Emma knew this was too true for contradiction, and therefore said nothing. He presently added, with a smile,

"I do not pretend to fix on times or places, but I must tell you that I have good reason to believe your little friend will soon hear of something to her advantage."

"Indeed! how so? of what sort?"

"A very serious sort, I assure you;" still smiling.

"Very serious! I can think of but one thing – Who is in love with her? Who makes you their confidant?"

Emma was more than half in hopes of Mr. Elton's having dropt a hint. Mr. Knightley was a sort of general friend and adviser, and she knew Mr. Elton looked up to him.

"I have reason to think," he replied, "that Harriet Smith will soon have an offer of marriage, and from a most unexceptionable quarter:– Robert Martin is the man. Her visit to Abbey-Mill, this summer, seems to have done his business. He is desperately in love and means to marry her."

"He is very obliging," said Emma; "but is he sure that Harriet means to marry him?"

"Well, well, means to make her an offer then. Will that do? He came to the Abbey two evenings ago, on purpose to consult me about it. He knows I have a thorough regard for him and all his family, and, I believe, considers me as one of his best friends. He came to ask me whether I thought it would be imprudent in him to settle so early; whether I thought her too young: in short, whether I approved his choice altogether; having some apprehension perhaps of her being considered (especially since *your* making so much of her) as in a line of society above him. I was very much pleased with all that he said. I never hear better sense from any one than Robert Martin. He always speaks to the purpose; open, straightforward, and very well judging. He told me every thing; his circumstances and plans, and what they all pro-posed doing in the event of his marriage. He is an excellent young man, both as son and brother. I had no hesitation in advising him to marry. He proved to me that he could afford it; and that being the case, I was convinced he could not do better. I praised the fair lady too, and altogether sent him away very happy. If he had never es-teemed my opinion before, he would have thought highly of me then; and, I dare say, left the house thinking me the best friend and counsellor man ever had. This happened the night before last. Now, as we may fairly suppose, he would not allow much time to pass before he spoke to the lady, and as he does not appear to have spoken yester-day, it is not unlikely that he should be at Mrs. Goddard's to-day; and she may be detained by a visitor, without thinking him at all a tiresome wretch."

"Pray, Mr. Knightley," said Emma, who had been smiling to herself through a great part of this speech, "how do you know that Mr. Martin did not speak yesterday?"

"Certainly," replied he, surprized, "I do not absolutely know it; but it may be inferred. Was not she the whole day with you?"

"Come," said she, "I will tell you something, in return for what you have told me. He did speak yesterday – that is, he wrote, and was refused."

This was obliged to be repeated before it could be believed; and Mr. Knightley actually looked red with surprize and displeasure, as he stood up, in tall indignation, and said,

"Then she is a greater simpleton than I ever believed her. What is the foolish girl about?"

"Oh! to be sure," cried Emma, "it is always incomprehensible to a man that a woman should ever refuse an offer of marriage. A man always imagines a woman to be ready for any body who asks her."

"Nonsense! a man does not imagine any such thing. But what is the meaning of this? Harriet Smith refuse Robert Martin? madness, if it is so; but I hope you are mistaken."

"I saw her answer! – nothing could be clearer."

"You saw her answer! – you wrote her answer too. Emma, this is your doing. You persuaded her to refuse him."

"And if I did, (which, however, I am far from allowing) I should not feel that I had done wrong. Mr. Martin is a very respectable young man, but I cannot admit him to be Harriet's equal; and am rather surprized indeed that he should have ventured to address her. By your account, he does seem to have had some scruples. It is a pity that they were ever got over."

"Not Harriet's equal!" exclaimed Mr. Knightley loudly and warmly; and with calmer asperity, added, a few moments afterwards, "No, he is not her equal indeed, for he is as much her superior in sense as in situation. Emma, your infatuation about that girl blinds you. What are Harriet Smith's claims, either of birth, nature or education, to any connexion higher than Robert Martin? She is the natural daughter of nobody knows whom, with probably no settled provision at all, and certainly no respectable relations. She is known only as parlour-boarder at a common school. She is not a sensible girl, nor a girl of any information. She has been taught nothing useful, and is too young and too simple to have acquired any thing herself. At her age she can have no experience, and with her little wit, is not very likely ever to have any that can avail her. She is pretty, and she is good tempered, and that is all. My only scruple in advising the match was on his account, as being beneath his deserts, and a bad connexion for him. I felt that, as to fortune, in all probability he might do much better; and that as to a rational companion or useful helpmate, he could not do worse. But I could not reason so to a man in love, and was willing to trust to there being no harm in her, to her having that sort of disposition, which, in good hands, like his, might be easily led aright and turn out very well. The advantage of the match I felt to be all on her side; and had not the smallest doubt (nor have I now) that there would be a general cry-out upon her extreme good luck. Even *your* satisfaction I made sure of. It crossed my mind immediately that you would not regret your friend's leaving Highbury, for the sake of her being settled so well. I remember saying to myself, 'Even Emma, with all her partiality for Harriet, will think this a good match.'"

"I cannot help wondering at your knowing so little of Emma as to say any such thing. What! think a farmer, (and with all his sense and all his merit Mr. Martin is nothing more,) a good match for my intimate friend! Not regret her leaving Highbury for the sake of marrying a man whom I could never admit as an acquaintance of my own! I wonder you should think it possible for me to have such feelings. I assure you mine are very different. I must think your statement by no means fair. You are not just to Harriet's claims. They would be estimated very differently by others as well as myself; Mr. Martin may be the richest of the two, but he is undoubtedly her inferior as to rank in society. – The sphere in which she moves is much above his. – It would be a degradation."

"A degradation to illegitimacy and ignorance, to be married to a respectable, intelligent gentleman-farmer!"

"As to the circumstances of her birth, though in a legal sense she may be called Nobody, it will not hold in common sense. She is not to pay for the offence of others, by being held below the level of those with whom she is brought up. – There can scarcely be a doubt that her father is a gentleman – and a gentleman of fortune. – Her allowance is very liberal; nothing has ever been grudged for her improvement or comfort. – That she is a gentleman's daughter, is indubitable to me; that she associates with gentlemen's daughters, no one, I apprehend, will deny. – She is superior to Mr. Robert Martin."

"Whoever might be her parents," said Mr. Knightley, "whoever may have had the charge of her, it does not appear to have been any part of their plan to introduce her into what you would call good society. After receiving a very indifferent education she is left in Mrs. Goddard's hands to shift as she can; – to move, in short, in Mrs. Goddard's line, to have Mrs.

Goddard's acquaintance. Her friends evidently thought this good enough for her; and it *was* good enough. She desired nothing better herself. Till you chose to turn her into a friend, her mind had no distaste for her own set, nor any ambition beyond it. She was as happy as possible with the Martins in the summer. She had no sense of superiority then. If she has it now, you have given it. You have been no friend to Harriet Smith, Emma. Robert Martin would never have proceeded so far, if he had not felt persuaded of her not being disinclined to him. I know him well. He has too much real feeling to address any woman on the haphazard of selfish passion. And as to conceit, he is the farthest from it of any man I know. Depend upon it he had encouragement."

It was most convenient to Emma not to make a direct reply to this assertion; she chose rather to take up her own line of the subject again.

"You are a very warm friend to Mr. Martin; but, as I said before, are unjust to Harriet. Harriet's claims to marry well are not so contemptible as you represent them. She is not a clever girl, but she has better sense than you are aware of, and does not deserve to have her understanding spoken of so slightingly. Waiving that point, however, and supposing her to be, as you describe her, only pretty and good-natured, let me tell you, that in the degree she possesses them, they are not trivial recommendations to the world in general, for she is, in fact, a beautiful girl, and must be thought so by ninety-nine people out of an hundred; and till it appears that men are much more philosophic on the subject of beauty than they are generally supposed; till they do fall in love with well-informed minds instead of handsome faces, a girl, with such loveliness as Harriet, has a certainty of being admired and sought after, of having the power of chusing from among many, consequently a claim to be nice. Her good-nature, too, is not so very slight a claim, comprehending, as it does, real, thorough sweetness of temper and manner, a very humble opinion of herself, and a great readiness to be pleased with other people. I am very much mistaken if your sex in general would not think such beauty, and such temper, the highest claims a woman could possess."

"Upon my word, Emma, to hear you abusing the reason you have, is almost enough to make me think so too. Better be without sense, than misapply it as you do."

"To be sure!" cried she playfully. "I know *that* is the feeling of you all. I know that such a girl as Harriet is exactly what every man delights in – what at once bewitches his senses and satisfies his judgment. Oh! Harriet may pick and chuse. Were you, yourself, ever to marry, she is the very woman for you. And is she, at seventeen, just entering into life, just beginning to be known, to be wondered at because she does not accept the first offer she receives? No – pray let her have time to look about her."

"I have always thought it a very foolish intimacy," said Mr. Knightley presently, "though I have kept my thoughts to myself; but I now perceive that it will be a very unfortunate one for Harriet. You will puff her up with such ideas of her own beauty, and of what she has a claim to, that, in a little while, nobody within her reach will be good enough for her. Vanity working on a weak head, produces every sort of mischief. Nothing so easy as for a young lady to raise her expectations too high. Miss

Harriet Smith may not find offers of marriage flow in so fast, though she is a very pretty girl. Men of sense, whatever you may chuse to say, do not want silly wives. Men of family would not be very fond of connecting themselves with a girl of such obscurity – and most prudent men would be afraid of the inconvenience and disgrace they might be involved in, when the mystery of her parentage came to be revealed. Let her marry Robert Martin, and she is safe, respectable, and happy for ever; but if you encourage her to expect to marry greatly, and teach her to be satisfied with nothing less than a man of consequence and large fortune, she may be a parlour-boarder at Mrs. Goddard's all the rest of her life – or, at least, (for Harriet Smith is a girl who will marry somebody or other,) till she grow desperate, and is glad to catch at the old writing-master's son."

"We think so very differently on this point, Mr. Knightley, that there can be no use in canvassing it. We shall only be making each other more angry. But as to my *letting* her marry Robert Martin, it is impossible; she has refused him, and so decidedly, I think, as must prevent any second application. She must abide by the evil of having refused him, whatever it may be; and as to the refusal itself, I will not pretend to say that I might not influence her a little; but I assure you there was very little for me or for any body to do. His appearance is so much against him, and his manner so bad, that if she ever were disposed to favour him, she is not now. I can imagine, that before she had seen any body superior, she might tolerate him. He was the brother of her friends, and he took pains to please her; and altogether, having seen nobody better (that must have been his great assistant) she might not, while she was at Abbey-Mill, find him disagreeable. But the case is altered now. She knows now what gentlemen are; and nothing but a gentleman in education and manner has any chance with Harriet."

"Nonsense, errant nonsense, as ever was talked!" cried Mr. Knightley. – "Robert Martin's manners have sense, sincerity, and good-humour to recommend them; and his mind has more true gentility than Harriet Smith could understand."

Emma made no answer, and tried to look cheerfully unconcerned, but was really feeling uncomfortable and wanting him very much to be gone. She did not repent what she had done; she still thought herself a better judge of such a point of female right and refinement than he could be; but yet she had a sort of habitual respect for his judgment in general, which made her dislike having it so loudly against her; and to have him sitting just opposite to her in angry state, was very disagreeable. Some minutes passed in this unpleasant silence, with only one attempt on Emma's side to talk of the weather, but he made no answer. He was thinking. The result of his thoughts appeared at last in these words.

"Robert Martin has no great loss – if he can but think so; and I hope it will not be long before he does. Your views for Harriet are best known to yourself; but as you make no secret of your love of match-making, it is fair to suppose that views, and plans, and projects you have; – and as a friend I shall just hint to you that if Elton is the man, I think it will be all labour in vain."

Emma laughed and disclaimed. He continued,

"Depend upon it, Elton will not do. Elton is a very good sort of man, and a very respectable vicar of Highbury, but not at all likely to make an imprudent match. He knows the value of a good income as well as any body. Elton may talk sentimentally, but he will act rationally. He is as well acquainted with his own claims, as you can be with Harriet's. He knows that he is a very handsome young man, and a great favourite wherever he goes; and from his general way of talking in unreserved moments, when there are only men present, I am convinced that he does not mean to throw himself away. I have heard him speak with great animation of a large family of young ladies that his sisters are intimate with, who have all twenty thousand pounds apiece."

"I am very much obliged to you," said Emma, laughing again. "If I had set my heart on Mr. Elton's marrying Harriet, it would have been very kind to open my eyes; but at present I only want to keep Harriet to myself. I have done with match-making indeed. I could never hope to equal my own doings at Randalls. I shall leave off while I am well."

"Good morning to you," – said he, rising and walking off abruptly. He was very much vexed. He felt the disappointment of the young man, and was mortified to have been the means of promoting it, by the sanction he had given; and the part which he was persuaded Emma had taken in the affair, was provoking him exceedingly.

Emma remained in a state of vexation too; but there was more indistinctness in the causes of her's, than in his. She did not always feel so absolutely satisfied with herself, so entirely convinced that her opinions were right and her adversary's wrong, as Mr. Knightley. He walked off in more complete self-approbation than he left for her. She was not so materially cast down, however, but that a little time and the return of Harriet were very adequate restoratives. Harriet's staying away so long was beginning to make her uneasy. The possibility of the young man's coming to Mrs. Goddard's that morning, and meeting with Harriet and pleading his own cause, gave alarming ideas. The dread of such a failure after all became the prominent uneasiness; and when Harriet appeared, and in very good spirits, and without having any such reason to give for her long absence, she felt a satisfaction which settled her with her own mind, and convinced her, that let Mr. Knightley think or say what he would, she had done nothing which woman's friendship and woman's feelings would not justify.

He had frightened her a little about Mr. Elton; but when she considered that Mr. Knightley could not have observed him as she had done, neither with the interest, nor (she must be allowed to tell herself, in spite of Mr. Knightley's pretensions) with the skill of such an observer on such a question as herself, that he had spoken it hastily and in anger, she was able to believe, that he had rather said what he wished resentfully to be true, than what he knew any thing about. He certainly might have heard Mr. Elton speak with more unreserve than she had ever done, and Mr. Elton might not be of an imprudent, inconsiderate disposition as to money matters; he might naturally be rather attentive than otherwise to them; but then, Mr. Knightley did not make due allowance for the influence of a strong passion at war with all interested motives. Mr. Knightley saw no such passion, and of course thought nothing of its effects; but she saw too much of it to feel a doubt of its overcoming any hesitations that a reasonable prudence might originally suggest; and more than a reasonable, becoming degree of prudence, she was very sure did not belong to Mr. Elton.

Harriet's cheerful look and manner established hers: she came back, not to think of Mr. Martin, but to talk of Mr. Elton. Miss Nash had been telling her something, which she repeated immediately with great delight. Mr. Perry had been to Mrs. Goddard's to attend a sick child, and Miss Nash had seen him, and he had told Miss Nash, that as he was coming back yesterday from Clayton Park, he had met Mr. Elton, and found to his great surprize, that Mr. Elton was actually on his road to London, and not meaning to return till the morrow, though it was the whist-club night, which he had been never known to miss before; and Mr. Perry had remonstrated with him about it, and told him how shabby it was in him, their best player, to absent himself, and tried very much to persuade him to put off his journey only one day; but it would not do; Mr. Elton had been determined to go on, and had said in a *very particular* way indeed, that he was going on business which he would not put off for any inducement in the world; and something about a very enviable commission, and being the bearer of something exceedingly precious. Mr. Perry could not quite understand him, but he was very sure there must be a *lady* in the case, and he told him so; and Mr. Elton only looked very conscious and smiling, and rode off in great spirits. Miss Nash had told her all this, and had talked a great deal more about Mr. Elton; and said, looking so very significantly at her, "that she did not pretend to understand what his business might be, but she only knew that any woman whom Mr. Elton could prefer, she should think the luckiest woman in the world; for, beyond a doubt, Mr. Elton had not his equal for beauty or agreeableness."

CHAPTER IX

Mr. Knightley might quarrel with her, but Emma could not quarrel with herself. He was so much displeased, that it was longer than usual before he came to Hartfield again; and when they did meet, his grave looks shewed that she was not forgiven. She was sorry, but could not repent. On the contrary, her plans and proceedings were more and more justified and endeared to her by the general appearances of the next few days.

The Picture, elegantly framed, came safely to hand soon after Mr. Elton's return, and being hung over the mantelpiece of the common sitting-room, he got up to look at it, and sighed out his half sentences of admiration just as he ought; and as for Harriet's feelings, they were visibly forming themselves into as strong and steady an attachment as her youth and sort of mind admitted. Emma was soon perfectly satisfied of Mr. Martin's being no otherwise remembered, than as he furnished a contrast with Mr. Elton, of the utmost advantage to the latter.

Her views of improving her little friend's mind, by a great deal of useful reading and conversation, had never yet led to more than a few first chapters, and the intention of going on to-morrow. It was much easier to chat than to study; much pleasanter to let her imagination range and work at Harriet's fortune, than to be labouring to enlarge her comprehension or exercise it on sober facts; and the only literary pursuit which engaged Harriet at present, the only mental provision she was making for the evening of life, was the collecting and transcribing all the riddles of every sort that she could meet with, into a thin quarto of hot-pressed paper, made up by her friend, and ornamented with ciphers and trophies.

In this age of literature, such collections on a very grand scale are not uncommon. Miss Nash, head-teacher at Mrs. Goddard's, had written out at least three hundred; and Harriet, who had taken the first hint of it from her, hoped, with Miss Woodhouse's help, to get a great many more. Emma assisted with her invention, memory and taste; and as Harriet wrote a very pretty hand, it was likely to be an arrangement of the first order, in form as well as quantity.

Mr. Woodhouse was almost as much interested in the business as the girls, and tried very often to recollect something worth their putting in. "So many clever riddles as there used to be when he was young – he wondered he could not remember them! but he hoped he should in time." And it always ended in "Kitty, a fair but frozen maid."

His good friend Perry, too, whom he had spoken to on the subject, did not at present recollect any thing of the riddle kind; but he had desired Perry to be upon the watch, and as he went about so much, something, he thought, might come from that quarter.

It was by no means his daughter's wish that the intellects of Highbury in general should be put under requisition. Mr. Elton was the only one whose assistance she asked. He was invited to contribute any really good enigmas, charades, or conundrums that he might recollect; and she had the pleasure of seeing him most intently at work with his recollections; and at the same time, as she could perceive, most earnestly careful that nothing ungallant, nothing that did not breathe a compliment to the sex should pass his lips. They owed to him their two or three politest puzzles; and the joy and exultation with which at last he recalled, and rather sentimentally recited, that well-known charade,

My first doth affliction denote,
Which my second is destin'd to feel
And my whole is the best antidote
That affliction to soften and heal.–

made her quite sorry to acknowledge that they had transcribed it some pages ago already.

"Why will not you write one yourself for us, Mr. Elton?" said she; "that is the only security for its freshness; and nothing could be easier to you."

"Oh no! he had never written, hardly ever, any thing of the kind in his life. The stupidest fellow! He was afraid not even Miss Woodhouse" – he stopt a moment – "or Miss Smith could inspire him."

The very next day however produced some proof of inspiration. He called for a few moments, just to leave a piece of paper on the table containing, as he said, a charade, which a friend of his had addressed to a young lady, the object of his admiration, but which, from his manner, Emma was immediately convinced must be his own.

"I do not offer it for Miss Smith's collection," said he. "Being my friend's, I have no right to expose it in any degree to the public eye, but perhaps you may not dislike looking at it."

The speech was more to Emma than to Harriet, which Emma could understand. There was deep consciousness about him, and he found it easier to meet her eye than her friend's. He was gone the next moment:– after another moment's pause,

"Take it," said Emma, smiling, and pushing the paper towards Harriet – "it is for you. Take your own."

But Harriet was in a tremor, and could not touch it; and Emma, never loth to be first, was obliged to examine it herself.

To Miss–

CHARADE

My first displays the wealth and pomp of kings,

Lords of the earth! their luxury and ease.
Another view of man, my second brings,
Behold him there, the monarch of the seas!

But ah! united, what reverse we have!
Man's boasted power and freedom, all are flown;
Lord of the earth and sea, he bends a slave,
And woman, lovely woman, reigns alone.

Thy ready wit the word will soon supply,
May its approval beam in that soft eye!

She cast her eye over it, pondered, caught the meaning, read it through again to be quite certain, and quite mistress of the lines, and then passing it to Harriet, sat happily smiling, and saying to herself, while Harriet was puzzling over the paper in all the confusion of hope and dulness, "Very well, Mr. Elton, very well indeed. I have read worse charades. *Courtship* a very good hint. I give you credit for it. This is feeling your way. This is saying very plainly – 'Pray, Miss Smith, give me leave to pay my addresses to you. Approve my charade and my intentions in the same glance.'

May its approval beam in that soft eye!

Harriet exactly. Soft is the very word for her eye – of all epithets, the justest that could be given.

Thy ready wit the word will soon supply.

Humph – Harriet's ready wit! All the better. A man must be very much in love, indeed, to describe her so. Ah! Mr. Knightley, I wish you had the benefit of this; I think this would convince you. For once in your life you would be obliged to own yourself mistaken. An excellent charade indeed! and very much to the purpose. Things must come to a crisis soon now."

She was obliged to break off from these very pleasant observations, which were otherwise of a sort to run into great length, by the eagerness of Harriet's wondering questions.

"What can it be, Miss Woodhouse? – what can it be? I have not an idea – I cannot guess it in the least. What can it possibly be? Do try to find it out, Miss Woodhouse. Do help me. I never saw any thing so hard. Is it kingdom? I wonder who the friend was – and who could be the young lady. Do you think it is a good one? Can it be woman?

And woman, lovely woman, reigns alone.

Can it be Neptune?

Behold him there, the monarch of the seas!

Or a trident? or a mermaid? or a shark? Oh, no! shark is only one syllable. It must be very clever, or he would not have brought it. Oh! Miss Woodhouse, do you think we shall ever find it out?"

"Mermaids and sharks! Nonsense! My dear Harriet, what are you thinking of? Where would be the use of his bringing us a charade made by a friend upon a mermaid or a shark? Give me the paper and listen.

For Miss –, read Miss Smith.

My first displays the wealth and pomp of kings,
    Lords of the earth! their luxury and ease.

That is *court*.

Another view of man, my second brings;
Behold him there, the monarch of the seas!

That is *ship*; – plain as it can be. – Now for the cream.

But ah! united, (courtship, you know,) what
reverse we have!
Man's boasted power and freedom, all are flown.
Lord of the earth and sea, he bends a slave,
And woman, lovely woman, reigns alone.

A very proper compliment! – and then follows the application, which I think, my dear Harriet, you cannot find much difficulty in comprehending. Read it in comfort to yourself. There can be no doubt of its being written for you and to you."

Harriet could not long resist so delightful a persuasion. She read the concluding lines, and was all flutter and happiness. She could not speak. But she was not wanted to speak. It was enough for her to feel. Emma spoke for her.

"There is so pointed, and so particular a meaning in this compliment," said she, "that I cannot have a doubt as to Mr. Elton's intentions. You are his object – and you will soon receive the completest proof of it. I thought it must be so. I thought I could not be so deceived; but now, it is clear; the state of his mind is as clear and decided, as my wishes on the subject have been ever since I knew you. Yes, Harriet, just so long have I been wanting the very circumstance to happen what has happened. I could never tell whether an attachment between you and Mr. Elton were most desirable or most natural. Its probability and its eligibility have really so equalled each other! I am very happy. I congratulate you, my dear Harriet, with all my heart. This is an attachment which a woman may well feel pride in creating. This is a connexion which offers nothing but good. It will give you every thing that you want – consideration, independence, a proper home – it will fix you in the centre of all your real friends, close to Hartfield and to me, and confirm our intimacy for ever. This, Harriet, is an alliance which can never raise a blush in either of us."

"Dear Miss Woodhouse!" – and "Dear Miss Woodhouse," was all that Harriet, with many tender embraces could articulate at first; but when they did arrive at something more like conversation, it was sufficiently clear to her friend that she saw, felt, anticipated, and remembered just as she ought. Mr. Elton's superiority had very ample acknowledgment.

"Whatever you say is always right," cried Harriet, "and therefore I suppose, and believe, and hope it must be so; but otherwise I could not have imagined it. It is so much beyond any thing I deserve. Mr. Elton, who might marry any body! There cannot be two opinions about *him*. He is so very superior. Only think of those sweet verses – 'To Miss –.' Dear me, how clever! – Could it really be meant for me?"

"I cannot make a question, or listen to a question about that. It is a certainty. Receive it on my judgment. It is a sort of prologue to the play, a motto to the chapter; and will be soon followed by matter-of-fact prose."

"It is a sort of thing which nobody could have expected. I am sure, a month ago, I had no more idea myself! – The strangest things do take place!"

"When Miss Smiths and Mr. Eltons get acquainted – they do indeed – and really it is strange; it is out of the common course that what is so evidently, so palpably desirable – what courts the pre-arrangement of other people, should so immediately shape itself into the proper form. You and Mr. Elton are by situation called together; you belong to one another by every circumstance of your respective homes. Your marrying will be equal to the match at Randalls. There does seem to be a something in the air of Hartfield which gives love exactly the right direction, and sends it into the very channel where it ought to flow.

The course of true love never did run smooth—

A Hartfield edition of Shakespeare would have a long note on that passage."

"That Mr. Elton should really be in love with me, – me, of all people, who did not know him, to speak to him, at Michaelmas! And he, the very handsomest man that ever was, and a man that every body looks up to, quite like Mr. Knightley! His company so sought after, that every body says he need not eat a single meal by himself if he does not chuse it; that he has more invitations than there are days in the week. And so excellent in the Church! Miss Nash has put down all the texts he has ever preached from since he came to Highbury. Dear me! When I look back to the first time I saw him! How little did I think! – The two Abbots and I ran into the front room and peeped through the blind when we heard he was going by, and Miss Nash came and scolded us away, and staid to look through herself; however, she called me back presently, and let me look too, which was very good-natured. And how beautiful we thought he looked! He was arm-in-arm with Mr. Cole."

"This is an alliance which, whoever – whatever your friends may be, must be agreeable to them, provided at least they have common sense; and we are not to be addressing our conduct to fools. If they are anxious to see you *happily* married, here is a man whose amiable character gives every assurance of it; – if they wish to have you settled in the same country and circle which they have chosen to place you in, here it will be accomplished; and if their only object is that you should, in the common phrase, be *well* married, here is the comfortable fortune, the respectable establishment, the rise in the world which must satisfy them."

"Yes, very true. How nicely you talk; I love to hear you. You understand every thing. You and Mr. Elton are one as clever as the other. This charade! – If I had studied a twelvemonth, I could never have made any thing like it."

"I thought he meant to try his skill, by his manner of declining it yesterday."

"I do think it is, without exception, the best charade I ever read."

"I never read one more to the purpose, certainly."

"It is as long again as almost all we have had before."

"I do not consider its length as particularly in its favour. Such things in general cannot be too short."

Harriet was too intent on the lines to hear. The most satisfactory comparisons were rising in her mind.

"It is one thing," said she, presently – her cheeks in a glow – "to have very good sense in a common way, like every body else, and if there is any thing to say, to sit down and write a letter, and say just what you must, in a short way; and another, to write verses and charades like this."

Emma could not have desired a more spirited rejection of Mr. Martin's prose.

"Such sweet lines!" continued Harriet – "these two last! – But how shall I ever be able to return the paper, or say I have found it out? – Oh! Miss Woodhouse, what can we do about that?"

"Leave it to me. You do nothing. He will be here this evening, I dare say, and then I will give it him back, and some nonsense or other will pass between us, and you shall not be committed. – Your soft eyes shall chuse their own time for beaming. Trust to me."

"Oh! Miss Woodhouse, what a pity that I must not write this beautiful charade into my book! I am sure I have not got one half so good."

"Leave out the two last lines, and there is no reason why you should not write it into your book."

"Oh! but those two lines are"–

– "The best of all. Granted; – for private enjoyment; and for private enjoyment keep them. They are not at all the less written you know, because you divide them. The couplet does not cease to be, nor does its meaning change. But take it away, and all *appropriation* ceases, and a very pretty gallant charade remains, fit for any collection. Depend upon it, he would not like to have his charade slighted, much better than his passion. A poet in love must be encouraged in both capacities, or neither. Give me the book, I will write it down, and then there can be no possible reflection on you."

Harriet submitted, though her mind could hardly separate the parts, so as to feel quite sure that her friend were not writing down a declaration of love. It seemed too precious an offering for any degree of publicity.

"I shall never let that book go out of my own hands," said she.

"Very well," replied Emma; "a most natural feeling; and the longer it lasts, the better I shall be pleased. But here is my father coming: you will not object to my reading the charade to him. It will be giving him so much pleasure! He loves any thing of the sort, and especially any thing that pays woman a compliment. He has the tenderest spirit of gallantry towards us all! – You must let me read it to him."

Harriet looked grave.

"My dear Harriet, you must not refine too much upon this charade. – You will betray your feelings improperly, if you are too conscious and too quick, and appear to affix more meaning, or even quite all the meaning which may be affixed to it. Do not be overpowered by such a little tribute of admiration. If he had been anxious for secrecy, he would not have left the paper while I was by; but he rather pushed it towards me than towards you. Do not let us be too solemn on the business. He has encouragement enough to proceed, without our sighing out our souls over this charade."

"Oh! no – I hope I shall not be ridiculous about it. Do as you please."

Mr. Woodhouse came in, and very soon led to the subject again, by the recurrence of his very frequent inquiry of "Well, my dears, how does your book go on? – Have you got any thing fresh?"

"Yes, papa; we have something to read you, something quite fresh. A piece of paper was found on the table this morning – (dropt, we suppose, by a fairy) – containing a very pretty charade, and we have just copied it in."

She read it to him, just as he liked to have any thing read, slowly and distinctly, and two or three times over, with explanations of every part as she proceeded – and he was very much pleased, and, as she had foreseen, especially struck with the complimentary conclusion.

"Aye, that's very just, indeed, that's very properly said. Very true. 'Woman, lovely woman.' It is such a pretty charade, my dear, that I can easily guess what fairy brought it. – Nobody could have written so prettily, but you, Emma."

Emma only nodded, and smiled. – After a little thinking, and a very tender sigh, he added,

"Ah! it is no difficulty to see who you take after! Your dear mother was so clever at all those things! If I had but her memory! But I can remember nothing; – not even that particular riddle which you have heard me mention; I can only recollect the first stanza; and there are several.

> Kitty, a fair but frozen maid,
> Kindled a flame I yet deplore,
> The hood-wink'd boy I called to aid,
> Though of his near approach afraid,
> So fatal to my suit before.

And that is all that I can recollect of it – but it is very clever all the way through. But I think, my dear, you said you had got it."

"Yes, papa, it is written out in our second page. We copied it from the Elegant Extracts. It was Garrick's, you know."

"Aye, very true. – I wish I could recollect more of it.

> Kitty, a fair but frozen maid.

The name makes me think of poor Isabella; for she was very near being christened Catherine after her grandmama. I hope we shall have her here next week. Have you thought, my dear, where you shall put her – and what room there will be for the children?”

“Oh! yes – she will have her own room, of course; the room she always has; – and there is the nursery for the children, – just as usual, you know. Why should there be any change?”

“I do not know, my dear – but it is so long since she was here! – not since last Easter, and then only for a few days. – Mr. John Knightley's being a lawyer is very inconvenient. – Poor Isabella! – she is sadly taken away from us all! – and how sorry she will be when she comes, not to see Miss Taylor here!”

“She will not be surprized, papa, at least.”

“I do not know, my dear. I am sure I was very much surprized when I first heard she was going to be married.”

“We must ask Mr. and Mrs. Weston to dine with us, while Isabella is here.”

“Yes, my dear, if there is time. – But – (in a very depressed tone) – she is coming for only one week. There will not be time for any thing."

"It is unfortunate that they cannot stay longer – but it seems a case of necessity. Mr. John Knightley must be in town again on the 28th, and we ought to be thankful, papa, that we are to have the whole of the time they can give to the country, that two or three days are not to be taken out for the Abbey. Mr. Knightley promises to give up his claim this Christmas – though you know it is longer since they were with him, than with us."

"It would be very hard, indeed, my dear, if poor Isabella were to be anywhere but at Hartfield."

Mr. Woodhouse could never allow for Mr. Knightley's claims on his brother, or any body's claims on Isabella, except his own. He sat musing a little while, and then said,

"But I do not see why poor Isabella should be obliged to go back so soon, though he does. I think, Emma, I shall try and persuade her to stay longer with us. She and the children might stay very well."

"Ah! papa – that is what you never have been able to accomplish, and I do not think you ever will. Isabella cannot bear to stay behind her husband."

This was too true for contradiction. Unwelcome as it was, Mr. Woodhouse could only give a submissive sigh; and as Emma saw his spirits affected by the idea of his daughter's attachment to her husband, she immediately led to such a branch of the subject as must raise them.

"Harriet must give us as much of her company as she can while my brother and sister are here. I am sure she will be pleased with the children. We are very proud of the children, are not we, papa? I wonder which she will think the handsomest, Henry or John?"

"Aye, I wonder which she will. Poor little dears, how glad they will be to come. They are very fond of being at Hartfield, Harriet."

"I dare say they are, sir. I am sure I do not know who is not."

"Henry is a fine boy, but John is very like his mama. Henry is the eldest, he was named after me, not after his father. John, the second, is named after his father. Some people are surprized, I believe, that the eldest was not, but Isabella would have him called Henry, which I thought very pretty of her. And he is a very clever boy, indeed. They are all remarkably clever; and they have so many pretty ways. They will come and stand by my chair, and say, 'Grandpapa, can you give me a bit of string?' and once Henry asked me for a knife, but I told him knives were only made for grandpapas. I think their father is too rough with them very often."

"He appears rough to you," said Emma, "because you are so very gentle yourself; but if you could compare him with other papas, you would not think him rough. He wishes his boys to be active and hardy; and if they misbehave, can give them a sharp word now and then; but he is an affectionate father – certainly Mr. John Knightley is an affectionate father. The children are all fond of him."

"And then their uncle comes in, and tosses them up to the ceiling in a very frightful way!"

"But they like it, papa; there is nothing they like so much. It is such enjoyment to them, that if their uncle did not lay down the rule of their taking turns, whichever began would never give way to the other."

"Well, I cannot understand it."

"That is the case with us all, papa. One half of the world cannot understand the pleasures of the other."

Later in the morning, and just as the girls were going to separate in preparation for the regular four o'clock dinner, the hero of this inimitable charade walked in again. Harriet turned away; but Emma could receive him with the usual smile, and her quick eye soon discerned in his the consciousness of having made a push – of having thrown a die; and she imagined he was come to see how it might turn up. His ostensible reason, however, was to ask whether Mr. Woodhouse's party could be made up in the evening without him, or whether he should be in the smallest degree necessary at Hartfield. If he were, every thing else must give way; but otherwise his friend Cole had been saying so much about his dining with him – had made such a point of it, that he had promised him conditionally to come.

Emma thanked him, but could not allow of his disappointing his friend on their account; her father was sure of his rubber. He re-urged – she re-declined; and he seemed then about to make his bow, when taking the paper from the table, she returned it–

"Oh! here is the charade you were so obliging as to leave with us; thank you for the sight of it. We admired it so much, that I have ventured to write it into Miss Smith's collection. Your friend will not take it amiss I hope. Of course I have not transcribed beyond the first eight lines."

Mr. Elton certainly did not very well know what to say. He looked rather doubtingly – rather confused; said something about "honour," – glanced at Emma and at Harriet, and then seeing the book open on the table, took it up, and examined it very attentively. With the view of passing off an awkward moment, Emma smilingly said,

"You must make my apologies to your friend; but so good a charade must not be confined to one or two. He may be sure of every woman's approbation while he writes with such gallantry."

"I have no hesitation in saying," replied Mr. Elton, though hesitating a good deal while he spoke; "I have no hesitation in saying – at least if my friend feels at all as *I* do – I have not the smallest doubt that, could he see his little effusion honoured as *I* see it, (looking at the book again, and replacing it on the table), he would consider it as the proudest moment of his life."

After this speech he was gone as soon as possible. Emma could not think it too soon; for with all his good and agreeable qualities, there was a sort of parade in his speeches which was very apt to incline her to laugh. She ran away to indulge the inclination, leaving the tender and the sublime of pleasure to Harriet's share.

CHAPTER X

Though now the middle of December, there had yet been no weather to prevent the young ladies from tolerably regular exercise; and on the morrow, Emma had a charitable visit to pay to a poor sick family, who lived a little way out of Highbury.

Their road to this detached cottage was down Vicarage Lane, a lane leading at right angles from the broad, though irregular, main street of the place; and, as may be inferred, containing the blessed abode of Mr. Elton. A few inferior dwellings were first to be passed, and then, about a quarter of a mile down the lane rose the Vicarage, an old and not very good house, almost as close to the road as it could be. It had no advantage of situation; but had been very much smartened up by the present proprietor; and, such as it was, there could be no possibility of the two friends passing it without a slackened pace and observing eyes. – Emma's remark was–

"There it is. There go you and your riddle-book one of these days." – Harriet's was–

"Oh, what a sweet house! – How very beautiful! – There are the yellow curtains that Miss Nash admires so much."

"I do not often walk this way *now*," said Emma, as they proceeded, "but *then* there will be an inducement, and I shall gradually get intimately acquainted with all the hedges, gates, pools and pollards of this part of Highbury."

Harriet, she found, had never in her life been within side the Vicarage, and her curiosity to see it was so extreme, that, considering exteriors and probabilities, Emma could only class it, as a proof of love, with Mr. Elton's seeing ready wit in her.

"I wish we could contrive it," said she; "but I cannot think of any tolerable pretence for going in; – no servant that I want to inquire about of his housekeeper – no message from my father."

She pondered, but could think of nothing. After a mutual silence of some minutes, Harriet thus began again–

"I do so wonder, Miss Woodhouse, that you should not be married, or going to be married! so charming as you are!"–

Emma laughed, and replied,

"My being charming, Harriet, is not quite enough to induce me to marry; I must find other people charming – one other person at least. And I am not only, not going to be married, at present, but have very little intention of ever marrying at all."

"Ah! – so you say; but I cannot believe it."

"I must see somebody very superior to any one I have seen yet, to be tempted; Mr. Elton, you know, (recollecting herself,) is out of the question: and I do – not – wish to see any such person. I would rather not be tempted. I cannot really change for the better. If I were to marry, I must expect to repent it."

"Dear me! – it is so odd to hear a woman talk so!"–

"I have none of the usual inducements of women to marry. Were I to fall in love, indeed, it would be a different thing! but I never have been in love; it is not my way, or my nature; and I do not think I ever shall. And, without love, I am sure I should be a fool to change such a situation as mine. Fortune I do not want; employment I do not want; consequence I do not want: I believe few married women are half as much mistress of their husband's house as I am of Hartfield; and never, never could I expect to be so truly beloved and important; so always first and always right in any man's eyes as I am in my father's."

"But then, to be an old maid at last, like Miss Bates!"

"That is as formidable an image as you could present, Harriet; and if I thought I should ever be like Miss Bates! so silly – so satisfied – so smiling – so prosing – so undistinguishing and unfastidious – and so apt to tell every thing relative to every body about me, I would marry to-morrow. But between us, I am convinced there never can be any likeness, except in being unmarried."

"But still, you will be an old maid! and that's so dreadful!"

"Never mind, Harriet, I shall not be a poor old maid; and it is poverty only which makes celibacy contemptible to a generous public! A single woman, with a very narrow income, must be a ridiculous, disagreeable old maid! the proper sport of boys and girls, but a single woman, of good fortune, is always respectable, and may be as sensible and pleasant as any body else. And the distinction is not quite so much against the candour and common sense of the world as appears at first; for a very narrow income has a tendency to contract the mind, and sour the temper. Those who can barely live, and who live perforce in a very small, and generally very inferior, society, may well be illiberal and cross. This does not apply, however, to Miss Bates; she is only too good natured and too silly to suit me; but, in general, she is very much to the taste of every body, though single and though poor. Poverty certainly has not contracted her mind: I really believe, if she had only a shilling in the world, she would be very likely to give away sixpence of it; and nobody is afraid of her: that is a great charm."

"Dear me! but what shall you do? how shall you employ yourself when you grow old?"

"If I know myself, Harriet, mine is an active, busy mind, with a great many independent resources; and I do not perceive why I should be more in want of employment at forty or fifty than one-and-twenty. Woman's usual occupations of hand and mind will be as open to me then as they are now; or with no important variation. If I draw less, I shall read more; if I give up music, I shall take to carpet-work. And as for objects of interest, objects for the affections, which is in truth the great point of inferiority, the want of which is really the great evil to be avoided in *not* marrying, I shall be very well off, with all the children of a sister I love so much, to care about. There will be enough of them, in all probability, to supply every sort of sensation that declining life can need. There will be enough for every hope and every fear; and though my attachment to none can equal that of a parent, it suits my ideas of comfort better than what is warmer and blinder. My nephews and nieces! – I shall often have a niece with me."

"Do you know Miss Bates's niece? That is, I know you must have seen her a hundred times – but are you acquainted?"

"Oh! yes; we are always forced to be acquainted whenever she comes to Highbury. By the bye, *that* is almost enough to put one out of conceit with a niece. Heaven forbid! at least, that I should ever bore people half so much about all the Knightleys together, as she does about Jane Fairfax. One is sick of the very name of Jane Fairfax. Every letter from her is read forty times over; her compliments to all friends go round and round again; and if she does but send her aunt the pattern of a stomacher, or knit a pair of garters for her grandmother, one hears of nothing else for a month. I wish Jane Fairfax very well; but she tires me to death."

They were now approaching the cottage, and all idle topics were superseded. Emma was very compassionate; and the distresses of the poor were as sure of relief from her personal attention and kindness, her counsel and her patience, as from her purse. She understood their ways, could allow for their ignorance and their temptations, had no romantic expectations of extraordinary virtue from those for whom education had done so little; entered into their troubles with ready sympathy, and always gave her assistance with as much intelligence as good-will. In the present instance, it was sickness and poverty together which she came to visit; and after remaining there as long as she could give comfort or advice, she quitted the cottage with such an impression of the scene as made her say to Harriet, as they walked away,

"These are the sights, Harriet, to do one good. How trifling they make every thing else appear! – I feel now as if I could think of nothing but these poor creatures all the rest of the day; and yet, who can say how soon it may all vanish from my mind?"

"Very true," said Harriet. "Poor creatures! one can think of nothing else."

"And really, I do not think the impression will soon be over," said Emma, as she crossed the low hedge, and tottering footstep which ended the narrow, slippery path through the cottage garden, and brought them into the lane again. "I do not think it will," stopping to look once more at all the outward wretchedness of the place, and recall the still greater within.

"Oh! dear, no," said her companion.

They walked on. The lane made a slight bend; and when that bend was passed, Mr. Elton was immediately in sight; and so near as to give Emma time only to say farther,

"Ah! Harriet, here comes a very sudden trial of our stability in good thoughts. Well, (smiling,) I hope it may be allowed that if compassion has produced exertion and relief to the sufferers, it has done all that is truly important. If we feel for the wretched, enough to do all we can for them, the rest is empty sympathy, only distressing to ourselves."

Harriet could just answer, "Oh! dear, yes," before the gentleman joined them. The wants and sufferings of the poor family, however, were the first subject on meeting. He had been going to call on them. His visit he would now defer; but they had a very interesting parley about what could be done and should be done. Mr. Elton then turned back to accompany them.

"To fall in with each other on such an errand as this," thought Emma; "to meet in a charitable scheme; this will bring a great increase of love on each side. I should not wonder if it were to bring on the declaration. It must, if I were not here. I wish I were anywhere else."

Anxious to separate herself from them as far as she could, she soon afterwards took possession of a narrow footpath, a little raised on one side of the lane, leaving them together in the main road. But she had not been there two minutes when she found that Harriet's habits of dependence and imitation were bringing her up too, and that, in short, they would both be soon after her. This would not do; she immediately stopped, under pretence of having some alteration to make in the lacing of her half-boot, and stooping down in complete occupation of the footpath, begged them to have the goodness to walk on, and she would follow in half a minute. They did as they were desired; and by the time she judged it reasonable to have done with her boot, she had the comfort of farther delay in her power, being overtaken by a child from the cottage, setting out, according to orders, with her pitcher, to fetch broth from Hartfield. To walk by the side of this child, and talk to and question her, was the most natural thing in the world, or would have been the most natural, had she been acting just then without design; and by this means the others were still able to keep ahead, without any obligation of waiting for her. She gained on them, however, involuntarily: the child's pace was quick, and theirs rather slow; and she was the more concerned at it, from their being evidently in a conversation which interested them. Mr. Elton was speaking with animation, Harriet listening with a very pleased attention; and Emma, having sent the child on, was beginning to think how she might draw back a little more, when they both looked around, and she was obliged to join them.

Mr. Elton was still talking, still engaged in some interesting detail; and Emma experienced some disappointment when she found that he was only giving his fair companion an account of the yesterday's party at his friend Cole's, and that she was come in herself for the Stilton cheese, the north Wiltshire, the butter, the cellery, the beet-root, and all the dessert.

"This would soon have led to something better, of course," was her consoling reflection; "any thing interests between those who love; and any thing will serve as introduction to what is near the heart. If I could but have kept longer away!"

They now walked on together quietly, till within view of the vicarage pales, when a sudden resolution, of at least getting Harriet into the house, made her again find something very much amiss about her boot, and fall behind to arrange it once more. She then broke the lace off short, and dexterously throwing it into a ditch, was presently obliged to entreat them to stop, and acknowledged her inability to put herself to rights so as to be able to walk home in tolerable comfort.

"Part of my lace is gone," said she, "and I do not know how I am to contrive. I really am a most troublesome companion to you both, but I hope I am not often so ill-equipped. Mr. Elton, I must beg leave to stop at your house, and ask your housekeeper for a bit of ribband or string, or any thing just to keep my boot on."

Mr. Elton looked all happiness at this proposition; and nothing could exceed his alertness and attention in conducting them into his house and endeavouring to make every thing appear to advantage. The room they were taken into was the one he chiefly occupied, and looking forwards; behind it was another with which it immediately communicated; the door between them was open, and Emma passed into it with the housekeeper to receive her assistance in the most comfortable manner. She was obliged to leave the door ajar as she found it; but she fully intended that Mr. Elton should close it. It was not closed, however, it still remained ajar; but by engaging the housekeeper in incessant conversation, she hoped to make it practicable for him to chuse his own subject in the adjoining room. For ten minutes she could hear nothing but herself. It could be protracted no longer. She was then obliged to be finished, and make her appearance.

The lovers were standing together at one of the windows. It had a most favourable aspect; and, for half a minute, Emma felt the glory of having schemed successfully. But it would not do; he had not come to the point. He had been most agreeable, most delightful; he had told Harriet that he had seen them go by, and had purposely followed them; other little gallantries and allusions had been dropt, but nothing serious.

"Cautious, very cautious," thought Emma; "he advances inch by inch, and will hazard nothing till he believes himself secure."

Still, however, though every thing had not been accomplished by her ingenious device, she could not but flatter herself that it had been the occasion of much present enjoyment to both, and must be leading them forward to the great event.

CHAPTER XI

Mr. Elton must now be left to himself. It was no longer in Emma's power to superintend his happiness or quicken his measures. The coming of her sister's family was so very near at hand, that first in anticipation, and then in reality, it became henceforth her prime object of interest; and during the ten days of their stay at Hartfield it was not to be expected – she did not herself expect – that any thing beyond occasional, fortuitous assistance could be afforded by her to the lovers. They might advance rapidly if they would, however; they must advance somehow or other whether they would or no. She hardly wished to have more leisure for them. There are people, who the more you do for them, the less they will do for themselves.

Mr. and Mrs. John Knightley, from having been longer than usual absent from Surry, were exciting of course rather more than the usual interest. Till this year, every long vacation since their marriage had been divided between Hartfield and Donwell Abbey; but all the holidays of this autumn had been given to sea-bathing for the children, and it was therefore many months since they had been seen in a regular way by their Surry connexions, or seen at all by Mr. Woodhouse, who could not be induced to get so far as London, even for poor Isabella's sake; and who consequently was now most nervously and apprehensively happy in fore-stalling this too short visit.

He thought much of the evils of the journey for her, and not a little of the fatigues of his own horses and coachman who were to bring some of the party the last half of the way; but his alarms were needless; the sixteen miles being happily accomplished, and Mr. and Mrs. John Knightley, their five children, and a competent number of nursery-maids, all reaching Hartfield in safety. The bustle and joy of such an arrival, the many to be talked to, welcomed, encouraged, and variously dispersed and disposed of, produced a noise and confusion which his nerves could not have borne under any other cause, nor have endured much longer even for this; but the ways of Hartfield and the feelings of her father were so respected by Mrs. John Knightley, that in spite of maternal solicitude for the immediate enjoyment of her little ones, and for their having instantly all the liberty and attendance, all the eating and drinking, and sleeping and playing, which they could possibly wish for, without the smallest delay, the children were never allowed to be long a disturbance to him, either in themselves or in any restless attendance on them.

Mrs. John Knightley was a pretty, elegant little woman, of gentle, quiet manners, and a disposition remarkably amiable and affectionate; wrapt up in her family; a devoted wife, a doating mother, and so tenderly attached to her father and sister that, but for these higher ties, a warmer love might have seemed impossible. She could never see a fault in any of them. She was not a woman of strong understanding or any quickness; and with this resemblance of her father, she inherited also much of his constitution; was delicate in her own health, over-careful of that of her children, had many fears and many nerves, and was as fond of her own Mr. Wingfield in town as her father could be of Mr. Perry. They were alike too, in a general benevolence of temper, and a strong habit of regard for every old acquaintance.

Mr. John Knightley was a tall, gentleman-like, and very clever man; rising in his profession, domestic, and respectable in his private character; but with reserved manners which prevented his being generally pleasing; and capable of being sometimes out of humour. He was not an ill-tempered man, not so often unreasonably cross as to deserve such a reproach; but his temper was not his great perfection; and, indeed, with such a worshipping wife, it was hardly possible that any natural defects in it should not be increased. The extreme sweetness of her temper must hurt his. He had all the clearness and quickness of mind which she wanted, and he could sometimes act an ungracious, or say a severe thing.

He was not a great favourite with his fair sister-in-law. Nothing wrong in him escaped her. She was quick in feeling the little injuries to Isabella, which Isabella never felt herself. Perhaps she might have passed over more had his manners been flattering to Isabella's sister, but they were only those of a calmly kind brother and friend, without praise and without blindness; but hardly any degree of personal compliment could have made her regardless of that greatest fault of all in her eyes which he sometimes fell into, the want of respectful forbearance towards her father. There he had not always the patience that could have been wished. Mr. Woodhouse's peculiarities and fidgetiness were sometimes provoking him to a rational remonstrance or sharp retort equally ill-bestowed. It did not often happen; for Mr. John Knightley had really a great regard for his father-in-law, and generally a strong sense of what was due to him; but it was too often for Emma's charity, especially as there was all the pain of apprehension frequently to be endured, though the offence came not. The beginning, however, of every visit displayed none but the properest feelings, and this being of necessity so short might be hoped to pass away in unsullied cordiality. They had not been long seated and composed when Mr. Woodhouse, with a melancholy shake of the head and a sigh, called his daughter's attention to the sad change at Hartfield since she had been there last.

"Ah, my dear," said he, "poor Miss Taylor – It is a grievous business."

"Oh yes, sir," cried she with ready sympathy, "how you must miss her! And dear Emma, too! – What a dreadful loss to you both! – I have been so grieved for you. – I could not imagine how you could possibly do without her. – It is a sad change indeed. – But I hope she is pretty well, sir."

"Pretty well, my dear – I hope – pretty well. – I do not know but that the place agrees with her tolerably."

Mr. John Knightley here asked Emma quietly whether there were any doubts of the air of Randalls.

"Oh! no – none in the least. I never saw Mrs. Weston better in my life – never looking so well. Papa is only speaking his own regret."

"Very much to the honour of both," was the handsome reply.

"And do you see her, sir, tolerably often?" asked Isabella in the plaintive tone which just suited her father.

Mr. Woodhouse hesitated. – "Not near so often, my dear, as I could wish."

"Oh! papa, we have missed seeing them but one entire day since they married. Either in the morning or evening of every day, excepting one, have we seen either Mr. Weston or Mrs. Weston, and generally both, either at Randalls or here –

and as you may suppose, Isabella, most frequently here. They are very, very kind in their visits. Mr. Weston is really as kind as herself. Papa, if you speak in that melancholy way, you will be giving Isabella a false idea of us all. Every body must be aware that Miss Taylor must be missed, but every body ought also to be assured that Mr. and Mrs. Weston do really prevent our missing her by any means to the extent we ourselves anticipated – which is the exact truth."

"Just as it should be," said Mr. John Knightley, "and just as I hoped it was from your letters. Her wish of shewing you attention could not be doubted, and his being a disengaged and social man makes it all easy. I have been always telling you, my love, that I had no idea of the change being so very material to Hartfield as you apprehended; and now you have Emma's account, I hope you will be satisfied."

"Why, to be sure," said Mr. Woodhouse – "yes, certainly – I cannot deny that Mrs. Weston, poor Mrs. Weston, does come and see us pretty often – but then – she is always obliged to go away again."

"It would be very hard upon Mr. Weston if she did not, papa. – You quite forget poor Mr. Weston."

"I think, indeed," said John Knightley pleasantly, "that Mr. Weston has some little claim. You and I, Emma, will venture to take the part of the poor husband. I, being a husband, and you not being a wife, the claims of the man may very likely strike us with equal force. As for Isabella, she has been married long enough to see the convenience of putting all the Mr. Westons aside as much as she can."

"Me, my love," cried his wife, hearing and understanding only in part. – "Are you talking about me? – I am sure nobody ought to be, or can be, a greater advocate for matrimony than I am; and if it had not been for the misery of her leaving Hartfield, I should never have thought of Miss Taylor but as the most fortunate woman in the world; and as to slighting Mr. Weston, that excellent Mr. Weston, I think there is nothing he does not deserve. I believe he is one of the very best-tempered men that ever existed. Excepting yourself and your brother, I do not know his equal for temper. I shall never forget his flying Henry's kite for him that very windy day last Easter – and ever since his particular kindness last September twelvemonth in writing that note, at twelve o'clock at night, on purpose to assure me that there was no scarlet fever at Cobham, I have been convinced there could not be a more feeling heart nor a better man in existence. – If any body can deserve him, it must be Miss Taylor."

"Where is the young man?" said John Knightley. "Has he been here on this occasion – or has he not?"

"He has not been here yet," replied Emma. "There was a strong expectation of his coming soon after the marriage, but it ended in nothing; and I have not heard him mentioned lately."

"But you should tell them of the letter, my dear," said her father. "He wrote a letter to poor Mrs. Weston, to congratulate her, and a very proper, handsome letter it was. She shewed it to me. I thought it very well done of him indeed. Whether it was his own idea you know, one cannot tell. He is but young, and his uncle, perhaps–"

"My dear papa, he is three-and-twenty. You forget how time passes."

"Three-and-twenty! – is he, indeed? – Well, I could not have thought it – and he was but two years old when he lost his poor mother! Well, time does fly indeed! – and my memory is very bad. However, it was an exceeding good, pretty letter, and gave Mr. and Mrs. Weston a great deal of pleasure. I remember it was written from Weymouth, and dated Sept. 28th – and began, 'My dear Madam,' but I forget how it went on; and it was signed 'F.C. Weston Churchill.' – I remember that perfectly."

"How very pleasing and proper of him!" cried the good-hearted Mrs. John Knightley. "I have no doubt of his being a most amiable young man. But how sad it is that he should not live at home with his father! There is something so shocking in a child's being taken away from his parents and natural home! I never could comprehend how Mr. Weston could part with him. To give up one's child! I really never could think well of any body who proposed such a thing to any body else."

"Nobody ever did think well of the Churchills, I fancy," observed Mr. John Knightley coolly. "But you need not imagine Mr. Weston to have felt what you would feel in giving up Henry or John. Mr.

Weston is rather an easy, cheerful-tempered man, than a man of strong feelings; he takes things as he finds them, and makes enjoyment of them somehow or other, depending, I suspect, much more upon what is called society for his comforts, that is, upon the power of eating and drinking, and playing whist with his neighbours five times a week, than upon family affection, or any thing that home affords."

Emma could not like what bordered on a reflection on Mr. Weston, and had half a mind to take it up; but she struggled, and let it pass. She would keep the peace if possible; and there was something honourable and valuable in the strong domestic habits, the all-sufficiency of home to himself, whence resulted her brother's disposition to look down on the common rate of social intercourse, and those to whom it was important. – It had a high claim to forbearance.

CHAPTER XII

Mr. Knightley was to dine with them – rather against the inclination of Mr. Woodhouse, who did not like that any one should share with him in Isabella's first day. Emma's sense of right however had decided it; and besides the consideration of what was due to each brother, she had particular pleasure, from the circumstance of the late disagreement between Mr. Knightley and herself, in procuring him the proper invitation.

She hoped they might now become friends again. She thought it was time to make up. Making-up indeed would not do. She certainly had not been in the wrong, and *he* would never own that he had. Concession must be out of the question; but it was time to appear to forget that they had ever quarrelled; and she hoped it might rather assist the restoration of friendship, that when he came into the room she had one of the children with her – the youngest, a nice little girl about eight months old, who was now making her first visit to Hartfield, and very happy to be danced about in her aunt's arms. It did assist; for though he began with grave looks and short questions, he was soon led on to talk of them all in the usual way, and to take the child out of her arms with all the unceremoniousness of perfect amity. Emma felt they were friends again; and the conviction giving her at first great satisfaction, and then a little sauciness, she could not help saying, as he was admiring the baby,

"What a comfort it is, that we think alike about our nephews and nieces. As to men and women, our opinions are sometimes very different; but with regard to these children, I observe we never disagree."

"If you were as much guided by nature in your estimate of men and women, and as little under the power of fancy and whim in your dealings with them, as you are where these children are concerned, we might always think alike."

"To be sure – our discordancies must always arise from my being in the wrong."

"Yes," said he, smiling – "and reason good. I was sixteen years old when you were born."

"A material difference then," she replied – "and no doubt you were much my superior in judgment at that period of our lives; but does not the lapse of one-and-twenty years bring our understandings a good deal nearer?"

"Yes – a good deal *nearer*."

"But still, not near enough to give me a chance of being right, if we think differently."

"I have still the advantage of you by sixteen years' experience, and by not being a pretty young woman and a spoiled child. Come, my dear Emma, let us be friends, and say no more about it. Tell your aunt, little Emma, that she ought to set you a better example than to be renewing old grievances, and that if she were not wrong before, she is now."

"That's true," she cried – "very true. Little Emma, grow up a better woman than your aunt. Be infinitely cleverer and not half so conceited. Now, Mr. Knightley, a word or two more, and I have done. As far as good intentions went, we were *both* right, and I must say that no effects on my side of the argument have yet proved wrong. I only want to know that Mr. Martin is not very, very bitterly disappointed."

"A man cannot be more so," was his short, full answer.

"Ah! – Indeed I am very sorry. – Come, shake hands with me."

This had just taken place and with great cordiality, when John Knightley made his appearance, and "How d'ye do, George?" and "John, how are you?" succeeded in the true English style, burying under a calmness that seemed all but indifference, the real attachment which would have led either of them, if requisite, to do every thing for the good of the other.

The evening was quiet and conversable, as Mr. Woodhouse declined cards entirely for the sake of comfortable talk with his dear Isabella, and the little party made two natural divisions; on one side he and his daughter; on the other the two Mr. Knightleys; their subjects totally distinct, or very rarely mixing – and Emma only occasionally joining in one or the other.

The brothers talked of their own concerns and pursuits, but principally of those of the elder, whose temper was by much the most communicative, and who was always the greater talker. As a magistrate, he had generally some point of law to consult John about, or, at least, some curious anecdote to give; and as a farmer, as keeping in hand the home-farm at Donwell, he had to tell what every field was to bear next year, and to give all such local information as could not fail of being interesting to a brother whose home it had equally been the longest part of his life, and whose attachments were strong. The plan of a drain, the change of a fence, the felling of a tree, and the destination of every acre for wheat, turnips, or spring corn, was entered into with as much equality of interest by John, as his cooler manners rendered possible; and if his willing brother ever left him any thing to inquire about, his inquiries even approached a tone of eagerness.

While they were thus comfortably occupied, Mr. Woodhouse was enjoying a full flow of happy regrets and fearful affection with his daughter.

"My poor dear Isabella," said he, fondly taking her hand, and interrupting, for a few moments, her busy labours for some one of her five children – "How long it is, how terribly long since you were here! And how tired you must be after your journey! You must go to bed early, my dear – and I recommend a little gruel to you before you go. – You and I will have a nice basin of gruel together. My dear Emma, suppose we all have a little gruel."

Emma could not suppose any such thing, knowing as she did, that both the Mr. Knightleys were as unpersuadable on that article as herself; – and two basins only were ordered. After a little more discourse in praise of gruel, with some wondering at its not being taken every evening by every body, he proceeded to say, with an air of grave reflection,

"It was an awkward business, my dear, your spending the autumn at South End instead of coming here. I never had much opinion of the sea air."

"Mr. Wingfield most strenuously recommended it, sir – or we should not have gone. He recommended it for all the children, but particularly for the weakness in little Bella's throat, – both sea air and bathing."

"Ah! my dear, but Perry had many doubts about the sea doing her any good; and as to myself, I have been long perfectly convinced, though perhaps I never told you so before, that the sea is very rarely of use to any body. I am sure it almost killed me once."

"Come, come," cried Emma, feeling this to be an unsafe subject, "I must beg you not to talk of the sea. It makes me envious and miserable; – I who have never seen it! South End is prohibited, if you please. My dear Isabella, I have not heard you make one inquiry about Mr. Perry yet; and he never forgets you."

"Oh! good Mr. Perry – how is he, sir?"

"Why, pretty well; but not quite well. Poor Perry is bilious, and he has not time to take care of himself – he tells me he has not time to take care of himself – which is very sad – but he is always wanted all round the country. I suppose there is not a man in such practice anywhere. But then there is not so clever a man any where."

"And Mrs. Perry and the children, how are they? do the children grow? I have a great regard for

Mr. Perry. I hope he will be calling soon. He will be so pleased to see my little ones."

"I hope he will be here to-morrow, for I have a question or two to ask him about myself of some consequence. And, my dear, whenever he comes, you had better let him look at little Bella's throat."

"Oh! my dear sir, her throat is so much better that I have hardly any uneasiness about it. Either bathing has been of the greatest service to her, or else it is to be attributed to an excellent embrocation of Mr. Wingfield's, which we have been applying at times ever since August."

"It is not very likely, my dear, that bathing should have been of use to her – and if I had known you were wanting an embrocation, I would have spoken to–

"You seem to me to have forgotten Mrs. and Miss Bates," said Emma, "I have not heard one inquiry after them."

"Oh! the good Bateses – I am quite ashamed of myself – but you mention them in most of your letters. I hope they are quite well. Good old Mrs.

Bates – I will call upon her to-morrow, and take my children. – They are always so pleased to see my children. – And that excellent Miss Bates! – such thorough worthy people! – How are they, sir?"

"Why, pretty well, my dear, upon the whole. But poor Mrs. Bates had a bad cold about a month ago."

"How sorry I am! But colds were never so prevalent as they have been this autumn. Mr. Wingfield told me that he has never known them more general or heavy – except when it has been quite an influenza."

"That has been a good deal the case, my dear; but not to the degree you mention. Perry says that colds have been very general, but not so heavy as he has very often known them in November. Perry does not call it altogether a sickly season."

"No, I do not know that Mr. Wingfield considers it very sickly except–

"Ah! my poor dear child, the truth is, that in London it is always a sickly season. Nobody is healthy in London, nobody can be. It is a dreadful thing to have you forced to live there! so far off! – and the air so bad!"

"No, indeed we are not at all in a bad air. Our part of London is very superior to most others! – You must not confound us with London in general, my dear sir. The neighbourhood of Brunswick Square is very different from almost all the rest. We are so very airy! I should be unwilling, I own, to live in any other part of the town; – there is hardly any other that I could be satisfied to have my children in: but *we* are so remarkably airy! – Mr. Wingfield thinks the vicinity of Brunswick Square decidedly the most favourable as to air."

"Ah! my dear, it is not like Hartfield. You make the best of it – but after you have been a week at Hartfield, you are all of you different creatures; you do not look like the same. Now I cannot say, that I think you are any of you looking well at present."

"I am sorry to hear you say so, sir; but I assure you, excepting those little nervous head-aches and palpitations which I am never entirely free from anywhere, I am quite well myself; and if the children were rather pale before they went to bed, it was only because they were a little more tired than usual, from their journey and the happiness of coming. I hope you will think better of their looks to-morrow; for I assure you Mr. Wingfield told me, that he did not believe he had ever sent us off altogether, in such good case. I trust, at least, that you do not think Mr. Knightley looking ill," turning her eyes with affectionate anxiety towards her husband.

"Middling, my dear; I cannot compliment you. I think Mr. John Knightley very far from looking well."

"What is the matter, sir? – Did you speak to me?" cried Mr. John Knightley, hearing his own name.

"I am sorry to find, my love, that my father does not think you looking well – but I hope it is only from being a little fatigued. I could have wished, however, as you know, that you had seen Mr. Wingfield before you left home."

"My dear Isabella," – exclaimed he hastily – "pray do not concern yourself about my looks.

Be satisfied with doctoring and coddling yourself and the children, and let me look as I chuse."

"I did not thoroughly understand what you were telling your brother," cried Emma, "about your friend Mr. Graham's intending to have a bailiff from Scotland, to look after his new estate. What will it answer? Will not the old prejudice be too strong?"

And she talked in this way so long and successfully that, when forced to give her attention again to her father and sister, she had nothing worse to hear than Isabella's kind inquiry after Jane Fairfax; and Jane Fairfax, though no great favourite with her in general, she was at that moment very happy to assist in praising.

"That sweet, amiable Jane Fairfax!" said Mrs. John Knightley. – "It is so long since I have seen her, except now and then for a moment accidentally in town! What happiness it must be to her good old grandmother and excellent aunt, when she comes to visit them! I always regret excessively on dear Emma's account that she cannot be more at Highbury; but now their daughter is married, I suppose Colonel and Mrs. Campbell will not be able to part with her at all. She would be such a delightful companion for Emma."

Mr. Woodhouse agreed to it all, but added,

"Our little friend Harriet Smith, however, is just such another pretty kind of young person. You will like Harriet. Emma could not have a better companion than Harriet."

"I am most happy to hear it – but only Jane Fairfax one knows to be so very accomplished and superior! – and exactly Emma's age."

This topic was discussed very happily, and others succeeded of similar moment, and passed away with similar harmony; but the evening did not close without a little return of agitation. The gruel came and supplied a great deal to be said – much praise and many comments – undoubting decision of its wholesomeness for every constitution, and pretty severe Philippics upon the many houses where it was never met with tolerable; – but, unfortunately, among the failures which the daughter had to instance, the most recent, and therefore most prominent, was in her own cook at South End, a young woman hired for the time, who never had been able to understand what she meant by a basin of nice smooth gruel, thin, but not too thin. Often as she had wished for and ordered it, she had never been able to get any thing tolerable. Here was a dangerous opening.

"Ah!" said Mr. Woodhouse, shaking his head and fixing his eyes on her with tender concern. – The ejaculation in Emma's ear expressed, "Ah! there is no end of the sad consequences of your going to South End. It does not bear talking of." And for a little while she hoped he would not talk of it, and that a silent rumination might suffice to restore him to the relish of his own smooth gruel. After an interval of some minutes, however, he began with,

"I shall always be very sorry that you went to the sea this autumn, instead of coming here."

"But why should you be sorry, sir? – I assure you, it did the children a great deal of good."

"And, moreover, if you must go to the sea, it had better not have been to South End. South End is an unhealthy place. Perry was surprized to hear you had fixed upon South End."

"I know there is such an idea with many people, but indeed it is quite a mistake, sir. – We all had our health perfectly well there, never found the least inconvenience from the mud; and Mr. Wingfield says it is entirely a mistake to suppose the place unhealthy; and I am sure he may be depended on, for he thoroughly understands the nature of the air, and his own brother and family have been there repeatedly."

"You should have gone to Cromer, my dear, if you went anywhere. – Perry was a week at Cromer once, and he holds it to be the best of all the sea-bathing places. A fine open sea, he says, and very pure air. And, by what I understand, you might have had lodgings there quite away from the sea – a quarter of a mile off – very comfortable. You should have consulted Perry."

"But, my dear sir, the difference of the journey; – only consider how great it would have been. – An hundred miles, perhaps, instead of forty."

"Ah! my dear, as Perry says, where health is at stake, nothing else should be considered; and if one is to travel, there is not much to chuse between forty miles and an hundred. – Better not move at all, better stay in London altogether than travel forty miles to get into a worse air. This is just what Perry said. It seemed to him a very ill-judged measure."

Emma's attempts to stop her father had been vain; and when he had reached such a point as this, she could not wonder at her brother-in-law's breaking out.

"Mr. Perry," said he, in a voice of very strong displeasure, "would do as well to keep his opinion till it is asked for. Why does he make it any business of his, to wonder at what I do? – at my taking my family to one part of the coast or another? – I may be allowed, I hope, the use of my judgment as well as Mr. Perry. – I want his directions no more than his drugs." He paused – and growing cooler in a moment, added, with only sarcastic dryness, "If Mr. Perry can tell me how to convey a wife and five children a distance of an hundred and thirty miles with no greater expense or inconvenience than a distance of forty, I should be as willing to prefer Cromer to South End as he could him-self."

"True, true," cried Mr. Knightley, with most ready interposition – "very true. That's a consideration indeed. – But John, as to what I was telling you of my idea of moving the path to Langham, of turning it more to the right that it may not cut through the home meadows, I cannot conceive any difficulty. I should not attempt it, if it were to be the means of inconvenience to the Highbury people, but if you call to mind exactly the present line of the path.... The only way of proving it, however, will be to turn to our maps. I shall see you at the Abbey to-morrow morning I hope, and then we will look them over, and you shall give me your opinion."

Mr. Woodhouse was rather agitated by such harsh reflections on his friend Perry, to whom he had, in fact, though unconsciously, been attributing many of his own feelings and expressions; – but the soothing attentions of his daughters gradually removed the present evil, and the immediate alertness of one brother, and better recollections of the other, prevented any renewal of it.

CHAPTER XIII

There could hardly be a happier creature in the world than Mrs. John Knightley, in this short visit to Hartfield, going about every morning among her old acquaintance with her five children, and talking over what she had done every evening with her father and sister. She had nothing to wish otherwise, but that the days did not pass so swiftly. It was a delightful visit; – perfect, in being much too short.

In general their evenings were less engaged with friends than their mornings; but one complete dinner engagement, and out of the house too, there was no avoiding, though at Christmas. Mr. Weston would take no denial; they must all dine at Randalls one day; – even Mr. Woodhouse was persuaded to think it a possible thing in preference to a division of the party.

How they were all to be conveyed, he would have made a difficulty if he could, but as his son and daughter's carriage and horses were actually at Hartfield, he was not able to make more than a simple question on that head; it hardly amounted to a doubt; nor did it occupy Emma long to convince him that they might in one of the carriages find room for Harriet also.

Harriet, Mr. Elton, and Mr. Knightley, their own especial set, were the only persons invited to meet them; – the hours were to be early, as well as the numbers few; Mr. Woodhouse's habits and inclination being consulted in every thing.

The evening before this great event (for it was a very great event that Mr. Woodhouse should dine out, on the 24th of December) had been spent by Harriet at Hartfield, and she had gone home so much indisposed with a cold, that, but for her own earnest wish of being nursed by Mrs. Goddard, Emma could not have allowed her to leave the house. Emma called on her the next day, and found her doom already signed with regard to Randalls. She was very feverish and had a bad sore throat: Mrs. Goddard was full of care and affection, Mr. Perry was talked of, and Harriet herself was too ill and low to resist the authority which excluded her from this delightful engagement, though she could not speak of her loss without many tears.

Emma sat with her as long as she could, to attend her in Mrs. Goddard's unavoidable absences, and raise her spirits by representing how much Mr. Elton's would be depressed when he knew her state; and left her at last tolerably comfortable, in the sweet dependence of his having a most comfortless visit, and of their all missing her very much. She had not advanced many yards from Mrs. Goddard's door, when she was met by Mr. Elton himself, evidently coming towards it, and as they walked on slowly together in conversation about the invalid – of whom he, on the rumour of considerable illness, had been going to inquire, that he might carry some report of her to Hartfield – they were overtaken by Mr. John Knightley returning from the daily visit to Donwell, with his two eldest boys, whose healthy, glowing faces shewed all the benefit of a country run, and seemed to ensure a quick despatch of the roast mutton and rice pudding they were hastening home for. They joined company and proceeded together. Emma was just describing the nature of her friend's complaint; – "a throat very much inflamed, with a great deal of heat about her, a quick, low pulse, &c. and she was sorry to find from Mrs. Goddard that Harriet was liable to very bad sore-throats, and had often alarmed her with them." Mr. Elton looked all alarm on the occasion, as he exclaimed,

"A sore-throat! – I hope not infectious. I hope not of a putrid infectious sort. Has Perry seen her? Indeed you should take care of yourself as well as of your friend. Let me entreat you to run no risks. Why does not Perry see her?"

Emma, who was not really at all frightened herself, tranquillised this excess of apprehension by assurances of Mrs. Goddard's experience and care; but as there must still remain a degree of uneasiness which she could not wish to reason away, which she would rather feed and assist than not, she added soon afterwards – as if quite another subject,

"It is so cold, so very cold – and looks and feels so very much like snow, that if it were to any other place or with any other party, I should really try not to go out to-day – and dissuade my father from venturing; but as he has made up his mind, and does not seem to feel the cold himself, I do not like to interfere, as I know it would be so great a disappointment to Mr. and Mrs. Weston. But, upon my word, Mr. Elton, in your case, I should certainly excuse myself. You appear to me a little hoarse already, and when you consider what demand of voice and what fatigues to-morrow will bring, I think it would be no more than common prudence to stay at home and take care of yourself to-night."

Mr. Elton looked as if he did not very well know what answer to make; which was exactly the case; for though very much gratified by the kind care of such a fair lady, and not liking to resist any advice of her's, he had not really the least inclination to give up the visit; – but Emma, too eager and busy in her own previous conceptions and views to hear him impartially, or see him with clear vision, was very well satisfied with his muttering acknowledgment of its being "very cold, certainly very cold," and walked on, rejoicing in having extricated him from Randalls, and secured him the power of sending to inquire after Harriet every hour of the evening.

"You do quite right," said she; – "we will make your apologies to Mr. and Mrs. Weston."

But hardly had she so spoken, when she found her brother was civilly offering a seat in his carriage, if the weather were Mr. Elton's only objection, and Mr. Elton actually accepting the offer with much prompt satisfaction. It was a done thing; Mr. Elton was to go, and never had his broad handsome face expressed more pleasure than at this moment; never had his smile been stronger, nor his eyes more exulting than when he next looked at her.

"Well," said she to herself, "this is most strange! After I had got him off so well, to chuse to go into company, and leave Harriet ill behind! – Most strange indeed! – But there is, I believe, in many men, especially single men, such an inclination – such a passion for dining out – a dinner engagement is so high in the class of their pleasures, their employments, their dignities, almost their duties, that any thing gives way to it – and this must be the case with Mr. Elton; a most valuable, amiable, pleasing young man undoubtedly, and very much in love with Harriet; but still, he cannot refuse an invitation, he must dine out wherever he is asked. What a strange thing love is! he can see ready wit in Harriet, but will not dine alone for her."

Soon afterwards Mr. Elton quitted them, and she could not but do him the justice of feeling that there was a great deal of sentiment in his manner of naming Harriet at parting; in the tone of his voice while assuring her that he should call at Mrs. Goddard's for news of her fair friend, the last thing before he prepared for the happiness of meeting her again, when he hoped to be able to give a better report; and he sighed and smiled himself off in a way that left the balance of approbation much in his favour.

After a few minutes of entire silence between them, John Knightley began with—

"I never in my life saw a man more intent on being agreeable than Mr. Elton. It is downright labour to him where ladies are concerned. With men he can be rational and unaffected, but when he has ladies to please, every feature works."

"Mr. Elton's manners are not perfect," replied Emma; "but where there is a wish to please, one ought to overlook, and one does overlook a great deal. Where a man does his best with only moderate powers, he will have the advantage over negligent superiority. There is such perfect good-temper and good-will in Mr. Elton as one cannot but value."

"Yes," said Mr. John Knightley presently, with some slyness, "he seems to have a great deal of good-will towards you."

"Me!" she replied with a smile of astonishment, "are you imagining me to be Mr. Elton's object?"

"Such an imagination has crossed me, I own, Emma; and if it never occurred to you before, you may as well take it into consideration now."

"Mr. Elton in love with me! – What an idea!"

"I do not say it is so; but you will do well to consider whether it is so or not, and to regulate your behaviour accordingly. I think your manners to him encouraging. I speak as a friend, Emma. You had better look about you, and ascertain what you do, and what you mean to do."

"I thank you; but I assure you you are quite mistaken. Mr. Elton and I are very good friends, and nothing more;" and she walked on, amusing herself in the consideration of the blunders which often arise from a partial knowledge of circumstances, of the mistakes which people of high pretensions to judgment are for ever falling into;

and not very well pleased with her brother for imagining her blind and ignorant, and in want of counsel. He said no more.

Mr. Woodhouse had so completely made up his mind to the visit, that in spite of the increasing coldness, he seemed to have no idea of shrinking from it, and set forward at last most punctually with his eldest daughter in his own carriage, with less apparent consciousness of the weather than either of the others; too full of the wonder of his own going, and the pleasure it was to afford at Randalls to see that it was cold, and too well wrapt up to feel it. The cold, however, was severe; and by the time the second carriage was in motion, a few flakes of snow were finding their way down, and the sky had the appearance of being so over-charged as to want only a milder air to produce a very white world in a very short time.

Emma soon saw that her companion was not in the happiest humour. The preparing and the going abroad in such weather, with the sacrifice of his children after dinner, were evils, were disagree-ables at least, which Mr. John Knightley did not by any means like; he anticipated nothing in the visit that could be at all worth the purchase; and the whole of their drive to the vicarage was spent by him in expressing his discontent.

"A man," said he, "must have a very good opinion of himself when he asks people to leave their own fireside, and encounter such a day as this, for the sake of coming to see him. He must think himself a most agreeable fellow; I could not do such a thing. It is the greatest absurdity – Actually snowing at this moment! – The folly of not allowing people to be comfortable at home – and the folly of people's not staying comfortably at home when they can! If we were obliged to go out such an evening as this, by any call of duty or business, what a hardship we should deem it; – and here are we, probably with rather thinner clothing than usual, setting forward voluntarily, without excuse, in defiance of the voice of nature, which tells man, in every thing given to his view or his feelings, to stay at home himself, and keep all under shelter that he can; – here are we setting forward to spend five dull hours in another man's house, with nothing to say or to hear that was not said and heard yesterday, and may not be said and heard again to-morrow. Going in dismal weather, to return probably in worse; – four horses and four servants taken out for nothing but to convey five idle, shivering creatures into colder rooms and worse company than they might have had at home."

Emma did not find herself equal to give the pleased assent, which no doubt he was in the habit of receiving, to emulate the "Very true, my love," which must have been usually administered by his travelling companion; but she had resolution enough to refrain from making any answer at all. She could not be complying, she dreaded being quarrelsome; her heroism reached only to silence. She allowed him to talk, and arranged the glasses, and wrapped herself up, without opening her lips.

They arrived, the carriage turned, the step was let down, and Mr. Elton, spruce, black, and smiling, was with them instantly. Emma thought with pleasure of some change of subject. Mr. Elton was all obligation and cheerfulness; he was so very cheerful in his civilities indeed, that she began to think he must have received a different account of Harriet from what had reached her. She had sent while dressing, and the answer had been, "Much the same – not better."

"*My* report from Mrs. Goddard's," said she presently, "was not so pleasant as I had hoped – 'Not better' was *my* answer."

His face lengthened immediately; and his voice was the voice of sentiment as he answered.

"Oh! no – I am grieved to find – I was on the point of telling you that when I called at Mrs. Goddard's door, which I did the very last thing before I returned to dress, I was told that Miss Smith was not better, by no means better, rather worse. Very much grieved and concerned – I had flattered myself that she must be better after such a cordial as I knew had been given her in the morning."

Emma smiled and answered – "My visit was of use to the nervous part of her complaint, I hope; but not even I can charm away a sore throat; it is a most severe cold indeed. Mr. Perry has been with her, as you probably heard."

"Yes – I imagined – that is – I did not–"

"He has been used to her in these complaints, and I hope to-morrow morning will bring us both a more comfortable report. But it is impossible not to feel uneasiness. Such a sad loss to our party to-day!"

"Dreadful! – Exactly so, indeed. – She will be missed every moment."

This was very proper; the sigh which accompanied it was really estimable; but it should have lasted longer. Emma was rather in dismay when only half a minute afterwards he began to speak of other things, and in a voice of the greatest alacrity and enjoyment.

"What an excellent device," said he, "the use of a sheepskin for carriages. How very comfortable they make it; – impossible to feel cold with such precautions. The contrivances of modern days indeed have rendered a gentleman's carriage per-fectly complete. One is so fenced and guarded from the weather, that not a breath of air can find its way unpermitted. Weather becomes absolutely of no consequence. It is a very cold afternoon – but in this carriage we know nothing of the matter. – Ha! snows a little I see."

"Yes," said John Knightley, "and I think we shall have a good deal of it."

"Christmas weather," observed Mr. Elton. "Quite seasonable; and extremely fortunate we may think ourselves that it did not begin yesterday, and prevent this day's party, which it might very possibly have done, for Mr. Woodhouse would hardly have ventured had there been much snow on the ground; but now it is of no consequence. This is quite the season indeed for friendly meetings. At Christmas every body invites their friends about them, and people think little of even the worst weather. I was snowed up at a friend's house once for a week. Nothing could be pleasanter. I went for only one night, and could not get away till that very day se'nnight."

Mr. John Knightley looked as if he did not comprehend the pleasure, but said only, coolly,

"I cannot wish to be snowed up a week at Randalls."

At another time Emma might have been amused, but she was too much astonished now at Mr. Elton's spirits for other feelings. Harriet seemed quite forgotten in the expectation of a pleasant party.

"We are sure of excellent fires," continued he, "and every thing in the greatest comfort. Charming people, Mr. and Mrs. Weston; – Mrs. Weston indeed is much beyond praise, and he is exactly what one values, so hospitable, and so fond of society; – it will be a small party, but where small parties are select, they are perhaps the most agreeable of any. Mr. Weston's dining-room does not accommodate more than ten comfortably; and for my part, I would rather, under such circumstances, fall short by two than exceed by two. I think you will agree with me, (turning with a soft air to Emma,) I think I shall certainly have your approbation, though Mr. Knightley perhaps, from being used to the large parties of London, may not quite enter into our feelings."

"I know nothing of the large parties of London, sir – I never dine with any body."

"Indeed! (in a tone of wonder and pity,) I had no idea that the law had been so great a slavery. Well, sir, the time must come when you will be paid for all this, when you will have little labour and great enjoyment."

"My first enjoyment," replied John Knightley, as they passed through the sweep-gate, "will be to find myself safe at Hartfield again."

CHAPTER XIV

Some change of countenance was necessary for each gentleman as they walked into Mrs. Weston's drawing-room; – Mr. Elton must compose his joyous looks, and Mr. John Knightley disperse his ill-humour. Mr. Elton must smile less, and Mr. John Knightley more, to fit them for the place. – Emma only might be as nature prompted, and shew herself just as happy as she was. To her it was real enjoyment to be with the Westons. Mr. Weston was a great favourite, and there was not a creature in the world to whom she spoke with such unreserve, as to his wife; not any one, to whom she related with such conviction of being listened to and understood, of being always interesting and always intelligible, the little affairs, arrangements, perplexities, and pleasures of her father and herself. She could tell nothing of Hartfield, in which Mrs. Weston had not a lively concern; and half an hour's uninterrupted communication of all those little matters on which the daily happiness of private life depends, was one of the first gratifications of each.

This was a pleasure which perhaps the whole day's visit might not afford, which certainly did not belong to the present half-hour; but the very sight of Mrs. Weston, her smile, her touch, her voice was grateful to Emma, and she determined to think as little as possible of Mr. Elton's oddities, or of any thing else unpleasant, and enjoy all that was enjoyable to the utmost.

The misfortune of Harriet's cold had been pretty well gone through before her arrival. Mr. Woodhouse had been safely seated long enough to give the history of it, besides all the history of his own and Isabella's coming, and of Emma's being to follow, and had indeed just got to the end of his satisfaction that James should come and see his daughter, when the others appeared, and Mrs. Weston, who had been almost wholly engrossed by her attentions to him, was able to turn away and welcome her dear Emma.

Emma's project of forgetting Mr. Elton for a while made her rather sorry to find, when they had all taken their places, that he was close to her. The difficulty was great of driving his strange insensibility towards Harriet, from her mind, while he not only sat at her elbow, but was continually obtruding his happy countenance on her notice, and solicitously addressing her upon every occasion. Instead of forgetting him, his behaviour was such that she could not avoid the internal suggestion of "Can it really be as my brother imagined? can it be possible for this man to be beginning to transfer his affections from Harriet to me? – Absurd and insufferable!" – Yet he would be so anxious for her being perfectly warm, would be so interested about her father, and so delighted with Mrs. Weston; and at last would begin admiring her drawings with so much zeal and so little knowledge as seemed terribly like a would-be lover, and made it some effort with her to preserve her good manners. For her own sake she could not be rude; and for Harriet's, in the hope that all would yet turn out right, she was even positively civil; but it was an effort; especially as something was going on amongst the others, in the most overpowering period of Mr. Elton's nonsense, which she particularly wished to listen to. She heard enough to know that Mr. Weston was giving some information about his son; she heard the words "my son," and "Frank," and "my son," repeated several times over; and, from a few other half-syllables very much suspected that he was announcing an early visit from his son; but before she could quiet Mr. Elton, the subject was so completely past that any reviving question from her would have been awkward.

Now, it so happened that in spite of Emma's resolution of never marrying, there was something in the name, in the idea of Mr. Frank Churchill, which always interested her. She had frequently thought – especially since his father's marriage with Miss Taylor – that if she *were* to marry, he was the very person to suit her in age, character and condition. He seemed by this connexion between the families, quite to belong to her. She could not but suppose it to be a match that every body who knew them must think of. That Mr. and Mrs. Weston did think of it, she was very strongly persuaded; and though not meaning to be induced by him, or by any body else, to give up a situation which she believed more replete with good than any she could change it for, she had a great curiosity to see him, a decided intention of finding him pleasant, of being liked by him to a certain degree, and a sort of pleasure in the idea of their being coupled in their friends' imaginations.

With such sensations, Mr. Elton's civilities were dreadfully ill-timed; but she had the comfort of appearing very polite, while feeling very cross – and of thinking that the rest of the visit could not possibly pass without bringing forward the same information again, or the substance of it, from the open-hearted Mr. Weston. – So it proved; – for when happily released from Mr. Elton, and seated by Mr. Weston, at dinner, he made use of the very first interval in the cares of hospitality, the very first leisure from the saddle of mutton, to say to her,

"We want only two more to be just the right number. I should like to see two more here, – your pretty little friend, Miss Smith, and my son – and then I should say we were quite complete. I believe you did not hear me telling the others in the drawing-room that we are expecting Frank. I had a letter from him this morning, and he will be with us within a fortnight."

Emma spoke with a very proper degree of pleasure; and fully assented to his proposition of Mr. Frank Churchill and Miss Smith making their party quite complete.

"He has been wanting to come to us," continued Mr. Weston, "ever since September: every letter has been full of it; but he cannot command his own time. He has those to please who must be pleased, and who (between ourselves) are sometimes to be pleased only by a good many sacrifices. But now I have no doubt of seeing him here about the second week in January."

"What a very great pleasure it will be to you! and Mrs. Weston is so anxious to be acquainted with him, that she must be almost as happy as yourself."

"Yes, she would be, but that she thinks there will be another put-off. She does not depend upon his coming so much as I do: but she does not know the parties so well as I do. The case, you see, is – (but this is quite between ourselves: I did not mention a syllable of it in the other room. There are secrets in all families, you know) – The case is, that a party of friends are invited to pay a visit at Enscombe in January; and that Frank's coming depends upon their being put off. If they are not put off, he cannot stir. But I know they will, because it is a family that a certain lady, of some consequence, at Enscombe, has a particular dislike to: and though it is thought necessary to invite them once in two or three years, they always are put off when it comes to the point. I have not the smallest doubt of the issue. I am as confident of seeing Frank here before the middle of January, as I am of being here myself: but your good friend there (nodding towards the upper end of the table) has so few vagaries herself, and has been so little used to them at Hartfield, that she cannot calculate on their effects, as I have been long in the practice of doing."

"I am sorry there should be any thing like doubt in the case," replied Emma; "but am disposed to side with you, Mr. Weston. If you think he will come, I shall think so too; for you know Enscombe."

"Yes – I have some right to that knowledge; though I have never been at the place in my life. – She is an odd woman! – But I never allow myself to speak ill of her, on Frank's account; for I do believe her to be very fond of him. I used to think she was not capable of being fond of any body, except herself: but she has always been kind to him (in her way – allowing for little whims and caprices, and expecting every thing to be as she likes). And it is no small credit, in my opinion, to him, that he should excite such an affection; for, though I would not say it to any body else, she has no more heart than a stone to people in general; and the devil of a temper."

Emma liked the subject so well, that she began upon it, to Mrs. Weston, very soon after their moving into the drawing-room: wishing her joy – yet observing, that she knew the first meeting must be rather alarming. – Mrs. Weston agreed to it; but added, that she should be very glad to be secure of undergoing the anxiety of a first meeting at the time talked of: "for I cannot depend upon his coming. I cannot be so sanguine as Mr. Weston. I am very much afraid that it will all end in nothing. Mr. Weston, I dare say, has been telling you exactly how the matter stands?"

"Yes – it seems to depend upon nothing but the ill-humour of Mrs. Churchill, which I imagine to be the most certain thing in the world."

"My Emma!" replied Mrs. Weston, smiling, "what is the certainty of caprice?" Then turning to Isabella, who had not been attending before – "You must know, my dear Mrs. Knightley, that we are by no means so sure of seeing Mr. Frank Churchill, in my opinion, as his father thinks. It depends entirely upon his aunt's spirits and pleasure; in short, upon her temper. To you – to my two daughters – I may venture on the truth. Mrs. Churchill rules at Enscombe, and is a very odd-tempered woman; and his coming now, depends upon her being willing to spare him."

"Oh, Mrs. Churchill; every body knows Mrs. Churchill," replied Isabella: "and I am sure I never think of that poor young man without the greatest compassion. To be constantly living with an ill-tempered person, must be dreadful. It is what we happily have never known any thing of; but it must be a life of misery. What a blessing, that she never had any children! Poor little creatures, how unhappy she would have made them!"

Emma wished she had been alone with Mrs. Weston. She should then have heard more: Mrs. Weston would speak to her, with a degree of unreserve which she would not hazard with Isabella; and, she really believed, would scarcely try to conceal any thing relative to the Churchills from her, excepting those views on the young man, of which her own imagination had already given her such instinctive knowledge. But at present there was nothing more to be said. Mr. Woodhouse very soon followed them into the drawing-room. To be sitting long after dinner, was a confinement that he could not endure. Neither wine nor conversation was any thing to him; and gladly did he move to those with whom he was always comfortable.

While he talked to Isabella, however, Emma found an opportunity of saying,

"And so you do not consider this visit from your son as by any means certain. I am sorry for it. The introduction must be unpleasant, whenever it takes place; and the sooner it could be over, the better."

"Yes; and every delay makes one more apprehensive of other delays. Even if this family, the Braithwaites, are put off, I am still afraid that some excuse may be found for disappointing us. I cannot bear to imagine any reluctance on his side; but I am sure there is a great wish on the Churchills' to keep him to themselves. There is jealousy. They are jealous even of his regard for his father. In short, I can feel no dependence on his coming, and I wish Mr. Weston were less sanguine."

"He ought to come," said Emma. "If he could stay only a couple of days, he ought to come; and one can hardly conceive a young man's not having it in his power to do as much as that. A young woman , if she fall into bad hands, may be teazed, and kept at a distance from those she wants to be with; but one cannot comprehend a young man's being under such restraint, as not to be able to spend a week with his father, if he likes it."

"One ought to be at Enscombe, and know the ways of the family, before one decides upon what he can do," replied Mrs. Weston. "One ought to use the same caution, perhaps, in judging of the conduct of any one individual of any one family; but Enscombe, I believe, certainly must not be judged by general rules: *she* is so very unreasonable; and every thing gives way to her."

"But she is so fond of the nephew: he is so very great a favourite. Now, according to my idea of Mrs. Churchill, it would be most natural, that while she makes no sacrifice for the comfort of the husband, to whom she owes every thing, while she exercises incessant caprice towards *him*, she should frequently be governed by the nephew, to whom she owes nothing at all."

"My dearest Emma, do not pretend, with your sweet temper, to understand a bad one, or to lay down rules for it: you must let it go its own way. I have no doubt of his having, at times, considerable influence; but it may be perfectly impossible for him to know beforehand *when* it will be."

Emma listened, and then coolly said, "I shall not be satisfied, unless he comes."

"He may have a great deal of influence on some points," continued Mrs. Weston, "and on others, very little: and among those, on which she is beyond his reach, it is but too likely, may be this very circumstance of his coming away from them to visit us."

CHAPTER XV

Mr. Woodhouse was soon ready for his tea; and when he had drank his tea he was quite ready to go home; and it was as much as his three companions could do, to entertain away his notice of the lateness of the hour, before the other gentlemen appeared. Mr. Weston was chatty and convivial, and no friend to early separations of any sort; but at last the drawing-room party did receive an augmentation. Mr. Elton, in very good spirits, was one of the first to walk in. Mrs. Weston and Emma were sitting together on a sofa. He joined them immediately, and, with scarcely an invitation, seated himself between them.

Emma, in good spirits too, from the amusement afforded her mind by the expectation of Mr. Frank Churchill, was willing to forget his late improprieties, and be as well satisfied with him as before, and on his making Harriet his very first subject, was ready to listen with most friendly smiles.

He professed himself extremely anxious about her fair friend – her fair, lovely, amiable friend. "Did she know? – had she heard any thing about her, since their being at Randalls? – he felt much anxiety – he must confess that the nature of her complaint alarmed him considerably." And in this style he talked on for some time very properly, not much attending to any answer, but altogether sufficiently awake to the terror of a bad sore throat; and Emma was quite in charity with him.

But at last there seemed a perverse turn; it seemed all at once as if he were more afraid of its being a bad sore throat on her account, than on Harriet's – more anxious that she should escape the infection, than that there should be no infection in the complaint. He began with great earnestness to entreat her to refrain from visiting the sick-chamber again, for the present – to entreat her to *promise him* not to venture into such hazard till he had seen Mr. Perry and learnt his opinion; and though she tried to laugh it off and bring the subject back into its proper course, there was no putting an end to his extreme solicitude about her. She was vexed. It did appear – there was no concealing it – exactly like the pretence of being in love with her, instead of Harriet; an inconstancy, if real, the most contemptible and abominable! and she had difficulty in behaving with temper. He turned to Mrs. Weston to implore her assistance, "Would not she give him her support? – would not she add her persuasions to his, to induce Miss Woodhouse not to go to Mrs. Goddard's till it were certain that Miss Smith's disorder had no infection? He could not be satisfied without a promise – would not she give him her influence in procuring it?"

"So scrupulous for others," he continued, "and yet so careless for herself! She wanted me to nurse my cold by staying at home to-day, and yet will not promise to avoid the danger of catching an ulcerated sore throat herself. Is this fair, Mrs. Weston? – Judge between us. Have not I some right to complain? I am sure of your kind support and aid."

Emma saw Mrs. Weston's surprize, and felt that it must be great, at an address which, in words and manner, was assuming to himself the right of first interest in her; and as for herself, she was too much provoked and offended to have the power of directly saying any thing to the purpose. She could only give him a look; but it was such a look as she thought must restore him to his senses, and then left the sofa, removing to a seat by her sister, and giving her all her attention.

She had not time to know how Mr. Elton took the reproof, so rapidly did another subject succeed; for Mr. John Knightley now came into the room from examining the weather, and opened on them all with the information of the ground being covered with snow, and of its still snowing fast, with a strong drifting wind; concluding with these words to Mr. Woodhouse:

"This will prove a spirited beginning of your winter engagements, sir. Something new for your coachman and horses to be making their way through a storm of snow."

Poor Mr. Woodhouse was silent from consternation; but every body else had something to say; every body was either surprized or not surprized, and had some question to ask, or some comfort to offer. Mrs. Weston and Emma tried earnestly to cheer him and turn his attention from his son-in-law, who was pursuing his triumph rather unfeelingly.

"I admired your resolution very much, sir," said he, "in venturing out in such weather, for of course you saw there would be snow very soon. Every body must have seen the snow coming on. I admired your spirit; and I dare say we shall get home very well. Another hour or two's snow can hardly make the road impassable; and we are two carriages; if one is blown over in the bleak part of the common field there will be the other at hand. I dare say we shall be all safe at Hartfield before midnight."

Mr. Weston, with triumph of a different sort, was confessing that he had known it to be snowing some time, but had not said a word, lest it should make Mr. Woodhouse uncomfortable, and be an excuse for his hurrying away. As to there being any quantity of snow fallen or likely to fall to impede their return, that was a mere joke; he was afraid they would find no difficulty. He wished the road might be impassable, that he might be able to keep them all at Randalls; and with the utmost good-will was sure that accommodation might be found for every body, calling on his wife to agree with him, that with a little contrivance, every body might be lodged, which she hardly knew how to do, from the consciousness of there being but two spare rooms in the house.

"What is to be done, my dear Emma? – what is to be done?" was Mr. Woodhouse's first exclamation, and all that he could say for some time. To her he looked for comfort; and her assurances of safety, her representation of the excellence of the horses, and of James, and of their having so many friends about them, revived him a little.

His eldest daughter's alarm was equal to his own. The horror of being blocked up at Randalls, while her children were at Hartfield, was full in her imagination; and fancying the road to be now just passable for adventurous people, but in a state that admitted no delay, she was eager to have it settled, that her father and Emma should remain at Randalls, while she and her husband set forward instantly through all the possible accumulations of drifted snow that might impede them.

"You had better order the carriage directly, my love," said she; "I dare say we shall be able to get along, if we set off directly; and if we do come to any thing very bad, I can get out and walk. I am not at all afraid. I should not mind walking half the way. I could change my shoes, you know, the moment I got home; and it is not the sort of thing that gives me cold."

"Indeed!" replied he. "Then, my dear Isabella, it is the most extraordinary sort of thing in the world, for in general every thing does give you cold. Walk home! – you are prettily shod for walking home, I dare say. It will be bad enough for the horses."

Isabella turned to Mrs. Weston for her approbation of the plan. Mrs. Weston could only approve. Isabella then went to Emma; but Emma could not so entirely give up the hope of their being all able to get away; and they were still discussing the point, when Mr. Knightley, who had left the room immediately after his brother's first report of the snow, came back again, and told them that he had been out of doors to examine, and could answer for there not being the smallest difficulty in their getting home, whenever they liked it, either now or an hour hence. He had gone beyond the sweep – some way along the Highbury road – the snow was nowhere above half an inch deep – in many places hardly enough to whiten the ground; a very few flakes were falling at present, but the clouds were parting, and there was every appearance of its being soon over. He had seen the coachmen, and they both agreed with him in there being nothing to apprehend.

To Isabella, the relief of such tidings was very great, and they were scarcely less acceptable to Emma on her father's account, who was immediately set as much at ease on the subject as his nervous constitution allowed; but the alarm that had been raised could not be appeased so as to admit of any comfort for him while he continued at Randalls. He was satisfied of there being no present danger in returning home, but no assurances could convince him that it was safe to stay; and while the others were variously urging and recommending, Mr. Knightley and Emma settled it in a few brief sentences: thus—

"Your father will not be easy; why do not you go?"

"I am ready, if the others are."

"Shall I ring the bell?"

"Yes, do."

And the bell was rung, and the carriages spoken for. A few minutes more, and Emma hoped to see one troublesome companion deposited in his own house, to get sober and cool, and the other recover his temper and happiness when this visit of hardship were over.

The carriage came: and Mr. Woodhouse, always the first object on such occasions, was carefully attended to his own by Mr. Knightley and Mr. Weston; but not all that either could say could prevent some renewal of alarm at the sight of the snow which had actually fallen, and the discovery of a much darker night than he had been prepared for. "He was afraid they should have a very bad drive. He was afraid poor Isabella would not like it. And there would be poor Emma in the carriage behind. He did not know what they had best do. They must keep as much together as they could;" and James was talked to, and given a charge to go very slow and wait for the other carriage.

Isabella stept in after her father; John Knightley, forgetting that he did not belong to their party, stept in after his wife very naturally; so that Emma found, on being escorted and followed into the second carriage by Mr. Elton, that the door was to be lawfully shut on them, and that they were to have a tete-a-tete drive. It would not have been the awkwardness of a moment, it would have been rather a pleasure, previous to the suspicions of this very day; she could have talked to him of Harriet, and the three-quarters of a mile would have seemed but one. But now, she would rather it had not happened. She believed he had been drinking too much of Mr. Weston's good wine, and felt sure that he would want to be talking nonsense.

To restrain him as much as might be, by her own manners, she was immediately preparing to speak with exquisite calmness and gravity of the weather and the night; but scarcely had she begun, scarcely had they passed the sweep-gate and joined the other carriage, than she found her subject cut up – her hand seized – her attention demanded, and Mr. Elton actually making violent love to her: availing himself of the precious opportunity, declaring sentiments which must be already well known, hoping – fearing – adoring – ready to die if she refused him; but flattering himself that his ardent attachment and unequalled love and unexampled passion could not fail of having some effect, and in short, very much resolved on being seriously accepted as soon as possible. It really was so. Without scruple – without apology –

without much apparent diffidence, Mr. Elton, the lover of Harriet, was professing himself *her* lover. She tried to stop him; but vainly; he would go on, and say it all. Angry as she was, the thought of the moment made her resolve to restrain herself when she did speak. She felt that half this folly must be drunkenness, and therefore could hope that it might belong only to the passing hour. Accordingly, with a mixture of the serious and the playful, which she hoped would best suit his half and half state, she replied,

"I am very much astonished, Mr. Elton. This to *me*! you forget yourself – you take me for my friend – any message to Miss Smith I shall be happy to deliver; but no more of this to *me*, if you please."

"Miss Smith! – message to Miss Smith! – What could she possibly mean!" – And he repeated her words with such assurance of accent, such boastful pretence of amazement, that she could not help replying with quickness,

"Mr. Elton, this is the most extraordinary conduct! and I can account for it only in one way; you are not yourself, or you could not speak either to me, or of Harriet, in such a manner. Command yourself enough to say no more, and I will endeavour to forget it."

But Mr. Elton had only drunk wine enough to elevate his spirits, not at all to confuse his intellects. He perfectly knew his own meaning; and having warmly protested against her suspicion as most injurious, and slightly touched upon his respect for Miss Smith as her friend, – but acknowledging his wonder that Miss Smith should be mentioned at all, – he resumed the subject of his own passion, and was very urgent for a favourable answer.

As she thought less of his inebriety, she thought more of his inconstancy and presumption; and with fewer struggles for politeness, replied,

"It is impossible for me to doubt any longer. You have made yourself too clear. Mr. Elton, my astonishment is much beyond any thing I can express. After such behaviour, as I have witnessed during the last month, to Miss Smith – such attentions as I have been in the daily habit of observing – to be addressing me in this manner – this is an unsteadiness of character, indeed, which I had not supposed possible! Believe me, sir, I am far, very far, from gratified in being the object of such professions."

"Good Heaven!" cried Mr. Elton, "what can be the meaning of this? – Miss Smith! – I never thought of Miss Smith in the whole course of my existence – never paid her any attentions, but as your friend: never cared whether she were dead or alive, but as your friend. If she has fancied otherwise, her own wishes have misled her, and I am very sorry – extremely sorry – But, Miss Smith, indeed! – Oh! Miss Woodhouse! who can think of Miss Smith, when Miss Woodhouse is near! No, upon my honour, there is no unsteadiness of character. I have thought only of you. I protest against having paid the smallest attention to any one else. Every thing that I have said or done, for many weeks past, has been with the sole view of marking my adoration of yourself. You cannot really, seriously, doubt it. No! – (in an accent meant to be insinuating) – I am sure you have seen and understood me."

It would be impossible to say what Emma felt, on hearing this – which of all her unpleasant sensations was uppermost. She was too completely overpowered to be immediately able to reply: and two moments of silence being ample encouragement for Mr. Elton's sanguine state of mind, he tried to take her hand again, as he joyously exclaimed–

"Charming Miss Woodhouse! allow me to interpret this interesting silence. It confesses that you have long understood me."

"No, sir," cried Emma, "it confesses no such thing. So far from having long understood you, I have been in a most complete error with respect to your views, till this moment. As to myself, I am very sorry that you should have been giving way to any feelings – Nothing could be farther from my wishes – your attachment to my friend Harriet – your pursuit of her, (pursuit, it appeared,) gave me great pleasure, and I have been very earnestly wishing you success: but had I supposed that she were not your attraction to Hartfield, I should certainly have thought you judged ill in making your visits so frequent. Am I to believe that you have never sought to recommend yourself particularly to Miss Smith? – that you have never thought seriously of her?"

"Never, madam," cried he, affronted in his turn: "never, I assure you. – I – think seriously of Miss Smith! – Miss Smith is a very good sort of girl; and I should be happy to see her respectably settled. I wish her extremely well: and, no doubt, there are men who might not object to – Every body has their level: but as for myself, I am not, I think, quite so much at a loss. I need not so totally despair of an equal alliance, as to be addressing myself to Miss Smith! – No, madam, my visits to Hartfield have been for yourself only; and the encouragement I received–"

"Encouragement! – I give you encouragement! – Sir, you have been entirely mistaken in supposing it. I have seen you only as the admirer of my friend. In no other light could you have been more to me than a common acquaintance. I am exceedingly sorry: but it is well that the mistake ends where it does. Had the same behaviour continued, Miss Smith might have been led into a misconception of your views; not being aware, probably, any more than myself, of the very great inequality which you are so sensible of. But, as it is, the disappointment is single, and, I trust, will not be lasting. I have no thoughts of matrimony at present."

He was too angry to say another word; her manner too decided to invite supplication; and in this state of swelling resentment, and mutually deep mortification, they had to continue together a few minutes longer, for the fears of Mr. Woodhouse had confined them to a foot-pace. If there had not been so much anger, there would have been desperate awkwardness; but their straightforward emotions left no room for the little zigzags of embarrassment. Without knowing when the carriage turned into Vicarage Lane, or when it stopped, they found themselves, all at once, at the door of his house; and he was out before another syllable passed. – Emma then felt it indispensable to wish him a good night. The compliment was just returned, coldly and proudly; and, under indescribable irritation of spirits, she was then conveyed to Hartfield.

There she was welcomed, with the utmost delight, by her father, who had been trembling for the dangers of a solitary drive from Vicarage Lane – turning a corner which he could never bear to think of – and in strange hands – a mere common coachman – no James; and there it seemed as if her return only were wanted to make every thing go well: for Mr. John Knightley, ashamed of his ill-humour, was now all kindness and attention; and so particularly solicitous for the comfort of her father, as to seem – if not quite ready to join him in a basin of gruel – perfectly sensible of its being exceedingly wholesome; and the day was concluding in peace and comfort to all their little party, except herself. – But her mind had never been in such perturbation; and it needed a very strong effort to appear attentive and cheerful till the usual hour of separating allowed her the relief of quiet reflection.

CHAPTER XVI

The hair was curled, and the maid sent away, and Emma sat down to think and be miserable. – It was a wretched business indeed! – Such an over-throw of every thing she had been wishing for! – Such a development of every thing most unwel-come! – Such a blow for Harriet! – that was the worst of all. Every part of it brought pain and humiliation, of some sort or other; but, compared with the evil to Harriet, all was light; and she would gladly have submitted to feel yet more mistaken – more in error – more disgraced by mis-judgment, than she actually was, could the effects of her blunders have been confined to herself.

"If I had not persuaded Harriet into liking the man, I could have borne any thing. He might have dou-bled his presumption to me – but poor Harriet!"

How she could have been so deceived! – He protested that he had never thought seriously of Harriet – never! She looked back as well as she could; but it was all confusion. She had taken up the idea, she supposed, and made every thing bend to it. His manners, however, must have been un-marked, wavering, dubious, or she could not have been so misled.

The picture! – How eager he had been about the picture! – and the charade! – and an hundred other circumstances; – how clearly they had seemed to point at Harriet. To be sure, the charade, with its "ready wit" – but then the "soft eyes" – in fact it suited neither; it was a jumble without taste or truth. Who could have seen through such thick-headed nonsense?

Certainly she had often, especially of late, thought his manners to herself unnecessarily gallant; but it had passed as his way, as a mere error of judgment, of knowledge, of taste, as one proof among others that he had not always lived in the best society, that with all the gentleness of his address, true elegance was sometimes wanting; but, till this very day, she had never, for an instant, suspected it to mean any thing but grateful respect to her as Harriet's friend.

To Mr. John Knightley was she indebted for her first idea on the subject, for the first start of its possibility. There was no denying that those brothers had penetration. She remembered what Mr. Knightley had once said to her about Mr. Elton, the caution he had given, the conviction he had professed that Mr. Elton would never marry indiscreetly; and blushed to think how much truer a knowledge of his character had been there shewn than any she had reached herself. It was dreadfully mortifying; but Mr. Elton was proving himself, in many respects, the very reverse of what she had meant and believed him; proud, assuming, conceited; very full of his own claims, and little concerned about the feelings of others.

Contrary to the usual course of things, Mr. Elton's wanting to pay his addresses to her had sunk him in her opinion. His professions and his proposals did him no service. She thought nothing of his attachment, and was insulted by his hopes. He wanted to marry well, and having the arrogance to raise his eyes to her, pretended to be in love; but she was perfectly easy as to his not suffering any disappointment that need be cared for. There had been no real affection either in his language or manners. Sighs and fine words had been given in abundance; but she could hardly devise any set of expressions, or fancy any tone of voice, less allied with real love. She need not trouble herself to pity him. He only wanted to aggrandise and enrich himself; and if Miss Woodhouse of Hartfield, the heiress of thirty thousand pounds, were not quite so easily obtained as he had fancied, he would soon try for Miss Somebody else with twenty, or with ten.

But – that he should talk of encouragement, should consider her as aware of his views, accepting his attentions, meaning (in short), to marry him! – should suppose himself her equal in connexion or mind! – look down upon her friend, so well understanding the gradations of rank below him, and be so blind to what rose above, as to fancy himself shewing no presumption in addressing her! – It was most provoking.

Perhaps it was not fair to expect him to feel how very much he was her inferior in talent, and all the elegancies of mind. The very want of such equality might prevent his perception of it; but he must know that in fortune and consequence she was greatly his superior. He must know that the Woodhouses had been settled for several generations at Hartfield, the younger branch of a very ancient family – and that the Eltons were nobody. The landed property of Hartfield certainly was inconsiderable, being but a sort of notch in the Donwell Abbey estate, to which all the rest of Highbury belonged; but their fortune, from other sources, was such as to make them scarcely secondary to Donwell Abbey itself, in every other kind of consequence; and the Woodhouses had long held a high place in the consideration of the neighbourhood which Mr. Elton had first entered not two years ago, to make his way as he could, without any alliances but in trade, or any thing to recommend him to notice but his situation and his civility. – But he had fancied her in love with him; that evidently must have been his dependence; and after raving a little about the seeming incongruity of gentle manners and a conceited head, Emma was obliged in common honesty to stop and admit that her own behaviour to him had been so complaisant and obliging, so full of courtesy and attention, as (supposing her real motive unperceived) might warrant a man of ordinary observation and delicacy, like Mr. Elton, in fancying himself a very decided favourite. If *she* had so misinterpreted his feelings, she had little right to wonder that *he*, with self-interest to blind him, should have mistaken hers.

The first error and the worst lay at her door. It was foolish, it was wrong, to take so active a part in bringing any two people together. It was adventuring too far, assuming too much, making light of what ought to be serious, a trick of what ought to be simple. She was quite concerned and ashamed, and resolved to do such things no more.

"Here have I," said she, "actually talked poor Harriet into being very much attached to this man. She might never have thought of him but for me; and certainly never would have thought of him with hope, if I had not assured her of his attachment, for she is as modest and humble as I used to think him. Oh! that I had been satisfied with persuading her not to accept young Martin. There I was quite right. That was well done of me; but there I should have stopped, and left the rest to time and chance. I was introducing her into good company, and giving her the opportunity of pleasing some one worth having; I ought not to have attempted more. But now, poor girl, her peace is cut up for some time. I have been but half a friend to her; and if she were *not* to feel this disappointment so very much, I am sure I have not an idea of any body else who would be at all desirable for her; – William Coxe – Oh! no, I could not endure William Coxe – a pert young lawyer."

She stopt to blush and laugh at her own relapse, and then resumed a more serious, more dispiriting cogitation upon what had been, and might be, and must be. The distressing explanation she had to make to Harriet, and all that poor Harriet would be suffering, with the awkwardness of future meetings, the difficulties of continuing or discontinuing the acquaintance, of subduing feelings, concealing resentment, and avoiding eclat, were enough to occupy her in most unmirthful reflections some time longer, and she went to bed at last with nothing settled but the conviction of her having blundered most dreadfully.

To youth and natural cheerfulness like Emma's, though under temporary gloom at night, the return of day will hardly fail to bring return of spirits. The youth and cheerfulness of morning are in happy analogy, and of powerful operation; and if the distress be not poignant enough to keep the eyes unclosed, they will be sure to open to sensations of softened pain and brighter hope.

Emma got up on the morrow more disposed for comfort than she had gone to bed, more ready to see alleviations of the evil before her, and to depend on getting tolerably out of it.

It was a great consolation that Mr. Elton should not be really in love with her, or so particularly amiable as to make it shocking to disappoint him – that Harriet's nature should not be of that superior sort in which the feelings are most acute and retentive – and that there could be no necessity for any body's knowing what had passed except the three principals, and especially for her father's being given a moment's uneasiness about it.

These were very cheering thoughts; and the sight of a great deal of snow on the ground did her further service, for any thing was welcome that might justify their all three being quite asunder at present.

The weather was most favourable for her; though Christmas Day, she could not go to church. Mr. Woodhouse would have been miserable had his daughter attempted it, and she was therefore safe from either exciting or receiving unpleasant and most unsuitable ideas. The ground covered with snow, and the atmosphere in that unsettled state between frost and thaw, which is of all others the most unfriendly for exercise, every morning beginning in rain or snow, and every evening setting in to freeze, she was for many days a most honourable prisoner. No intercourse with Harriet possible but by note; no church for her on Sunday any more than on Christmas Day; and no need to find excuses for Mr. Elton's absenting himself.

It was weather which might fairly confine every body at home; and though she hoped and believed him to be really taking comfort in some society or other, it was very pleasant to have her father so well satisfied with his being all alone in his own house, too wise to stir out; and to hear him say to Mr. Knightley, whom no weather could keep entirely from them,–

"Ah! Mr. Knightley, why do not you stay at home like poor Mr. Elton?"

These days of confinement would have been, but for her private perplexities, remarkably comfortable, as such seclusion exactly suited her brother, whose feelings must always be of great importance to his companions; and he had, besides, so thoroughly cleared off his ill-humour at Randalls, that his amiableness never failed him during the rest of his stay at Hartfield. He was always agreeable and obliging, and speaking pleasantly of every body. But with all the hopes of cheerfulness, and all the present comfort of delay, there was still such an evil hanging over her in the hour of explanation with Harriet, as made it impossible for Emma to be ever perfectly at ease.

CHAPTER XVII

Mr. and Mrs. John Knightley were not detained long at Hartfield. The weather soon improved enough for those to move who must move; and Mr. Woodhouse having, as usual, tried to persuade his daughter to stay behind with all her children, was obliged to see the whole party set off, and return to his lamentations over the destiny of poor Isabella; – which poor Isabella, passing her life with those she doated on, full of their merits, blind to their faults, and always innocently busy, might have been a model of right feminine happiness.

The evening of the very day on which they went brought a note from Mr. Elton to Mr. Woodhouse, a long, civil, ceremonious note, to say, with Mr. Elton's best compliments, "that he was proposing to leave Highbury the following morning in his way to Bath; where, in compliance with the pressing entreaties of some friends, he had engaged to spend a few weeks, and very much regretted the impossibility he was under, from various circumstances of weather and business, of taking a personal leave of Mr. Woodhouse, of whose friendly civilities he should ever retain a grateful sense – and had Mr. Woodhouse any commands, should be happy to attend to them."

Emma was most agreeably surprized. – Mr. Elton's absence just at this time was the very thing to be desired. She admired him for contriving it, though not able to give him much credit for the manner in which it was announced. Resentment could not have been more plainly spoken than in a civility to her father, from which she was so pointedly excluded. She had not even a share in his opening compliments. – Her name was not mentioned; – and there was so striking a change in all this, and such an ill-judged solemnity of leave-taking in his graceful acknowledgments, as she thought, at first, could not escape her father's suspicion.

It did, however. – Her father was quite taken up with the surprize of so sudden a journey, and his fears that Mr. Elton might never get safely to the end of it, and saw nothing extraordinary in his language. It was a very useful note, for it supplied them with fresh matter for thought and conversation during the rest of their lonely evening. Mr. Woodhouse talked over his alarms, and Emma was in spirits to persuade them away with all her usual promptitude.

She now resolved to keep Harriet no longer in the dark. She had reason to believe her nearly recovered from her cold, and it was desirable that she should have as much time as possible for getting the better of her other complaint before the gentleman's return. She went to Mrs. Goddard's accordingly the very next day, to undergo the necessary penance of communication; and a severe one it was. – She had to destroy all the hopes which she had been so industriously feeding – to appear in the ungracious character of the one preferred – and acknowledge herself grossly mistaken and mis-judging in all her ideas on one subject, all her observations, all her convictions, all her prophecies for the last six weeks.

The confession completely renewed her first shame – and the sight of Harriet's tears made her think that she should never be in charity with herself again.

Harriet bore the intelligence very well – blaming nobody – and in every thing testifying such an ingenuousness of disposition and lowly opinion of herself, as must appear with particular advantage at that moment to her friend.

Emma was in the humour to value simplicity and modesty to the utmost; and all that was amiable, all that ought to be attaching, seemed on Harriet's side, not her own. Harriet did not consider herself as having any thing to complain of. The affection of such a man as Mr. Elton would have been too great a distinction. – She never could have deserved him – and nobody but so partial and kind a friend as Miss Woodhouse would have thought it possible.

Her tears fell abundantly – but her grief was so truly artless, that no dignity could have made it more respectable in Emma's eyes – and she listened to her and tried to console her with all her heart and understanding – really for the time convinced that Harriet was the superior creature of the two – and that to resemble her would be more for her own welfare and happiness than all that genius or intelligence could do.

It was rather too late in the day to set about being simple-minded and ignorant; but she left her with every previous resolution confirmed of being humble and discreet, and repressing imagination all the rest of her life. Her second duty now, inferior only to her father's claims, was to promote Harriet's comfort, and endeavour to prove her own affection in some better method than by match-making. She got her to Hartfield, and shewed her the most unvarying kindness, striving to occupy and amuse her, and by books and conversation, to drive Mr. Elton from her thoughts.

Time, she knew, must be allowed for this being thoroughly done; and she could suppose herself but an indifferent judge of such matters in general, and very inadequate to sympathise in an attachment to Mr. Elton in particular; but it seemed to her reasonable that at Harriet's age, and with the entire extinction of all hope, such a progress might be made towards a state of composure by the time of Mr. Elton's return, as to allow them all to meet again in the common routine of acquaintance, without any danger of betraying sentiments or increasing them.

Harriet did think him all perfection, and maintained the non-existence of any body equal to him in person or goodness – and did, in truth, prove herself more resolutely in love than Emma had foreseen; but yet it appeared to her so natural, so inevitable to strive against an inclination of that sort *unrequited*, that she could not comprehend its continuing very long in equal force.

If Mr. Elton, on his return, made his own indifference as evident and indubitable as she could not doubt he would anxiously do, she could not imagine Harriet's persisting to place her happiness in the sight or the recollection of him.

Their being fixed, so absolutely fixed, in the same place, was bad for each, for all three. Not one of them had the power of removal, or of effecting any material change of society. They must encounter each other, and make the best of it.

Harriet was farther unfortunate in the tone of her companions at Mrs. Goddard's; Mr. Elton being the adoration of all the teachers and great girls in the school; and it must be at Hartfield only that she could have any chance of hearing him spoken of with cooling moderation or repellent truth. Where the wound had been given, there must the cure be found if anywhere; and Emma felt that, till she saw her in the way of cure, there could be no true peace for herself.

CHAPTER XVIII

Mr. Frank Churchill did not come. When the time proposed drew near, Mrs. Weston's fears were justified in the arrival of a letter of excuse. For the present, he could not be spared, to his "very great mortification and regret; but still he looked forward with the hope of coming to Randalls at no distant period."

Mrs. Weston was exceedingly disappointed – much more disappointed, in fact, than her husband, though her dependence on seeing the young man had been so much more sober: but a sanguine temper, though for ever expecting more good than occurs, does not always pay for its hopes by any proportionate depression. It soon flies over the present failure, and begins to hope again. For half an hour Mr. Weston was surprized and sorry; but then he began to perceive that Frank's coming two or three months later would be a much better plan; better time of year; better weather; and that he would be able, without any doubt, to stay considerably longer with them than if he had come sooner.

These feelings rapidly restored his comfort, while Mrs. Weston, of a more apprehensive disposition, foresaw nothing but a repetition of excuses and delays; and after all her concern for what her husband was to suffer, suffered a great deal more herself.

Emma was not at this time in a state of spirits to care really about Mr. Frank Churchill's not coming, except as a disappointment at Randalls. The acquaintance at present had no charm for her. She wanted, rather, to be quiet, and out of temptation; but still, as it was desirable that she should appear, in general, like her usual self, she took care to express as much interest in the circumstance, and enter as warmly into Mr. and Mrs. Weston's disappointment, as might naturally belong to their friendship.

She was the first to announce it to Mr. Knightley; and exclaimed quite as much as was necessary, (or, being acting a part, perhaps rather more,) at the conduct of the Churchills, in keeping him away. She then proceeded to say a good deal more than she felt, of the advantage of such an addition to their confined society in Surry; the pleasure of looking at somebody new;

the gala-day to Highbury entire, which the sight of him would have made; and ending with reflections on the Churchills again, found herself directly involved in a disagreement with Mr. Knightley; and, to her great amusement, perceived that she was taking the other side of the question from her real opinion, and making use of Mrs. Weston's arguments against herself.

"The Churchills are very likely in fault," said Mr. Knightley, coolly; "but I dare say he might come if he would."

"I do not know why you should say so. He wishes exceedingly to come; but his uncle and aunt will not spare him."

"I cannot believe that he has not the power of coming, if he made a point of it. It is too unlikely, for me to believe it without proof."

"How odd you are! What has Mr. Frank Churchill done, to make you suppose him such an unnatural creature?"

"I am not supposing him at all an unnatural creature, in suspecting that he may have learnt to be above his connexions, and to care very little for any thing but his own pleasure, from living with those who have always set him the example of it. It is a great deal more natural than one could wish, that a young man, brought up by those who are proud, luxurious, and selfish, should be proud, luxurious, and selfish too. If Frank Churchill had wanted to see his father, he would have contrived it between September and January. A man at his age – what is he? – three or four-and-twenty – cannot be without the means of doing as much as that. It is impossible."

"That's easily said, and easily felt by you, who have always been your own master. You are the worst judge in the world, Mr. Knightley, of the difficulties of dependence. You do not know what it is to have tempers to manage."

"It is not to be conceived that a man of three or four-and-twenty should not have liberty of mind or limb to that amount. He cannot want money – he cannot want leisure. We know, on the contrary, that he has so much of both, that he is glad to get rid of them at the idlest haunts in the kingdom. We hear of him for ever at some watering-place or other. A little while ago, he was at

Weymouth. This proves that he can leave the Churchills.”

“Yes, sometimes he can.”

“And those times are whenever he thinks it worth his while; whenever there is any temptation of pleasure.”

“It is very unfair to judge of any body's conduct, without an intimate knowledge of their situation. Nobody, who has not been in the interior of a family, can say what the difficulties of any individual of that family may be. We ought to be acquainted with Enscombe, and with Mrs. Churchill's temper, before we pretend to decide upon what her nephew can do. He may, at times, be able to do a great deal more than he can at others.”

“There is one thing, Emma, which a man can always do, if he chuses, and that is, his duty; not by manoeuvring and finessing, but by vigour and resolution. It is Frank Churchill's duty to pay this attention to his father. He knows it to be so, by his promises and messages; but if he wished to do it, it might be done. A man who felt rightly would say at once, simply and resolutely, to Mrs. Churchill – 'Every sacrifice of mere pleasure you will always find me ready to make to your convenience; but I must go and see my father immediately. I know he would be hurt by my failing in such a mark of respect to him on the present occasion. I shall, therefore, set off to-morrow.' – If he would say so to her at once, in the tone of decision becoming a man, there would be no opposition made to his going.”

“No,” said Emma, laughing; “but perhaps there might be some made to his coming back again. Such language for a young man entirely dependent, to use! – Nobody but you, Mr. Knightley, would imagine it possible. But you have not an idea of what is requisite in situations directly opposite to your own. Mr. Frank Churchill to be making such a speech as that to the uncle and aunt, who have brought him up, and are to provide for him! – Standing up in the middle of the room, I suppose, and speaking as loud as he could! – How can you imagine such conduct practicable?”

“Depend upon it, Emma, a sensible man would find no difficulty in it. He would feel himself in the right; and the declaration – made, of course, as a man of sense would make it, in a proper manner – would do him more good, raise him higher, fix his interest stronger with the people he depended on, than all that a line of shifts and expedients can ever do. Respect would be added to affection. They would feel that they could trust him; that the nephew who had done rightly by his father, would do rightly by them; for they know, as well as he does, as well as all the world must know, that he ought to pay this visit to his father; and while meanly exerting their power to delay it, are in their hearts not thinking the better of him for submitting to their whims. Respect for right conduct is felt by every body. If he would act in this sort of manner, on principle, consistently, regularly, their little minds would bend to his."

"I rather doubt that. You are very fond of bending little minds; but where little minds belong to rich people in authority, I think they have a knack of swelling out, till they are quite as unmanageable as great ones. I can imagine, that if you, as you are, Mr. Knightley, were to be transported and placed all at once in Mr. Frank Churchill's situation, you would be able to say and do just what you have been recommending for him; and it might have a very good effect. The Churchills might not have a word to say in return; but then, you would have no habits of early obedience and long observance to break through. To him who has, it might not be so easy to burst forth at once into perfect independence, and set all their claims on his gratitude and regard at nought. He may have as strong a sense of what would be right, as you can have, without being so equal, under particular circumstances, to act up to it."

"Then it would not be so strong a sense. If it failed to produce equal exertion, it could not be an equal conviction."

"Oh, the difference of situation and habit! I wish you would try to understand what an amiable young man may be likely to feel in directly opposing those, whom as child and boy he has been looking up to all his life."

"Our amiable young man is a very weak young man, if this be the first occasion of his carrying through a resolution to do right against the will of others. It ought to have been a habit with him by this time, of following his duty, instead of consulting expediency. I can allow for the fears of the child, but not of the man. As he became rational, he ought to have roused himself and shaken off all that was unworthy in their authority. He ought to have opposed the first attempt on their side to make him slight his father. Had he begun as he ought, there would have been no difficulty now."

"We shall never agree about him," cried Emma; "but that is nothing extraordinary. I have not the least idea of his being a weak young man: I feel sure that he is not. Mr. Weston would not be blind to folly, though in his own son; but he is very likely to have a more yielding, complying, mild disposition than would suit your notions of man's perfection. I dare say he has; and though it may cut him off from some advantages, it will secure him many others."

"Yes; all the advantages of sitting still when he ought to move, and of leading a life of mere idle pleasure, and fancying himself extremely expert in finding excuses for it. He can sit down and write a fine flourishing letter, full of professions and falsehoods, and persuade himself that he has hit upon the very best method in the world of preserving peace at home and preventing his father's having any right to complain. His letters disgust me."

"Your feelings are singular. They seem to satisfy every body else."

"I suspect they do not satisfy Mrs. Weston. They hardly can satisfy a woman of her good sense and quick feelings: standing in a mother's place, but without a mother's affection to blind her. It is on her account that attention to Randalls is doubly due, and she must doubly feel the omission. Had she been a person of consequence herself, he would have come I dare say; and it would not have signified whether he did or no. Can you think your friend behindhand in these sort of considerations? Do you suppose she does not often say all this to herself? No, Emma, your amiable young man can be amiable only in French, not in English. He may be very 'aimable,' have very good manners, and be very agreeable; but he can have no English delicacy towards the feelings of other people: nothing really amiable about him."

"You seem determined to think ill of him."

"Me! – not at all," replied Mr. Knightley, rather displeased; "I do not want to think ill of him. I should be as ready to acknowledge his merits as any other man; but I hear of none, except what are merely personal; that he is well-grown and good-looking, with smooth, plausible manners."

"Well, if he have nothing else to recommend him, he will be a treasure at Highbury. We do not often look upon fine young men, well-bred and agreeable. We must not be nice and ask for all the virtues into the bargain. Cannot you imagine, Mr. Knightley, what a *sensation* his coming will produce? There will be but one subject throughout the parishes of Donwell and Highbury; but one interest – one object of curiosity; it will be all Mr. Frank Churchill; we shall think and speak of nobody else."

"You will excuse my being so much over-powered. If I find him conversable, I shall be glad of his acquaintance; but if he is only a chattering coxcomb, he will not occupy much of my time or thoughts."

"My idea of him is, that he can adapt his conversation to the taste of every body, and has the power as well as the wish of being universally agreeable. To you, he will talk of farming; to me, of drawing or music; and so on to every body, having that general information on all subjects which will enable him to follow the lead, or take the lead, just as propriety may require, and to speak extremely well on each; that is my idea of him."

"And mine," said Mr. Knightley warmly, "is, that if he turn out any thing like it, he will be the most insufferable fellow breathing! What! at three-and-twenty to be the king of his company – the great man – the practised politician, who is to read every body's character, and make every body's talents conduce to the display of his own superiority; to be dispensing his flatteries around, that he may make all appear like fools compared with himself! My dear Emma, your own good sense could not endure such a puppy when it came to the point."

"I will say no more about him," cried Emma, "you turn every thing to evil. We are both prejudiced; you against, I for him; and we have no chance of agreeing till he is really here."

"Prejudiced! I am not prejudiced."

"But I am very much, and without being at all ashamed of it. My love for Mr. and Mrs. Weston gives me a decided prejudice in his favour."

"He is a person I never think of from one month's end to another," said Mr. Knightley, with a degree of vexation, which made Emma immediately talk of something else, though she could not comprehend why he should be angry.

To take a dislike to a young man, only because he appeared to be of a different disposition from himself, was unworthy the real liberality of mind which she was always used to acknowledge in him; for with all the high opinion of himself, which she had often laid to his charge, she had never before for a moment supposed it could make him unjust to the merit of another.

VOLUME II

CHAPTER I

Emma and Harriet had been walking together one morning, and, in Emma's opinion, had been talking enough of Mr. Elton for that day. She could not think that Harriet's solace or her own sins required more; and she was therefore industriously getting rid of the subject as they returned; – but it burst out again when she thought she had succeeded, and after speaking some time of what the poor must suffer in winter, and receiving no other answer than a very plaintive – "Mr. Elton is so good to the poor!" she found something else must be done.

They were just approaching the house where lived Mrs. and Miss Bates. She determined to call upon them and seek safety in numbers. There was always sufficient reason for such an attention; Mrs. and Miss Bates loved to be called on, and she knew she was considered by the very few who presumed ever to see imperfection in her, as rather negligent in that respect, and as not contributing what she ought to the stock of their scanty comforts.

She had had many a hint from Mr. Knightley and some from her own heart, as to her deficiency – but none were equal to counteract the persuasion of its being very disagreeable, – a waste of time – tiresome women – and all the horror of being in danger of falling in with the second-rate and third-rate of Highbury, who were calling on them for ever, and therefore she seldom went near them. But now she made the sudden resolution of not passing their door without going in – observing, as she proposed it to Harriet, that, as well as she could calculate, they were just now quite safe from any letter from Jane Fairfax.

The house belonged to people in business. Mrs. and Miss Bates occupied the drawing-room floor; and there, in the very moderate-sized apartment, which was every thing to them, the visitors were most cordially and even gratefully welcomed; the quiet neat old lady, who with her knitting was seated in the warmest corner, wanting even to give up her place to Miss Woodhouse, and her more active, talking daughter, almost ready to overpower them with care and kindness, thanks for their visit, solicitude for their shoes, anxious inquiries after Mr. Woodhouse's health, cheerful communications about her mother's, and sweet-cake from the beaufet – "Mrs. Cole had just been there, just called in for ten minutes, and had been so good as to sit an hour with them, and *she* had taken a piece of cake and been so kind as to say she liked it very much; and, therefore, she hoped Miss Woodhouse and Miss Smith would do them the favour to eat a piece too."

The mention of the Coles was sure to be followed by that of Mr. Elton. There was intimacy between them, and Mr. Cole had heard from Mr. Elton since his going away. Emma knew what was coming; they must have the letter over again, and settle how long he had been gone, and how much he was engaged in company, and what a favourite he was wherever he went, and how full the Master of the Ceremonies' ball had been; and she went through it very well, with all the interest and all the commendation that could be requisite, and always putting forward to prevent Harriet's being obliged to say a word.

This she had been prepared for when she entered the house; but meant, having once talked him handsomely over, to be no farther incommoded by any troublesome topic, and to wander at large amongst all the Mistresses and Misses of Highbury, and their card-parties. She had not been prepared to have Jane Fairfax succeed Mr. Elton; but he was actually hurried off by Miss Bates, she jumped away from him at last abruptly to the Coles, to usher in a letter from her niece.

"Oh! yes – Mr. Elton, I understand – certainly as to dancing – Mrs. Cole was telling me that dancing at the rooms at Bath was – Mrs. Cole was so kind as to sit some time with us, talking of Jane; for as soon as she came in, she began inquiring after her, Jane is so very great a favourite there. Whenever she is with us, Mrs. Cole does not know how to shew her kindness enough; and I must say that Jane deserves it as much as any body can. And so she began inquiring after her directly, saying, 'I know you cannot have heard from Jane lately, because it is not her time for writing;' and when I immediately said, 'But indeed we have, we had a letter this very morning,' I do not know that I ever saw any body more surprized. 'Have you, upon your honour?' said she; 'well, that is quite unexpected. Do let me hear what she says.'"

Emma's politeness was at hand directly, to say, with smiling interest–

"Have you heard from Miss Fairfax so lately? I am extremely happy. I hope she is well?"

"Thank you. You are so kind!" replied the happily deceived aunt, while eagerly hunting for the letter. – "Oh! here it is. I was sure it could not be far off; but I had put my huswife upon it, you see, without being aware, and so it was quite hid, but I had it in my hand so very lately that I was almost sure it must be on the table. I was reading it to Mrs. Cole, and since she went away, I was reading it again to my mother, for it is such a pleasure to her – a letter from Jane – that she can never hear it often enough; so I knew it could not be far off, and here it is, only just under my huswife – and since you are so kind as to wish to hear what she says; – but, first of all, I really must, in justice to Jane, apologise for her writing so short a letter – only two pages you see – hardly two – and in general she fills the whole paper and crosses half. My mother often wonders that I can make it out so well. She often says, when the letter is first opened, 'Well, Hetty, now I think you will be put to it to make out all that checker-work' – don't you, ma'am? – And then I tell her, I am sure she would contrive to make it out herself, if she had nobody to do it for her – every word of it – I am sure she would pore over it till she had made out every word. And, indeed, though my mother's eyes are not so good as they were, she can see amazingly well still, thank God! with the help of spectacles. It is such a blessing! My mother's are really very good indeed. Jane often says, when she is here, 'I am sure, grandmama, you must have had very strong eyes to see as you do – and so much fine work as you have done too! – I only wish my eyes may last me as well.'"

All this spoken extremely fast obliged Miss Bates to stop for breath; and Emma said something very civil about the excellence of Miss Fairfax's handwriting.

"You are extremely kind," replied Miss Bates, highly gratified; "you who are such a judge, and write so beautifully yourself. I am sure there is nobody's praise that could give us so much pleasure as Miss Woodhouse's. My mother does not hear; she is a little deaf you know. Ma'am," addressing her, "do you hear what Miss Woodhouse is so obliging to say about Jane's handwriting?"

And Emma had the advantage of hearing her own silly compliment repeated twice over before the good old lady could comprehend it. She was pondering, in the meanwhile, upon the possibility, without seeming very rude, of making her escape from Jane Fairfax's letter, and had almost resolved on hurrying away directly under some slight excuse, when Miss Bates turned to her again and seized her attention.

"My mother's deafness is very trifling you see – just nothing at all. By only raising my voice, and saying any thing two or three times over, she is sure to hear; but then she is used to my voice. But it is very remarkable that she should always hear Jane better than she does me. Jane speaks so distinct! However, she will not find her grandmama at all deafer than she was two years ago; which is saying a great deal at my mother's time of life – and it really is full two years, you know, since she was here. We never were so long without seeing her before, and as I was telling Mrs. Cole, we shall hardly know how to make enough of her now."

"Are you expecting Miss Fairfax here soon?"

"Oh yes; next week."

"Indeed! – that must be a very great pleasure."

"Thank you. You are very kind. Yes, next week. Every body is so surprized; and every body says the same obliging things. I am sure she will be as happy to see her friends at Highbury, as they can be to see her. Yes, Friday or Saturday; she cannot say which, because Colonel Campbell will be wanting the carriage himself one of those days. So very good of them to send her the whole way! But they always do, you know. Oh yes, Friday or Saturday next. That is what she writes about. That is the reason of her writing out of rule, as we call it; for, in the common course, we should not have heard from her before next Tuesday or Wednesday."

"Yes, so I imagined. I was afraid there could be little chance of my hearing any thing of Miss Fairfax to-day."

"So obliging of you! No, we should not have heard, if it had not been for this particular circumstance, of her being to come here so soon. My mother is so delighted! – for she is to be three months with us at least. Three months, she says so, positively, as I am going to have the pleasure of reading to you. The case is, you see, that the Campbells are going to Ireland. Mrs. Dixon has persuaded her father and mother to come over and see her directly. They had not intended to go over till the summer, but she is so impatient to see them again – for till she married, last October, she was never away from them so much as a week, which must make it very strange to be in different kingdoms, I was going to say, but however different countries, and so she wrote a very urgent letter to her mother – or her father, I declare I do not know which it was, but we shall see presently in Jane's letter – wrote in Mr. Dixon's name as well as her own, to press their coming over directly, and they would give them the meeting in Dublin, and take them back to their country seat, Baly-craig, a beautiful place, I fancy. Jane has heard a great deal of its beauty; from Mr. Dixon, I mean – I do not know that she ever heard about it from any body else; but it was very natural, you know, that he should like to speak of his own place while he was paying his addresses – and as Jane used to be very often walking out with them – for Colonel and Mrs. Campbell were very particular about their daughter's not walking out often with only Mr. Dixon, for which I do not at all blame them; of course she heard every thing he might be telling Miss Campbell about his own home in Ireland; and I think she wrote us word that he had shewn them some drawings of the place, views that he had taken himself. He is a most amiable, charming young man, I believe. Jane was quite longing to go to Ireland, from his account of things."

At this moment, an ingenious and animating suspicion entering Emma's brain with regard to Jane Fairfax, this charming Mr. Dixon, and the not going to Ireland, she said, with the insidious design of farther discovery,

"You must feel it very fortunate that Miss Fairfax should be allowed to come to you at such a time. Considering the very particular friendship between her and Mrs. Dixon, you could hardly have expected her to be excused from accompanying Colonel and Mrs. Campbell."

"Very true, very true, indeed. The very thing that we have always been rather afraid of; for we should not have liked to have her at such a distance from us, for months together – not able to come if any thing was to happen. But you see, every thing turns out for the best. They want her (Mr. and Mrs. Dixon) excessively to come over with Colonel and Mrs. Campbell; quite depend upon it; nothing can be more kind or pressing than their *joint* invitation, Jane says, as you will hear presently; Mr. Dixon does not seem in the least backward in any attention. He is a most charming young man. Ever since the service he rendered Jane at Weymouth, when they were out in that party on the water, and she, by the sudden whirling round of something or other among the sails, would have been dashed into the sea at once, and actually was all but gone, if he had not, with the greatest presence of mind, caught hold of her habit – (I can never think of it without trembling!) – But ever since we had the history of that day, I have been so fond of Mr. Dixon!"

"But, in spite of all her friends' urgency, and her own wish of seeing Ireland, Miss Fairfax prefers devoting the time to you and Mrs. Bates?"

"Yes – entirely her own doing, entirely her own choice; and Colonel and Mrs. Campbell think she does quite right, just what they should recommend; and indeed they particularly *wish* her to try her native air, as she has not been quite so well as usual lately."

"I am concerned to hear of it. I think they judge wisely. But Mrs. Dixon must be very much disappointed. Mrs. Dixon, I understand, has no remarkable degree of personal beauty; is not, by any means, to be compared with Miss Fairfax."

"Oh! no. You are very obliging to say such things – but certainly not. There is no comparison between them. Miss Campbell always was absolutely plain – but extremely elegant and amiable."

"Yes, that of course."

"Jane caught a bad cold, poor thing! so long ago as the 7th of November, (as I am going to read to you,) and has never been well since. A long time, is not it, for a cold to hang upon her? She never mentioned it before, because she would not alarm us. Just like her! so considerate! – But however, she is so far from well, that her kind friends the Campbells think she had better come home, and try an air that always agrees with her; and they have no doubt that three or four months at Highbury will entirely cure her – and it is certainly a great deal better that she should come here, than go to Ireland, if she is unwell. Nobody could nurse her, as we should do."

"It appears to me the most desirable arrangement in the world."

"And so she is to come to us next Friday or Saturday, and the Campbells leave town in their way to Holyhead the Monday following – as you will find from Jane's letter. So sudden! – You may guess, dear Miss Woodhouse, what a flurry it has thrown me in! If it was not for the drawback of her illness – but I am afraid we must expect to see her grown thin, and looking very poorly. I must tell you what an unlucky thing happened to me, as to that. I always make a point of reading Jane's letters through to myself first, before I read them aloud to my mother, you know, for fear of there being any thing in them to distress her. Jane desired me to do it, so I always do: and so I began to-day with my usual caution; but no sooner did I come to the mention of her being unwell, than I burst out, quite frightened, with 'Bless me! poor Jane is ill!' – which my mother, being on the watch, heard distinctly, and was sadly alarmed at. However, when I read on, I found it was not near so bad as I had fancied at first; and I make so light of it now to her, that she does not think much about it. But I cannot imagine how I could be so off my guard. If Jane does not get well soon, we will call in Mr. Perry. The expense shall not be thought of; and though he is so liberal, and so fond of Jane that I dare say he would not mean to charge any thing for attendance, we could not suffer it to be so, you know. He has a wife and family to maintain, and is not to be giving away his time. Well, now I have just given you a hint of what Jane writes about, we will turn to her letter, and I am sure she tells her own story a great deal better than I can tell it for her."

"I am afraid we must be running away," said Emma, glancing at Harriet, and beginning to rise – "My father will be expecting us. I had no intention, I thought I had no power of staying more than five minutes, when I first entered the house. I merely called, because I would not pass the door without inquiring after Mrs. Bates; but I have been so pleasantly detained! Now, however, we must wish you and Mrs. Bates good morning."

And not all that could be urged to detain her succeeded. She regained the street – happy in this, that though much had been forced on her against her will, though she had in fact heard the whole substance of Jane Fairfax's letter, she had been able to escape the letter itself.

CHAPTER II

Jane Fairfax was an orphan, the only child of Mrs. Bates's youngest daughter.

The marriage of Lieut. Fairfax of the – regiment of infantry, and Miss Jane Bates, had had its day of fame and pleasure, hope and interest; but nothing now remained of it, save the melancholy remembrance of him dying in action abroad – of his widow sinking under consumption and grief soon afterwards – and this girl.

By birth she belonged to Highbury: and when at three years old, on losing her mother, she became the property, the charge, the consolation, the fondling of her grandmother and aunt, there had seemed every probability of her being permanently fixed there; of her being taught only what very limited means could command, and growing up with no advantages of connexion or improvement, to be engrafted on what nature had given her in a pleasing person, good understanding, and warm-hearted, well-meaning relations.

But the compassionate feelings of a friend of her father gave a change to her destiny. This was Colonel Campbell, who had very highly regarded Fairfax, as an excellent officer and most deserving young man; and farther, had been indebted to him for such attentions, during a severe camp-fever, as he believed had saved his life. These were claims which he did not learn to overlook, though some years passed away from the death of poor Fairfax, before his own return to England put any thing in his power. When he did return, he sought out the child and took notice of her. He was a married man, with only one living child, a girl, about Jane's age: and Jane became their guest, paying them long visits and growing a favourite with all; and before she was nine years old, his daughter's great fondness for her, and his own wish of being a real friend, united to produce an offer from Colonel Campbell of undertaking the whole charge of her education. It was accepted; and from that period Jane had belonged to Colonel Campbell's family, and had lived with them entirely, only visiting her grandmother from time to time.

The plan was that she should be brought up for educating others; the very few hundred pounds which she inherited from her father making independence impossible. To provide for her otherwise was out of Colonel Campbell's power; for though his income, by pay and appointments, was handsome, his fortune was moderate and must be all his daughter's; but, by giving her an education, he hoped to be supplying the means of respectable subsistence hereafter.

Such was Jane Fairfax's history. She had fallen into good hands, known nothing but kindness from the Campbells, and been given an excellent education. Living constantly with right-minded and well-informed people, her heart and understanding had received every advantage of discipline and culture; and Colonel Campbell's residence being in London, every lighter talent had been done full justice to, by the attendance of first-rate masters. Her disposition and abilities were equally worthy of all that friendship could do; and at eighteen or nineteen she was, as far as such an early age can be qualified for the care of children, fully competent to the office of instruction herself; but she was too much beloved to be parted with. Neither father nor mother could promote, and the daughter could not endure it. The evil day was put off. It was easy to decide that she was still too young; and Jane remained with them, sharing, as another daughter, in all the rational pleasures of an elegant society, and a judicious mixture of home and amusement, with only the drawback of the future, the sobering suggestions of her own good understanding to remind her that all this might soon be over.

The affection of the whole family, the warm attachment of Miss Campbell in particular, was the more honourable to each party from the circumstance of Jane's decided superiority both in beauty and acquirements. That nature had given it in feature could not be unseen by the young woman, nor could her higher powers of mind be unfelt by the parents. They continued together with unabated regard however, till the marriage of Miss Campbell, who by that chance, that luck which so often defies anticipation in matrimonial affairs, giving attraction to what is moderate rather than to what is superior, engaged the affections of Mr. Dixon, a young man, rich and agreeable, almost as soon as they were acquainted; and was eligibly and happily settled, while Jane Fairfax had yet her bread to earn.

This event had very lately taken place; too lately for any thing to be yet attempted by her less fortunate friend towards entering on her path of duty; though she had now reached the age which her own judgment had fixed on for beginning. She had long resolved that one-and-twenty should be the period. With the fortitude of a devoted novitiate, she had resolved at one-and-twenty to complete the sacrifice, and retire from all the pleasures of life, of rational intercourse, equal society, peace and hope, to penance and mortification for ever.

The good sense of Colonel and Mrs. Campbell could not oppose such a resolution, though their feelings did. As long as they lived, no exertions would be necessary, their home might be hers for ever; and for their own comfort they would have retained her wholly; but this would be selfishness:– what must be at last, had better be soon. Perhaps they began to feel it might have been kinder and wiser to have resisted the temptation of any delay, and spared her from a taste of such enjoyments of ease and leisure as must now be relinquished. Still, however, affection was glad to catch at any reasonable excuse for not hurrying on the wretched moment. She had never been quite well since the time of their daughter's marriage; and till she should have completely recovered her usual strength, they must forbid her engaging in duties, which, so far from being compatible with a weakened frame and varying spirits, seemed, under the most favourable circumstances, to require something more than human perfection of body and mind to be discharged with tolerable comfort.

With regard to her not accompanying them to Ireland, her account to her aunt contained nothing but truth, though there might be some truths not told. It was her own choice to give the time of their absence to Highbury; to spend, perhaps, her last months of perfect liberty with those kind relations to whom she was so very dear: and the Campbells, whatever might be their motive or motives, whether single, or double, or treble, gave the arrangement their ready sanction, and said, that they depended more on a few months spent in her native air, for the recovery of her health, than on any thing else. Certain it was that she was to come; and that Highbury, instead of welcoming that perfect novelty which had been so long promised it – Mr. Frank Churchill – must put up for the present with Jane Fairfax, who could bring only the freshness of a two years' absence.

Emma was sorry; – to have to pay civilities to a person she did not like through three long months! – to be always doing more than she wished, and less than she ought! Why she did not like Jane Fairfax might be a difficult question to answer; Mr. Knightley had once told her it was because she saw in her the really accomplished young woman, which she wanted to be thought herself; and though the accusation had been eagerly refuted at the time, there were moments of self-examination in which her conscience could not quite acquit her. But "she could never get acquainted with her: she did not know how it was, but there was such coldness and reserve – such apparent indifference whether she pleased or not – and then, her aunt was such an eternal talker! – and she was made such a fuss with by every body! – and it had been always imagined that they were to be so intimate – because their ages were the same, every body had supposed they must be so fond of each other." These were her reasons – she had no better.

It was a dislike so little just – every imputed fault was so magnified by fancy, that she never saw Jane Fairfax the first time after any considerable absence, without feeling that she had injured her;

and now, when the due visit was paid, on her arrival, after a two years' interval, she was particularly struck with the very appearance and manners, which for those two whole years she had been depreciating. Jane Fairfax was very elegant, remarkably elegant; and she had herself the highest value for elegance. Her height was pretty, just such as almost every body would think tall, and nobody could think very tall; her figure particularly graceful; her size a most becoming medium, between fat and thin, though a slight appearance of ill-health seemed to point out the likeliest evil of the two. Emma could not but feel all this; and then, her face – her features – there was more beauty in them altogether than she had remembered; it was not regular, but it was very pleasing beauty. Her eyes, a deep grey, with dark eyelashes and eyebrows, had never been denied their praise; but the skin, which she had been used to cavil at, as wanting colour, had a clearness and delicacy which really needed no fuller bloom. It was a style of beauty, of which elegance was the reigning character, and as such, she must, in honour, by all her principles, admire it:– elegance, which, whether of person or of mind, she saw so little in Highbury. There, not to be vulgar, was distinction, and merit.

In short, she sat, during the first visit, looking at Jane Fairfax with twofold complacency; the sense of pleasure and the sense of rendering justice, and was determining that she would dislike her no longer. When she took in her history, indeed, her situation, as well as her beauty; when she considered what all this elegance was destined to, what she was going to sink from, how she was going to live, it seemed impossible to feel any thing but compassion and respect; especially, if to every well-known particular entitling her to interest, were added the highly probable circumstance of an attachment to Mr. Dixon, which she had so naturally started to herself. In that case, nothing could be more pitiable or more honourable than the sacrifices she had resolved on. Emma was very willing now to acquit her of having seduced Mr. Dixon's actions from his wife, or of any thing mischievous which her imagination had suggested at first. If it were love, it might be simple, single, successless love on her side alone. She might have been unconsciously sucking in the sad poison, while a sharer of his conversation with her friend; and from the best, the purest of motives, might now be denying herself this visit to Ireland, and resolving to divide herself effectually from him and his connexions by soon beginning her career of laborious duty.

Upon the whole, Emma left her with such softened, charitable feelings, as made her look around in walking home, and lament that Highbury afforded no young man worthy of giving her independence; nobody that she could wish to scheme about for her.

These were charming feelings – but not lasting. Before she had committed herself by any public profession of eternal friendship for Jane Fairfax, or done more towards a recantation of past prejudices and errors, than saying to Mr. Knightley, "She certainly is handsome; she is better than handsome!" Jane had spent an evening at Hartfield with her grandmother and aunt, and every thing was relapsing much into its usual state. Former provocations reappeared. The aunt was as tiresome as ever; more tiresome, because anxiety for her health was now added to admiration of her powers; and they had to listen to the description of exactly how little bread and butter she ate for breakfast, and how small a slice of mutton for dinner, as well as to see exhibitions of new caps and new workbags for her mother and herself; and Jane's offences rose again. They had music; Emma was obliged to play; and the thanks and praise which necessarily followed appeared to her an affectation of candour, an air of greatness, meaning only to shew off in higher style her own very superior performance. She was, besides, which was the worst of all, so cold, so cautious! There was no getting at her real opinion. Wrapt up in a cloak of politeness, she seemed determined to hazard nothing. She was disgustingly, was suspiciously reserved.

If any thing could be more, where all was most, she was more reserved on the subject of Weymouth and the Dixons than any thing. She seemed bent on giving no real insight into Mr. Dixon's character, or her own value for his company, or opinion of the suitableness of the match. It was all general approbation and smoothness; nothing delineated or distinguished. It did her no service however. Her caution was thrown away. Emma saw its artifice, and returned to her first surmises. There probably *was* something more to conceal than her own preference; Mr. Dixon, perhaps, had been very near changing one friend for the other, or been fixed only to Miss Campbell, for the sake of the future twelve thousand pounds.

The like reserve prevailed on other topics. She and Mr. Frank Churchill had been at Weymouth at the same time. It was known that they were a little acquainted; but not a syllable of real information could Emma procure as to what he truly was. "Was he handsome?" – "She believed he was reckoned a very fine young man." "Was he agreeable?" – "He was generally thought so." "Did he appear a sensible young man; a young man of information?" – "At a watering-place, or in a common London acquaintance, it was difficult to decide on such points. Manners were all that could be safely judged of, under a much longer knowledge than they had yet had of Mr. Churchill. She believed every body found his manners pleasing." Emma could not forgive her.

CHAPTER III

Emma could not forgive her; – but as neither provocation nor resentment were discerned by Mr. Knightley, who had been of the party, and had seen only proper attention and pleasing behaviour on each side, he was expressing the next morning, being at Hartfield again on business with Mr. Woodhouse, his approbation of the whole; not so openly as he might have done had her father been out of the room, but speaking plain enough to be very intelligible to Emma. He had been used to think her unjust to Jane, and had now great pleasure in marking an improvement.

"A very pleasant evening," he began, as soon as Mr. Woodhouse had been talked into what was necessary, told that he understood, and the papers swept away; – "particularly pleasant. You and Miss Fairfax gave us some very good music. I do not know a more luxurious state, sir, than sitting at one's ease to be entertained a whole evening by two such young women; sometimes with music and sometimes with conversation. I am sure Miss Fairfax must have found the evening pleasant, Emma. You left nothing undone. I was glad you made her play so much, for having no instrument at her grandmother's, it must have been a real indulgence."

"I am happy you approved," said Emma, smiling; "but I hope I am not often deficient in what is due to guests at Hartfield."

"No, my dear," said her father instantly; "*that* I am sure you are not. There is nobody half so attentive and civil as you are. If any thing, you are too attentive. The muffin last night – if it had been handed round once, I think it would have been enough."

"No," said Mr. Knightley, nearly at the same time; "you are not often deficient; not often deficient either in manner or comprehension. I think you understand me, therefore."

An arch look expressed – "I understand you well enough;" but she said only, "Miss Fairfax is re-served."

"I always told you she was – a little; but you will soon overcome all that part of her reserve which ought to be overcome, all that has its foundation in diffidence. What arises from discretion must be honoured."

"You think her diffident. I do not see it."

"My dear Emma," said he, moving from his chair into one close by her, "you are not going to tell me, I hope, that you had not a pleasant evening."

"Oh! no; I was pleased with my own perseverance in asking questions; and amused to think how little information I obtained."

"I am disappointed," was his only answer.

"I hope every body had a pleasant evening," said Mr. Woodhouse, in his quiet way. "I had. Once, I felt the fire rather too much; but then I moved back my chair a little, a very little, and it did not disturb me. Miss Bates was very chatty and good-humoured, as she always is, though she speaks rather too quick. However, she is very agreeable, and Mrs. Bates too, in a different way. I like old friends; and Miss Jane Fairfax is a very pretty sort of young lady, a very pretty and a very well-behaved young lady indeed. She must have found the evening agreeable, Mr. Knightley, because she had Emma."

"True, sir; and Emma, because she had Miss Fairfax."

Emma saw his anxiety, and wishing to appease it, at least for the present, said, and with a sincerity which no one could question—

"She is a sort of elegant creature that one cannot keep one's eyes from. I am always watching her to admire; and I do pity her from my heart."

Mr. Knightley looked as if he were more gratified than he cared to express; and before he could make any reply, Mr. Woodhouse, whose thoughts were on the Bates's, said—

"It is a great pity that their circumstances should be so confined! a great pity indeed! and I have often wished – but it is so little one can venture to do – small, trifling presents, of any thing uncommon – Now we have killed a porker, and Emma thinks of sending them a loin or a leg; it is very small and delicate – Hartfield pork is not like any other pork – but still it is pork – and, my dear Emma, unless one could be sure of their making it into steaks, nicely fried, as ours are fried, without the smallest grease, and not roast it, for no stomach can bear roast pork – I think we had better send the leg – do not you think so, my dear?"

"My dear papa, I sent the whole hind-quarter. I knew you would wish it. There will be the leg to be salted, you know, which is so very nice, and the loin to be dressed directly in any manner they like."

"That's right, my dear, very right. I had not thought of it before, but that is the best way. They must not over-salt the leg; and then, if it is not over-salted, and if it is very thoroughly boiled, just as Serle boils ours, and eaten very moderately of, with a boiled turnip, and a little carrot or parsnip, I do not consider it unwholesome."

"Emma," said Mr. Knightley presently, "I have a piece of news for you. You like news – and I heard an article in my way hither that I think will interest you."

"News! Oh! yes, I always like news. What is it? – why do you smile so? – where did you hear it? – at Randalls?"

He had time only to say,

"No, not at Randalls; I have not been near Randalls," when the door was thrown open, and Miss Bates and Miss Fairfax walked into the room. Full of thanks, and full of news, Miss Bates knew not which to give quickest. Mr. Knightley soon saw that he had lost his moment, and that not another syllable of communication could rest with him.

"Oh! my dear sir, how are you this morning? My dear Miss Woodhouse – I come quite over-powered. Such a beautiful hind-quarter of pork! You are too bountiful! Have you heard the news? Mr. Elton is going to be married."

Emma had not had time even to think of Mr. Elton, and she was so completely surprized that she could not avoid a little start, and a little blush, at the sound.

"There is my news:– I thought it would interest you," said Mr. Knightley, with a smile which implied a conviction of some part of what had passed between them.

"But where could *you* hear it?" cried Miss Bates. "Where could you possibly hear it, Mr. Knightley? For it is not five minutes since I received Mrs. Cole's note – no, it cannot be more than five – or at least ten – for I had got my bonnet and spencer on, just ready to come out – I was only gone down to speak to Patty again about the pork – Jane was standing in the passage – were not you, Jane? – for my mother was so afraid that we had not any salting-pan large enough. So I said I would go down and see, and Jane said, 'Shall I go down instead? for I think you have a little cold, and Patty has been washing the kitchen.' – 'Oh! my dear,' said I – well, and just then came the note. A Miss Hawkins – that's all I know. A Miss Hawkins of Bath. But, Mr. Knightley, how could you possibly have heard it? for the very moment Mr. Cole told Mrs. Cole of it, she sat down and wrote to me. A Miss Hawkins–"

"I was with Mr. Cole on business an hour and a half ago. He had just read Elton's letter as I was shewn in, and handed it to me directly."

"Well! that is quite – I suppose there never was a piece of news more generally interesting. My dear sir, you really are too bountiful. My mother desires her very best compliments and regards, and a thousand thanks, and says you really quite oppress her."

"We consider our Hartfield pork," replied Mr. Woodhouse – "indeed it certainly is, so very superior to all other pork, that Emma and I cannot have a greater pleasure than–"

"Oh! my dear sir, as my mother says, our friends are only too good to us. If ever there were people who, without having great wealth themselves, had every thing they could wish for, I am sure it is us. We may well say that 'our lot is cast in a goodly heritage.' Well, Mr. Knightley, and so you actually saw the letter; well–"

"It was short – merely to announce – but cheerful, exulting, of course." – Here was a sly glance at Emma. "He had been so fortunate as to – I forget the precise words – one has no business to remember them. The information was, as you state, that he was going to be married to a Miss

Hawkins. By his style, I should imagine it just settled."

"Mr. Elton going to be married!" said Emma, as soon as she could speak. "He will have every body's wishes for his happiness."

"He is very young to settle," was Mr. Woodhouse's observation. "He had better not be in a hurry. He seemed to me very well off as he was. We were always glad to see him at Hartfield."

"A new neighbour for us all, Miss Woodhouse!" said Miss Bates, joyfully; "my mother is so pleased! – she says she cannot bear to have the poor old Vicarage without a mistress. This is great news, indeed. Jane, you have never seen Mr. Elton! – no wonder that you have such a curiosity to see him."

Jane's curiosity did not appear of that absorbing nature as wholly to occupy her.

"No – I have never seen Mr. Elton," she replied, starting on this appeal; "is he – is he a tall man?"

"Who shall answer that question?" cried Emma. "My father would say 'yes,' Mr. Knightley 'no;' and Miss Bates and I that he is just the happy medium. When you have been here a little longer, Miss Fairfax, you will understand that Mr. Elton is the standard of perfection in Highbury, both in person and mind."

"Very true, Miss Woodhouse, so she will. He is the very best young man – But, my dear Jane, if you remember, I told you yesterday he was precisely the height of Mr. Perry. Miss Hawkins, – I dare say, an excellent young woman. His extreme attention to my mother – wanting her to sit in the vicarage pew, that she might hear the better, for my mother is a little deaf, you know – it is not much, but she does not hear quite quick. Jane says that Colonel Campbell is a little deaf. He fancied bathing might be good for it – the warm bath – but she says it did him no lasting benefit. Colonel Campbell, you know, is quite our angel. And Mr. Dixon seems a very charming young man, quite worthy of him. It is such a happiness when good people get together – and they always do. Now, here will be Mr. Elton and Miss Hawkins; and there are the Coles, such very good people; and the Perrys – I suppose there never was a happier or a better couple than Mr. and Mrs. Perry. I say, sir," turning to Mr. Woodhouse, "I think there are few places with such society as Highbury. I always say, we are quite blessed in our neighbours. – My dear sir, if there is one thing my mother loves better than another, it is pork – a roast loin of pork–"

"As to who, or what Miss Hawkins is, or how long he has been acquainted with her," said Emma, "nothing I suppose can be known. One feels that it cannot be a very long acquaintance. He has been gone only four weeks."

Nobody had any information to give; and, after a few more wonderings, Emma said,

"You are silent, Miss Fairfax – but I hope you mean to take an interest in this news. You, who have been hearing and seeing so much of late on these subjects, who must have been so deep in the business on Miss Campbell's account – we shall not excuse your being indifferent about Mr. Elton and Miss Hawkins."

"When I have seen Mr. Elton," replied Jane, "I dare say I shall be interested – but I believe it requires *that* with me. And as it is some months since Miss Campbell married, the impression may be a little worn off."

"Yes, he has been gone just four weeks, as you observe, Miss Woodhouse," said Miss Bates, "four weeks yesterday. – A Miss Hawkins! – Well, I had always rather fancied it would be some young lady hereabouts; not that I ever – Mrs. Cole once whispered to me – but I immediately said, 'No, Mr. Elton is a most worthy young man – but' – In short, I do not think I am particularly quick at those sort of discoveries. I do not pretend to it. What is before me, I see. At the same time, nobody could wonder if Mr. Elton should have aspired – Miss Woodhouse lets me chatter on, so good-humouredly. She knows I would not offend for the world. How does Miss Smith do? She seems quite recovered now. Have you heard from Mrs. John Knightley lately? Oh! those dear little children. Jane, do you know I always fancy Mr. Dixon like Mr. John Knightley. I mean in person – tall, and with that sort of look – and not very talkative."

"Quite wrong, my dear aunt; there is no likeness at all."

"Very odd! but one never does form a just idea of any body beforehand. One takes up a notion, and runs away with it. Mr. Dixon, you say, is not, strictly speaking, handsome?"

"Handsome! Oh! no – far from it – certainly plain. I told you he was plain."

"My dear, you said that Miss Campbell would not allow him to be plain, and that you yourself–"

"Oh! as for me, my judgment is worth nothing. Where I have a regard, I always think a person well-looking. But I gave what I believed the general opinion, when I called him plain."

"Well, my dear Jane, I believe we must be running away. The weather does not look well, and grandmama will be uneasy. You are too obliging, my dear Miss Woodhouse; but we really must take leave. This has been a most agreeable piece of news indeed. I shall just go round by Mrs. Cole's; but I shall not stop three minutes: and, Jane, you had better go home directly – I would not have you out in a shower! – We think she is the better for Highbury already. Thank you, we do indeed. I shall not attempt calling on Mrs.

Goddard, for I really do not think she cares for any thing but *boiled* pork: when we dress the leg it will be another thing. Good morning to you, my dear sir. Oh! Mr. Knightley is coming too. Well, that is so very! – I am sure if Jane is tired, you will be so kind as to give her your arm. – Mr. Elton, and Miss Hawkins! – Good morning to you."

Emma, alone with her father, had half her attention wanted by him while he lamented that young people would be in such a hurry to marry – and to marry strangers too – and the other half she could give to her own view of the subject. It was to herself an amusing and a very welcome piece of news, as proving that Mr. Elton could not have suffered long; but she was sorry for Harriet: Harriet must feel it – and all that she could hope was, by giving the first information herself, to save her from hearing it abruptly from others. It was now about the time that she was likely to call. If she were to meet Miss Bates in her way! – and upon its beginning to rain, Emma was obliged to expect that the weather would be detaining her at Mrs. Goddard's, and that the intelligence would undoubtedly rush upon her without preparation.

The shower was heavy, but short; and it had not been over five minutes, when in came Harriet, with just the heated, agitated look which hurrying thither with a full heart was likely to give; and the "Oh! Miss Woodhouse, what do you think has happened!" which instantly burst forth, had all the evidence of corresponding perturbation. As the blow was given, Emma felt that she could not now shew greater kindness than in listening; and Harriet, unchecked, ran eagerly through what she had to tell. "She had set out from Mrs. Goddard's half an hour ago – she had been afraid it would rain – she had been afraid it would pour down every moment – but she thought she might get to Hartfield first – she had hurried on as fast as possible; but then, as she was passing by the house where a young woman was making up a gown for her, she thought she would just step in and see how it went on; and though she did not seem to stay half a moment there, soon after she came out it began to rain, and she did not know what to do; so she ran on directly, as fast as she could, and took shelter at Ford's." – Ford's was the principal woollen-draper, linen-draper, and haberdasher's shop united; the shop first in size and fashion in the place. – "And so, there she had set, without an idea of any thing in the world, full ten minutes, perhaps – when, all of a sudden, who should come in – to be sure it was so very odd! – but they always dealt at Ford's – who should come in, but Elizabeth Martin and her brother! – Dear Miss Woodhouse! only think. I thought I should have fainted. I did not know what to do. I was sitting near the door – Elizabeth saw me directly; but he did not; he was busy with the umbrella. I am sure she saw me, but she looked away directly, and took no notice; and they both went to quite the farther end of the shop; and I kept sitting near the door! – Oh! dear; I was so miserable! I am sure I must have been as white as my gown. I could not go away you know, because of the rain; but I did so wish myself anywhere in the world but there. – Oh! dear, Miss Woodhouse – well, at last, I fancy, he looked round and saw me; for instead of going on with her buyings, they began whispering to one another. I am sure they were talking of me; and I could not help thinking that he was persuading her to speak to me – (do you think he was, Miss Woodhouse?) – for presently she came forward – came quite up to me, and asked me how I did, and seemed ready to shake hands, if I would. She did not do any of it in the same way that she used; I could see she was altered; but, however, she seemed to *try* to be very friendly, and we shook hands, and stood talking some time; but I know no more what I said – I was in such a tremble! – I remember she said she was sorry we never met now; which I thought almost too kind! Dear, Miss Woodhouse, I was absolutely miserable! By that time, it was beginning to hold up, and I was determined that nothing should stop me from getting away – and then – only think! – I found he was coming up towards me too – slowly you know, and as if he did not quite know what to do; and so he came and spoke, and I answered – and I stood for a minute, feeling dreadfully, you know, one can't tell how; and then I took courage, and said it did not rain, and I must go; and so off I set; and I had not got three yards from the door, when he came after me, only to say, if I was going to Hartfield, he thought I had much better go round by Mr. Cole's stables, for I should find the near way quite floated by this rain. Oh! dear, I thought it would have been the death of me! So I said, I was very much obliged to him: you know I could not do less; and then he went back to Elizabeth, and I came round by the stables – I believe I did – but I hardly knew where I was, or any thing about it. Oh! Miss Woodhouse, I would rather done any thing than have it happen: and yet, you know, there was a sort of satisfaction in seeing him behave so pleasantly and so kindly. And Elizabeth, too. Oh! Miss Woodhouse, do talk to me and make me comfortable again."

Very sincerely did Emma wish to do so; but it was not immediately in her power. She was obliged to stop and think. She was not thoroughly comfortable herself. The young man's conduct, and his sister's, seemed the result of real feeling, and she could not but pity them. As Harriet described it, there had been an interesting mixture of wounded affection and genuine delicacy in their behaviour. But she had believed them to be well-meaning, worthy people before; and what difference did this make in the evils of the connexion? It was folly to be disturbed by it. Of course, he must be sorry to lose her – they must be all sorry. Ambition, as well as love, had probably been mortified. They might all have hoped to rise by Harriet's acquaintance: and besides, what was the value of Harriet's description? – So easily pleased – so little discerning; – what signified her praise?

She exerted herself, and did try to make her comfortable, by considering all that had passed as a mere trifle, and quite unworthy of being dwelt on,

"It might be distressing, for the moment," said she; "but you seem to have behaved extremely well; and it is over – and may never – can never, as a first meeting, occur again, and therefore you need not think about it."

Harriet said, "very true," and she "would not think about it;" but still she talked of it – still she could talk of nothing else; and Emma, at last, in order to put the Martins out of her head, was obliged to hurry on the news, which she had meant to give with so much tender caution; hardly knowing herself whether to rejoice or be angry, ashamed or only amused, at such a state of mind in poor Harriet – such a conclusion of Mr. Elton's importance with her!

Mr. Elton's rights, however, gradually revived. Though she did not feel the first intelligence as she might have done the day before, or an hour before, its interest soon increased; and before their first conversation was over, she had talked herself into all the sensations of curiosity, wonder and regret, pain and pleasure, as to this fortunate Miss Hawkins, which could conduce to place the Martins under proper subordination in her fancy.

Emma learned to be rather glad that there had been such a meeting. It had been serviceable in deadening the first shock, without retaining any influence to alarm. As Harriet now lived, the Martins could not get at her, without seeking her, where hitherto they had wanted either the courage or the condescension to seek her; for since her refusal of the brother, the sisters never had been at Mrs. Goddard's; and a twelvemonth might pass without their being thrown together again, with any necessity, or even any power of speech.

CHAPTER IV

Human nature is so well disposed towards those who are in interesting situations, that a young person, who either marries or dies, is sure of being kindly spoken of.

A week had not passed since Miss Hawkins's name was first mentioned in Highbury, before she was, by some means or other, discovered to have every recommendation of person and mind; to be handsome, elegant, highly accomplished, and perfectly amiable: and when Mr. Elton himself arrived to triumph in his happy prospects, and circulate the fame of her merits, there was very little more for him to do, than to tell her Christian name, and say whose music she principally played.

Mr. Elton returned, a very happy man. He had gone away rejected and mortified – disappointed in a very sanguine hope, after a series of what appeared to him strong encouragement; and not only losing the right lady, but finding himself debased to the level of a very wrong one. He had gone away deeply offended – he came back engaged to another – and to another as superior, of course, to the first, as under such circumstances what is gained always is to what is lost. He came back gay and self-satisfied, eager and busy, caring nothing for Miss Woodhouse, and defying Miss Smith.

The charming Augusta Hawkins, in addition to all the usual advantages of perfect beauty and merit, was in possession of an independent fortune, of so many thousands as would always be called ten; a point of some dignity, as well as some convenience: the story told well; he had not thrown himself away – he had gained a woman of 10,000*l.* or thereabouts; and he had gained her with such delightful rapidity – the first hour of introduction had been so very soon followed by distinguishing notice; the history which he had to give Mrs. Cole of the rise and progress of the affair was so glorious – the steps so quick, from the accidental rencontre, to the dinner at Mr. Green's, and the party at Mrs. Brown's – smiles and blushes rising in importance – with consciousness and agitation richly scattered – the lady had been so easily impressed – so sweetly disposed – had in short, to use a most intelligible phrase, been so very ready to have him, that vanity and prudence were equally contented.

He had caught both substance and shadow – both fortune and affection, and was just the happy man he ought to be; talking only of himself and his own concerns – expecting to be congratulated – ready to be laughed at – and, with cordial, fearless smiles, now addressing all the young ladies of the place, to whom, a few weeks ago, he would have been more cautiously gallant.

The wedding was no distant event, as the parties had only themselves to please, and nothing but the necessary preparations to wait for; and when he set out for Bath again, there was a general expectation, which a certain glance of Mrs. Cole's did not seem to contradict, that when he next entered Highbury he would bring his bride.

During his present short stay, Emma had barely seen him; but just enough to feel that the first meeting was over, and to give her the impression of his not being improved by the mixture of pique and pretension, now spread over his air. She was, in fact, beginning very much to wonder that she had ever thought him pleasing at all; and his sight was so inseparably connected with some very dis-agreeable feelings, that, except in a moral light, as a penance, a lesson, a source of profitable humiliation to her own mind, she would have been thankful to be assured of never seeing him again. She wished him very well; but he gave her pain, and his welfare twenty miles off would administer most satisfaction.

The pain of his continued residence in Highbury, however, must certainly be lessened by his marriage. Many vain solicitudes would be prevented – many awkwardnesses smoothed by it. A *Mrs.* Elton would be an excuse for any change of intercourse; former intimacy might sink without remark. It would be almost beginning their life of civility again.

Of the lady, individually, Emma thought very little. She was good enough for Mr. Elton, no doubt; accomplished enough for Highbury – handsome enough – to look plain, probably, by Harriet's side. As to connexion, there Emma was perfectly easy; persuaded, that after all his own vaunted claims and disdain of Harriet, he had done nothing. On that article, truth seemed attainable. *What* she was, must be uncertain; but *who* she was, might be found out; and setting aside the 10,000*l.*, it did not appear that she was at all Harriet's superior. She brought no name, no blood, no alliance. Miss

Hawkins was the youngest of the two daughters of a Bristol – merchant, of course, he must be called; but, as the whole of the profits of his mercantile life appeared so very moderate, it was not unfair to guess the dignity of his line of trade had been very moderate also. Part of every winter she had been used to spend in Bath; but Bristol was her home, the very heart of Bristol; for though the father and mother had died some years ago, an uncle remained – in the law line – nothing more distinctly honourable was hazarded of him, than that he was in the law line; and with him the daughter had lived. Emma guessed him to be the drudge of some attorney, and too stupid to rise. And all the grandeur of the connexion seemed dependent on the elder sister, who was *very well married*, to a gentleman in a *great way*, near Bristol, who kept two carriages! That was the wind-up of the history; that was the glory of Miss Hawkins.

Could she but have given Harriet her feelings about it all! She had talked her into love; but, alas! she was not so easily to be talked out of it. The charm of an object to occupy the many vacancies of Harriet's mind was not to be talked away. He might be superseded by another; he certainly would indeed; nothing could be clearer; even a Robert Martin would have been sufficient; but nothing else, she feared, would cure her. Harriet was one of those, who, having once begun, would be always in love. And now, poor girl! she was considerably worse from this reappearance of Mr. Elton. She was always having a glimpse of him somewhere or other. Emma saw him only once; but two or three times every day Harriet was sure *just* to meet with him, or *just* to miss him, *just* to hear his voice, or see his shoulder, *just* to have something occur to preserve him in her fancy, in all the favouring warmth of surprize and conjecture. She was, moreover, perpetually hearing about him; for, excepting when at Hartfield, she was always among those who saw no fault in Mr. Elton, and found nothing so interesting as the discussion of his concerns; and every report, therefore, every guess – all that had already occurred, all that might occur in the arrangement of his affairs, comprehending income, servants, and furniture, was continually in agitation around her. Her regard was receiving strength by invariable praise of him, and her regrets kept alive, and feelings irritated by ceaseless repetitions of Miss Hawkins's happiness, and continual observation of, how much he seemed attached! – his air as he walked by the house – the very sitting of his hat, being all in proof of how much he was in love!

Had it been allowable entertainment, had there been no pain to her friend, or reproach to herself, in the waverings of Harriet's mind, Emma would have been amused by its variations. Sometimes Mr. Elton predominated, sometimes the Martins; and each was occasionally useful as a check to the other. Mr. Elton's engagement had been the cure of the agitation of meeting Mr. Martin. The unhappiness produced by the knowledge of that engagement had been a little put aside by Elizabeth Martin's calling at Mrs. Goddard's a few days afterwards. Harriet had not been at home; but a note had been prepared and left for her, written in the very style to touch; a small mixture of reproach, with a great deal of kindness; and till Mr. Elton himself appeared, she had been much occupied by it, continually pondering over what could be done in return, and wishing to do more than she dared to confess. But Mr. Elton, in person, had driven away all such cares. While he staid, the Martins were forgotten; and on the very morning of his setting off for Bath again, Emma, to dissipate some of the distress it occasioned, judged it best for her to return Elizabeth Martin's visit.

How that visit was to be acknowledged – what would be necessary – and what might be safest, had been a point of some doubtful consideration. Absolute neglect of the mother and sisters, when invited to come, would be ingratitude. It must not be: and yet the danger of a renewal of the acquaintance!–

After much thinking, she could determine on nothing better, than Harriet's returning the visit; but in a way that, if they had understanding, should convince them that it was to be only a formal acquaintance. She meant to take her in the carriage, leave her at the Abbey Mill, while she drove a little farther, and call for her again so soon, as to allow no time for insidious applications or dangerous recurrences to the past, and give the most decided proof of what degree of intimacy was chosen for the future.

She could think of nothing better: and though there was something in it which her own heart could not approve – something of ingratitude, merely glossed over – it must be done, or what would become of Harriet?

CHAPTER V

Small heart had Harriet for visiting. Only half an hour before her friend called for her at Mrs. Goddard's, her evil stars had led her to the very spot where, at that moment, a trunk, directed to – The Rev. Philip Elton, White-Hart, *Bath*, was to be seen under the operation of being lifted into the butcher's cart, which was to convey it to where the coaches past; and every thing in this world, excepting that trunk and the direction, was consequently a blank.

She went, however; and when they reached the farm, and she was to be put down, at the end of the broad, neat gravel walk, which led between espalier apple-trees to the front door, the sight of every thing which had given her so much pleasure the autumn before, was beginning to revive a little local agitation; and when they parted, Emma observed her to be looking around with a sort of fearful curiosity, which determined her not to allow the visit to exceed the proposed quarter of an hour. She went on herself, to give that portion of time to an old servant who was married, and settled in Donwell.

The quarter of an hour brought her punctually to the white gate again; and Miss Smith receiving her summons, was with her without delay, and unattended by any alarming young man. She came solitarily down the gravel walk – a Miss Martin just appearing at the door, and parting with her seemingly with ceremonious civility.

Harriet could not very soon give an intelligible account. She was feeling too much; but at last Emma collected from her enough to understand the sort of meeting, and the sort of pain it was creating. She had seen only Mrs. Martin and the two girls. They had received her doubtingly, if not coolly; and nothing beyond the merest commonplace had been talked almost all the time – till just at last, when Mrs. Martin's saying, all of a sudden, that she thought Miss Smith was grown, had brought on a more interesting subject, and a warmer manner. In that very room she had been measured last September, with her two friends. There were the pencilled marks and memorandums on the wainscot by the window. *He* had done it. They all seemed to remember the day, the hour, the party, the occasion – to feel the same consciousness, the same regrets – to be ready to return to the same good understanding; and they were just growing again like themselves, (Harriet, as Emma must suspect, as ready as the best of them to be cordial and happy,) when the carriage reappeared, and all was over. The style of the visit, and the shortness of it, were then felt to be decisive. Fourteen minutes to be given to those with whom she had thankfully passed six weeks not six months ago! – Emma could not but picture it all, and feel how justly they might resent, how naturally Harriet must suffer. It was a bad business. She would have given a great deal, or endured a great deal, to have had the Martins in a higher rank of life. They were so deserving, that a *little* higher should have been enough: but as it was, how could she have done otherwise? – Impossible! – She could not repent. They must be separated; but there was a great deal of pain in the process – so much to herself at this time, that she soon felt the necessity of a little consolation, and resolved on going home by way of Randalls to procure it. Her mind was quite sick of Mr. Elton and the Martins. The refreshment of Randalls was absolutely necessary.

It was a good scheme; but on driving to the door they heard that neither "master nor mistress was at home;" they had both been out some time; the man believed they were gone to Hartfield.

"This is too bad," cried Emma, as they turned away. "And now we shall just miss them; too provoking! – I do not know when I have been so disappointed." And she leaned back in the corner, to indulge her murmurs, or to reason them away; probably a little of both – such being the commonest process of a not ill-disposed mind. Presently the carriage stopt; she looked up; it was stopt by Mr. and Mrs. Weston, who were standing to speak to her. There was instant pleasure in the sight of them, and still greater pleasure was conveyed in sound – for Mr. Weston immediately accosted her with,

"How d'ye do? – how d'ye do? – We have been sitting with your father – glad to see him so well. Frank comes to-morrow – I had a letter this morning – we see him to-morrow by dinner-time to a certainty – he is at Oxford to-day, and he comes for a whole fortnight; I knew it would be so. If he had come at Christmas he could not have staid three days; I was always glad he did not come at Christmas; now we are going to have just the right weather for him, fine, dry, settled weather. We shall enjoy him completely; every thing has turned out exactly as we could wish."

There was no resisting such news, no possibility of avoiding the influence of such a happy face as Mr. Weston's, confirmed as it all was by the words and the countenance of his wife, fewer and quieter, but not less to the purpose. To know that *she* thought his coming certain was enough to make Emma consider it so, and sincerely did she rejoice in their joy. It was a most delightful reanimation of exhausted spirits. The worn-out past was sunk in the freshness of what was coming; and in the rapidity of half a moment's thought, she hoped Mr. Elton would now be talked of no more.

Mr. Weston gave her the history of the engagements at Enscombe, which allowed his son to answer for having an entire fortnight at his command, as well as the route and the method of his journey; and she listened, and smiled, and congratulated.

"I shall soon bring him over to Hartfield," said he, at the conclusion.

Emma could imagine she saw a touch of the arm at this speech, from his wife.

"We had better move on, Mr. Weston," said she, "we are detaining the girls."

"Well, well, I am ready;" – and turning again to Emma, "but you must not be expecting such a *very* fine young man; you have only had *my* account you know; I dare say he is really nothing extraordinary:" – though his own sparkling eyes at the moment were speaking a very different conviction.

Emma could look perfectly unconscious and innocent, and answer in a manner that appropriated nothing.

"Think of me to-morrow, my dear Emma, about four o'clock," was Mrs. Weston's parting injunction; spoken with some anxiety, and meant only for her.

"Four o'clock! – depend upon it he will be here by three," was Mr. Weston's quick amendment; and so ended a most satisfactory meeting. Emma's spirits were mounted quite up to happiness; every thing wore a different air; James and his horses seemed not half so sluggish as before. When she looked at the hedges, she thought the elder at least must soon be coming out; and when she turned round to Harriet, she saw something like a look of spring, a tender smile even there.

"Will Mr. Frank Churchill pass through Bath as well as Oxford?" – was a question, however, which did not augur much.

But neither geography nor tranquillity could come all at once, and Emma was now in a humour to resolve that they should both come in time.

The morning of the interesting day arrived, and Mrs. Weston's faithful pupil did not forget either at ten, or eleven, or twelve o'clock, that she was to think of her at four.

"My dear, dear anxious friend," – said she, in mental soliloquy, while walking downstairs from her own room, "always overcareful for every body's comfort but your own; I see you now in all your little fidgets, going again and again into his room, to be sure that all is right." The clock struck twelve as she passed through the hall. "'Tis twelve; I shall not forget to think of you four hours hence; and by this time to-morrow, perhaps, or a little later, I may be thinking of the possibility of their all calling here. I am sure they will bring him soon."

She opened the parlour door, and saw two gentlemen sitting with her father – Mr. Weston and his son. They had been arrived only a few minutes, and Mr. Weston had scarcely finished his explanation of Frank's being a day before his time, and her father was yet in the midst of his very civil welcome and congratulations, when she appeared, to have her share of surprize, introduction, and pleasure.

The Frank Churchill so long talked of, so high in interest, was actually before her – he was presented to her, and she did not think too much had been said in his praise; he was a *very* good looking young man; height, air, address, all were unexceptionable, and his countenance had a great deal of the spirit and liveliness of his father's; he looked quick and sensible. She felt immediately that she should like him; and there was a well-bred ease of manner, and a readiness to talk, which convinced her that he came intending to be acquainted with her, and that acquainted they soon must be.

He had reached Randalls the evening before. She was pleased with the eagerness to arrive which had made him alter his plan, and travel earlier, later, and quicker, that he might gain half a day.

"I told you yesterday," cried Mr. Weston with exultation, "I told you all that he would be here before the time named. I remembered what I used to do myself. One cannot creep upon a journey; one cannot help getting on faster than one has planned; and the pleasure of coming in upon one's friends before the look-out begins, is worth a great deal more than any little exertion it needs."

"It is a great pleasure where one can indulge in it," said the young man, "though there are not many houses that I should presume on so far; but in coming *home* I felt I might do any thing."

The word *home* made his father look on him with fresh complacency. Emma was directly sure that he knew how to make himself agreeable; the conviction was strengthened by what followed. He was very much pleased with Randalls, thought it a most admirably arranged house, would hardly allow it even to be very small, admired the situation, the walk to Highbury, Highbury itself, Hartfield still more, and professed himself to have always felt the sort of interest in the country which none but one's *own* country gives, and the greatest curiosity to visit it. That he should never have been able to indulge so amiable a feeling before, passed suspiciously through Emma's brain; but still, if it were a falsehood, it was a pleasant one, and pleasantly handled. His manner had no air of study or exaggeration. He did really look and speak as if in a state of no common enjoyment.

Their subjects in general were such as belong to an opening acquaintance. On his side were the inquiries, – "Was she a horsewoman? – Pleasant rides? – Pleasant walks? – Had they a large neighbourhood? – Highbury, perhaps, afforded society enough? – There were several very pretty houses in and about it. – Balls – had they balls? – Was it a musical society?"

But when satisfied on all these points, and their acquaintance proportionably advanced, he contrived to find an opportunity, while their two fathers were engaged with each other, of introducing his mother-in-law, and speaking of her with so much handsome praise, so much warm admiration, so much gratitude for the happiness she secured to his father, and her very kind reception of himself, as was an additional proof of his knowing how to please – and of his certainly thinking it worth while to try to please her. He did not advance a word of praise beyond what she knew to be thoroughly deserved by Mrs. Weston; but, undoubtedly he could know very little of the matter. He understood what would be welcome; he could be sure of little else. "His father's marriage," he said, "had been the wisest measure, every friend must rejoice in it; and the family from whom he had received such a blessing must be ever considered as having conferred the highest obligation on him."

He got as near as he could to thanking her for Miss Taylor's merits, without seeming quite to forget that in the common course of things it was to be rather supposed that Miss Taylor had formed Miss Woodhouse's character, than Miss Woodhouse Miss Taylor's. And at last, as if resolved to qualify his opinion completely for travelling round to its object, he wound it all up with astonishment at the youth and beauty of her person.

"Elegant, agreeable manners, I was prepared for," said he; "but I confess that, considering every thing, I had not expected more than a very tolerably well-looking woman of a certain age; I did not know that I was to find a pretty young woman in Mrs. Weston."

"You cannot see too much perfection in Mrs. Weston for my feelings," said Emma; "were you to guess her to be *eighteen*, I should listen with pleasure; but *she* would be ready to quarrel with you for using such words. Don't let her imagine that you have spoken of her as a pretty young woman."

"I hope I should know better," he replied; "no, depend upon it, (with a gallant bow,) that in addressing Mrs. Weston I should understand whom I might praise without any danger of being thought extravagant in my terms."

Emma wondered whether the same suspicion of what might be expected from their knowing each other, which had taken strong possession of her mind, had ever crossed his; and whether his compliments were to be considered as marks of acquiescence, or proofs of defiance. She must see more of him to understand his ways; at present she only felt they were agreeable.

She had no doubt of what Mr. Weston was often thinking about. His quick eye she detected again and again glancing towards them with a happy expression; and even, when he might have determined not to look, she was confident that he was often listening.

Her own father's perfect exemption from any thought of the kind, the entire deficiency in him of all such sort of penetration or suspicion, was a most comfortable circumstance. Happily he was not farther from approving matrimony than from foreseeing it. – Though always objecting to every marriage that was arranged, he never suffered beforehand from the apprehension of any; it seemed as if he could not think so ill of any two persons' understanding as to suppose they meant to marry till it were proved against them. She blessed the favouring blindness. He could now, without the drawback of a single unpleasant surmise, without a glance forward at any possible treachery in his guest, give way to all his natural kind-hearted civility in solicitous inquiries after Mr. Frank Churchill's accommodation on his journey, through the sad evils of sleeping two nights on the road, and express very genuine unmixed anxiety to know that he had certainly escaped catching cold – which, however, he could not allow him to feel quite assured of himself till after another night.

A reasonable visit paid, Mr. Weston began to move. – "He must be going. He had business at the Crown about his hay, and a great many errands for Mrs. Weston at Ford's, but he need not hurry any body else." His son, too well bred to hear the hint, rose immediately also, saying,

"As you are going farther on business, sir, I will take the opportunity of paying a visit, which must be paid some day or other, and therefore may as well be paid now. I have the honour of being acquainted with a neighbour of yours, (turning to Emma,) a lady residing in or near Highbury; a family of the name of Fairfax. I shall have no difficulty, I suppose, in finding the house; though Fairfax, I believe, is not the proper name – I should rather say Barnes, or Bates. Do you know any family of that name?"

"To be sure we do," cried his father; "Mrs. Bates – we passed her house – I saw Miss Bates at the window. True, true, you are acquainted with Miss Fairfax; I remember you knew her at Weymouth, and a fine girl she is. Call upon her, by all means."

"There is no necessity for my calling this morning," said the young man; "another day would do as well; but there was that degree of acquaintance at Weymouth which–"

"Oh! go to-day, go to-day. Do not defer it. What is right to be done cannot be done too soon. And, besides, I must give you a hint, Frank; any want of attention to her *here* should be carefully avoided. You saw her with the Campbells, when she was the equal of every body she mixed with, but here she is with a poor old grandmother, who has barely enough to live on. If you do not call early it will be a slight."

The son looked convinced.

"I have heard her speak of the acquaintance," said Emma; "she is a very elegant young woman."

He agreed to it, but with so quiet a "Yes," as inclined her almost to doubt his real concurrence; and yet there must be a very distinct sort of elegance for the fashionable world, if Jane Fairfax could be thought only ordinarily gifted with it.

"If you were never particularly struck by her manners before," said she, "I think you will to-day. You will see her to advantage; see her and hear her – no, I am afraid you will not hear her at all, for she has an aunt who never holds her tongue."

"You are acquainted with Miss Jane Fairfax, sir, are you?" said Mr. Woodhouse, always the last to make his way in conversation; "then give me leave to assure you that you will find her a very agreeable young lady. She is staying here on a visit to her grandmama and aunt, very worthy people; I have known them all my life. They will be extremely glad to see you, I am sure; and one of my servants shall go with you to shew you the way."

"My dear sir, upon no account in the world; my father can direct me."

"But your father is not going so far; he is only going to the Crown, quite on the other side of the street, and there are a great many houses; you might be very much at a loss, and it is a very dirty walk, unless you keep on the footpath; but my coachman can tell you where you had best cross the street."

Mr. Frank Churchill still declined it, looking as serious as he could, and his father gave his hearty support by calling out, "My good friend, this is quite unnecessary; Frank knows a puddle of water when he sees it, and as to Mrs. Bates's, he may get there from the Crown in a hop, step, and jump."

They were permitted to go alone; and with a cordial nod from one, and a graceful bow from the other, the two gentlemen took leave. Emma remained very well pleased with this beginning of the acquaintance, and could now engage to think of them all at Randalls any hour of the day, with full confidence in their comfort.

CHAPTER VI

The next morning brought Mr. Frank Churchill again. He came with Mrs. Weston, to whom and to Highbury he seemed to take very cordially. He had been sitting with her, it appeared, most companionably at home, till her usual hour of exercise; and on being desired to chuse their walk, immediately fixed on Highbury. – "He did not doubt there being very pleasant walks in every direction, but if left to him, he should always chuse the same. Highbury, that airy, cheerful, happy-looking Highbury, would be his constant attraction." – Highbury, with Mrs. Weston, stood for Hartfield; and she trusted to its bearing the same construction with him. They walked thither directly.

Emma had hardly expected them: for Mr. Weston, who had called in for half a minute, in order to hear that his son was very handsome, knew nothing of their plans; and it was an agreeable surprize to her, therefore, to perceive them walking up to the house together, arm in arm. She was wanting to see him again, and especially to see him in company with Mrs. Weston, upon his behaviour to whom her opinion of him was to depend. If he were deficient there, nothing should make amends for it. But on seeing them together, she became perfectly satisfied. It was not merely in fine words or hyperbolical compliment that he paid his duty; nothing could be more proper or pleasing than his whole manner to her – nothing could more agreeably denote his wish of considering her as a friend and securing her affection. And there was time enough for Emma to form a reasonable judgment, as their visit included all the rest of the morning. They were all three walking about together for an hour or two – first round the shrubberies of Hartfield, and afterwards in Highbury. He was delighted with every thing; admired Hartfield sufficiently for Mr. Woodhouse's ear; and when their going farther was resolved on, confessed his wish to be made acquainted with the whole village, and found matter of commendation and interest much oftener than Emma could have supposed.

Some of the objects of his curiosity spoke very amiable feelings. He begged to be shewn the house which his father had lived in so long, and which had been the home of his father's father; and on recollecting that an old woman who had nursed him was still living, walked in quest of her cottage from one end of the street to the other; and though in some points of pursuit or observation there was no positive merit, they shewed, altogether, a good-will towards Highbury in general, which must be very like a merit to those he was with.

Emma watched and decided, that with such feelings as were now shewn, it could not be fairly supposed that he had been ever voluntarily absenting himself; that he had not been acting a part, or making a parade of insincere professions; and that Mr. Knightley certainly had not done him justice.

Their first pause was at the Crown Inn, an inconsiderable house, though the principal one of the sort, where a couple of pair of post-horses were kept, more for the convenience of the neighbourhood than from any run on the road; and his companions had not expected to be detained by any interest excited there; but in passing it they gave the history of the large room visibly added; it had been built many years ago for a ball-room, and while the neighbourhood had been in a particularly populous, dancing state, had been occasionally used as such; – but such brilliant days had long passed away, and now the highest purpose for which it was ever wanted was to accommodate a whist club established among the gentlemen and half-gentlemen of the place. He was immediately interested. Its character as a ball-room caught him; and instead of passing on, he stopt for several minutes at the two superior sashed windows which were open, to look in and contemplate its capabilities, and lament that its original purpose should have ceased. He saw no fault in the room, he would acknowledge none which they suggested. No, it was long enough, broad enough, handsome enough. It would hold the very number for comfort. They ought to have balls there at least every fortnight through the winter. Why had not Miss Woodhouse revived the former good old days of the room? – She who could do any thing in Highbury! The want of proper families in the place, and the conviction that none beyond the place and its immediate environs could be tempted to attend, were mentioned; but he was not satisfied. He could not be persuaded that so many good-looking houses as he saw around him, could not furnish numbers enough for such a meeting; and even when particulars were given and families described, he was still unwilling to admit that the inconvenience of such a mixture would be any thing, or that there would be the smallest difficulty in every body's returning into their proper place the next morning. He argued like a young man very much bent on dancing; and Emma was rather surprized to see the constitution of the Weston prevail so decidedly against the habits of the Churchills. He seemed to have all the life and spirit, cheerful feelings, and social inclinations of his father, and nothing of the pride or reserve of Enscombe. Of pride, indeed, there was, perhaps, scarcely enough; his indifference to a confusion of rank, bordered too much on inelegance of mind. He could be no judge, however, of the evil he was holding cheap. It was but an effusion of lively spirits.

At last he was persuaded to move on from the front of the Crown; and being now almost facing the house where the Bateses lodged, Emma recollected his intended visit the day before, and asked him if he had paid it.

"Yes, oh! yes" – he replied; "I was just going to mention it. A very successful visit:– I saw all the three ladies; and felt very much obliged to you for your preparatory hint. If the talking aunt had taken me quite by surprize, it must have been the death of me. As it was, I was only betrayed into paying a most unreasonable visit. Ten minutes would have been all that was necessary, perhaps all that was proper; and I had told my father I should certainly be at home before him – but there was no getting away, no pause; and, to my utter astonishment, I found, when he (finding me nowhere else) joined me there at last, that I had been actually sitting with them very nearly three-quarters of an hour. The good lady had not given me the possibility of escape before."

"And how did you think Miss Fairfax looking?"

"Ill, very ill – that is, if a young lady can ever be allowed to look ill. But the expression is hardly admissible, Mrs. Weston, is it? Ladies can never look ill. And, seriously, Miss Fairfax is naturally so pale, as almost always to give the appearance of ill health. – A most deplorable want of complex-ion."

Emma would not agree to this, and began a warm defence of Miss Fairfax's complexion. "It was certainly never brilliant, but she would not allow it to have a sickly hue in general; and there was a softness and delicacy in her skin which gave peculiar elegance to the character of her face." He listened with all due deference; acknowledged that he had heard many people say the same – but yet he must confess, that to him nothing could make amends for the want of the fine glow of health. Where features were indifferent, a fine complexion gave beauty to them all; and where they were good, the effect was – fortunately he need not attempt to describe what the effect was.

"Well," said Emma, "there is no disputing about taste. – At least you admire her except her complexion."

He shook his head and laughed. – "I cannot separate Miss Fairfax and her complexion."

"Did you see her often at Weymouth? Were you often in the same society?"

At this moment they were approaching Ford's, and he hastily exclaimed, "Ha! this must be the very shop that every body attends every day of their lives, as my father informs me. He comes to Highbury himself, he says, six days out of the seven, and has always business at Ford's. If it be not inconvenient to you, pray let us go in, that I may prove myself to belong to the place, to be a true citizen of Highbury. I must buy something at

Ford's. It will be taking out my freedom. – I dare say they sell gloves."

"Oh! yes, gloves and every thing. I do admire your patriotism. You will be adored in Highbury. You were very popular before you came, because you were Mr. Weston's son – but lay out half a guinea at Ford's, and your popularity will stand upon your own virtues."

They went in; and while the sleek, well-tied parcels of "Men's Beavers" and "York Tan" were bringing down and displaying on the counter, he said – "But I beg your pardon, Miss Woodhouse, you were speaking to me, you were saying something at the very moment of this burst of my *amor patriae*. Do not let me lose it. I assure you the utmost stretch of public fame would not make me amends for the loss of any happiness in private life."

"I merely asked, whether you had known much of Miss Fairfax and her party at Weymouth."

"And now that I understand your question, I must pronounce it to be a very unfair one. It is always the lady's right to decide on the degree of acquaintance. Miss Fairfax must already have given her account. – I shall not commit myself by claiming more than she may chuse to allow."

"Upon my word! you answer as discreetly as she could do herself. But her account of every thing leaves so much to be guessed, she is so very reserved, so very unwilling to give the least information about any body, that I really think you may say what you like of your acquaintance with her."

"May I, indeed? – Then I will speak the truth, and nothing suits me so well. I met her frequently at Weymouth. I had known the Campbells a little in town; and at Weymouth we were very much in the same set. Colonel Campbell is a very agreeable man, and Mrs. Campbell a friendly, warm-hearted woman. I like them all."

"You know Miss Fairfax's situation in life, I conclude; what she is destined to be?"

"Yes – (rather hesitatingly) – I believe I do."

"You get upon delicate subjects, Emma," said Mrs. Weston smiling; "remember that I am here. – Mr. Frank Churchill hardly knows what to say when you speak of Miss Fairfax's situation in life. I will move a little farther off."

"I certainly do forget to think of *her*," said Emma, "as having ever been any thing but my friend and my dearest friend."

He looked as if he fully understood and honoured such a sentiment.

When the gloves were bought, and they had quitted the shop again, "Did you ever hear the young lady we were speaking of, play?" said Frank Churchill.

"Ever hear her!" repeated Emma. "You forget how much she belongs to Highbury. I have heard her every year of our lives since we both began. She plays charmingly."

"You think so, do you? – I wanted the opinion of some one who could really judge. She appeared to me to play well, that is, with considerable taste, but I know nothing of the matter myself. – I am excessively fond of music, but without the smallest skill or right of judging of any body's performance. – I have been used to hear her's admired;

and I remember one proof of her being thought to play well:– a man, a very musical man, and in love with another woman – engaged to her – on the point of marriage – would yet never ask that other woman to sit down to the instrument, if the lady in question could sit down instead – never seemed to like to hear one if he could hear the other. That, I thought, in a man of known musical talent, was some proof."

"Proof indeed!" said Emma, highly amused. – "Mr. Dixon is very musical, is he? We shall know more about them all, in half an hour, from you, than Miss Fairfax would have vouchsafed in half a year."

"Yes, Mr. Dixon and Miss Campbell were the persons; and I thought it a very strong proof."

"Certainly – very strong it was; to own the truth, a great deal stronger than, if *I* had been Miss Campbell, would have been at all agreeable to me. I could not excuse a man's having more music than love – more ear than eye – a more acute sensibility to fine sounds than to my feelings. How did Miss Campbell appear to like it?"

"It was her very particular friend, you know."

"Poor comfort!" said Emma, laughing. "One would rather have a stranger preferred than one's very particular friend – with a stranger it might not recur again – but the misery of having a very particular friend always at hand, to do every thing better than one does oneself! – Poor Mrs. Dixon! Well, I am glad she is gone to settle in Ireland."

"You are right. It was not very flattering to Miss Campbell; but she really did not seem to feel it."

"So much the better – or so much the worse:– I do not know which. But be it sweetness or be it stupidity in her – quickness of friendship, or dulness of feeling – there was one person, I think, who must have felt it: Miss Fairfax herself. She must have felt the improper and dangerous distinction."

"As to that – I do not–"

"Oh! do not imagine that I expect an account of Miss Fairfax's sensations from you, or from any body else. They are known to no human being, I guess, but herself. But if she continued to play whenever she was asked by Mr. Dixon, one may guess what one chuses."

"There appeared such a perfectly good under-standing among them all –" he began rather quickly, but checking himself, added, "however, it is impossible for me to say on what terms they really were – how it might all be behind the scenes. I can only say that there was smoothness outwardly. But you, who have known Miss Fairfax from a child, must be a better judge of her character, and of how she is likely to conduct herself in critical situations, than I can be."

"I have known her from a child, undoubtedly; we have been children and women together; and it is natural to suppose that we should be inti-mate, – that we should have taken to each other whenever she visited her friends. But we never did. I hardly know how it has happened; a little, perhaps, from that wickedness on my side which was prone to take disgust towards a girl so idolized and so cried up as she always was, by her aunt and grandmother, and all their set. And then, her reserve – I never could attach myself to any one so completely reserved."

"It is a most repulsive quality, indeed," said he. "Oftentimes very convenient, no doubt, but never pleasing. There is safety in reserve, but no attraction. One cannot love a reserved person."

"Not till the reserve ceases towards oneself; and then the attraction may be the greater. But I must be more in want of a friend, or an agreeable companion, than I have yet been, to take the trouble of conquering any body's reserve to procure one. Intimacy between Miss Fairfax and me is quite out of the question. I have no reason to think ill of her – not the least – except that such extreme and perpetual cautiousness of word and manner, such a dread of giving a distinct idea about any body, is apt to suggest suspicions of there being something to conceal."

He perfectly agreed with her: and after walking together so long, and thinking so much alike, Emma felt herself so well acquainted with him, that she could hardly believe it to be only their second meeting. He was not exactly what she had expected; less of the man of the world in some of his notions, less of the spoiled child of fortune, therefore better than she had expected. His ideas seemed more moderate – his feelings warmer. She was particularly struck by his manner of considering Mr. Elton's house, which, as well as the church, he would go and look at, and would not join them in finding much fault with. No, he could not believe it a bad house; not such a house as a man was to be pitied for having. If it were to be shared with the woman he loved, he could not think any man to be pitied for having that house. There must be ample room in it for every real comfort. The man must be a blockhead who wanted more.

Mrs. Weston laughed, and said he did not know what he was talking about. Used only to a large house himself, and without ever thinking how many advantages and accommodations were attached to its size, he could be no judge of the privations inevitably belonging to a small one. But Emma, in her own mind, determined that he *did* know what he was talking about, and that he shewed a very amiable inclination to settle early in life, and to marry, from worthy motives. He might not be aware of the inroads on domestic peace to be occasioned by no housekeeper's room, or a bad butler's pantry, but no doubt he did perfectly feel that Enscombe could not make him happy, and that whenever he were attached, he would willingly give up much of wealth to be allowed an early establishment.

CHAPTER VII

Emma's very good opinion of Frank Churchill was a little shaken the following day, by hearing that he was gone off to London, merely to have his hair cut. A sudden freak seemed to have seized him at breakfast, and he had sent for a chaise and set off, intending to return to dinner, but with no more important view that appeared than having his hair cut. There was certainly no harm in his travelling sixteen miles twice over on such an errand; but there was an air of foppery and nonsense in it which she could not approve. It did not accord with the rationality of plan, the moderation in expense, or even the unselfish warmth of heart, which she had believed herself to discern in him yesterday. Vanity, extravagance, love of change, restlessness of temper, which must be doing something, good or bad; heedlessness as to the pleasure of his father and Mrs. Weston, indifferent as to how his conduct might appear in general; he became liable to all these charges. His father only called him a coxcomb, and thought it a very good story; but that Mrs. Weston did not like it, was clear enough, by her passing it over as quickly as possible, and making no other comment than that "all young people would have their little whims."

With the exception of this little blot, Emma found that his visit hitherto had given her friend only good ideas of him. Mrs. Weston was very ready to say how attentive and pleasant a companion he made himself – how much she saw to like in his disposition altogether. He appeared to have a very open temper – certainly a very cheerful and lively one; she could observe nothing wrong in his notions, a great deal decidedly right; he spoke of his uncle with warm regard, was fond of talking of him – said he would be the best man in the world if he were left to himself; and though there was no being attached to the aunt, he acknowledged her kindness with gratitude, and seemed to mean always to speak of her with respect. This was all very promising; and, but for such an unfortunate fancy for having his hair cut, there was nothing to denote him unworthy of the distinguished honour which her imagination had given him; the honour, if not of being really in love with her, of being at least very near it, and saved only by her own indifference – (for still her resolution held of never marrying) – the honour, in short, of being marked out for her by all their joint acquaintance.

Mr. Weston, on his side, added a virtue to the account which must have some weight. He gave her to understand that Frank admired her extremely – thought her very beautiful and very charming; and with so much to be said for him altogether, she found she must not judge him harshly. As Mrs. Weston observed, "all young people would have their little whims."

There was one person among his new acquaintance in Surry, not so leniently disposed. In general he was judged, throughout the parishes of Donwell and Highbury, with great candour; liberal allowances were made for the little excesses of such a handsome young man – one who smiled so often and bowed so well; but there was one spirit among them not to be softened, from its power of censure, by bows or smiles – Mr. Knightley. The circumstance was told him at Hartfield; for the moment, he was silent; but Emma heard him almost immediately afterwards say to himself, over a newspaper he held in his hand, "Hum! just the trifling, silly fellow I took him for." She had half a mind to resent; but an instant's observation convinced her that it was really said only to relieve his own feelings, and not meant to provoke; and therefore she let it pass.

Although in one instance the bearers of not good tidings, Mr. and Mrs. Weston's visit this morning was in another respect particularly opportune. Something occurred while they were at Hartfield, to make Emma want their advice; and, which was still more lucky, she wanted exactly the advice they gave.

This was the occurrence:– The Coles had been settled some years in Highbury, and were very good sort of people – friendly, liberal, and unpretending; but, on the other hand, they were of low origin, in trade, and only moderately genteel. On their first coming into the country, they had lived in proportion to their income, quietly, keeping little company, and that little unexpensively; but the last year or two had brought them a considerable increase of means – the house in town had yielded greater profits, and fortune in general had smiled on them. With their wealth, their views increased; their want of a larger house, their inclination for more company. They added to their house, to their number of servants, to their expenses of every sort; and by this time were, in fortune and style of living, second only to the family at Hartfield. Their love of society, and their new dining-room, prepared every body for their keeping dinner-company; and a few parties, chiefly among the single men, had already taken place. The regular and best families Emma could hardly suppose they would presume to invite – neither Donwell, nor Hartfield, nor Randalls. Nothing should tempt – her – to go, if they did; and she regretted that her father's known habits would be giving her refusal less meaning than she could wish. The Coles were very respectable in their way, but they ought to be taught that it was not for them to arrange the terms on which the superior families would visit them. This lesson, she very much feared, they would receive only from herself; she had little hope of Mr. Knightley, none of Mr. Weston.

But she had made up her mind how to meet this presumption so many weeks before it appeared, that when the insult came at last, it found her very differently affected. Donwell and Randalls had received their invitation, and none had come for her father and herself; and Mrs. Weston's accounting for it with "I suppose they will not take the liberty with you; they know you do not dine out," was not quite sufficient. She felt that she should like to have had the power of refusal; and afterwards, as the idea of the party to be assembled there, consisting precisely of those whose society was dearest to her, occurred again and again, she did not know that she might not have been tempted to accept. Harriet was to be there in the evening, and the Bateses. They had been speaking of it as they walked about Highbury the day before, and Frank Churchill had most earnestly lamented her absence. Might not the evening end in a dance? had been a question of his. The bare possibility of it acted as a farther irritation on her spirits; and her being left in solitary grandeur, even supposing the omission to be intended as a compliment, was but poor comfort.

It was the arrival of this very invitation while the Westons were at Hartfield, which made their presence so acceptable; for though her first remark, on reading it, was that "of course it must be declined," she so very soon proceeded to ask them what they advised her to do, that their advice for her going was most prompt and successful.

She owned that, considering every thing, she was not absolutely without inclination for the party. The Coles expressed themselves so properly – there was so much real attention in the manner of it – so much consideration for her father. "They would have solicited the honour earlier, but had been waiting the arrival of a folding-screen from London, which they hoped might keep Mr. Woodhouse from any draught of air, and therefore induce him the more readily to give them the honour of his company." Upon the whole, she was very persuadable; and it being briefly settled among themselves how it might be done without neglecting his comfort – how certainly Mrs. Goddard, if not Mrs. Bates, might be depended on for bearing him company – Mr. Woodhouse was to be talked into an acquiescence of his daughter's going out to dinner on a day now near at hand, and spending the whole evening away from him. As for *his* going, Emma did not wish him to think it possible, the hours would be too late, and the party too numerous. He was soon pretty well resigned.

"I am not fond of dinner-visiting," said he – "I never was. No more is Emma. Late hours do not agree with us. I am sorry Mr. and Mrs. Cole should have done it. I think it would be much better if they would come in one afternoon next summer, and take their tea with us – take us in their afternoon walk; which they might do, as our hours are so reasonable, and yet get home without being out in the damp of the evening. The dews of a summer evening are what I would not expose any body to. However, as they are so very desirous to have dear Emma dine with them, and as you will both be there, and Mr. Knightley too, to take care of her, I cannot wish to prevent it, provided the weather be what it ought, neither damp, nor cold, nor windy." Then turning to Mrs. Weston, with a look of gentle reproach – "Ah! Miss Taylor, if you had not married, you would have staid at home with me."

"Well, sir," cried Mr. Weston, "as I took Miss Taylor away, it is incumbent on me to supply her place, if I can; and I will step to Mrs. Goddard in a moment, if you wish it."

But the idea of any thing to be done in a *moment*, was increasing, not lessening, Mr. Woodhouse's agitation. The ladies knew better how to allay it. Mr. Weston must be quiet, and every thing deliberately arranged.

With this treatment, Mr. Woodhouse was soon composed enough for talking as usual. "He should be happy to see Mrs. Goddard. He had a great regard for Mrs. Goddard; and Emma should write a line, and invite her. James could take the note. But first of all, there must be an answer written to Mrs. Cole."

"You will make my excuses, my dear, as civilly as possible. You will say that I am quite an invalid, and go no where, and therefore must decline their obliging invitation; beginning with my compliments , of course. But you will do every thing right. I need not tell you what is to be done. We must remember to let James know that the carriage will be wanted on Tuesday. I shall have no fears for you with him. We have never been there above once since the new approach was made; but still I have no doubt that James will take you very safely. And when you get there, you must tell him at what time you would have him come for you again; and you had better name an early hour. You will not like staying late. You will get very tired when tea is over."

"But you would not wish me to come away before I am tired, papa?"

"Oh! no, my love; but you will soon be tired. There will be a great many people talking at once. You will not like the noise."

"But, my dear sir," cried Mr. Weston, "if Emma comes away early, it will be breaking up the party."

"And no great harm if it does," said Mr. Woodhouse. "The sooner every party breaks up, the better."

"But you do not consider how it may appear to the Coles. Emma's going away directly after tea might be giving offence. They are good-natured people, and think little of their own claims; but still they must feel that any body's hurrying away is no great compliment; and Miss Woodhouse's doing it would be more thought of than any other person's in the room. You would not wish to disappoint and mortify the Coles, I am sure, sir; friendly, good sort of people as ever lived, and who have been your neighbours these *ten* years."

"No, upon no account in the world, Mr. Weston; I am much obliged to you for reminding me. I should be extremely sorry to be giving them any pain. I know what worthy people they are. Perry tells me that Mr. Cole never touches malt liquor. You would not think it to look at him, but he is bilious – Mr. Cole is very bilious. No, I would not be the means of giving them any pain. My dear Emma, we must consider this. I am sure, rather than run the risk of hurting Mr. and Mrs. Cole, you would stay a little longer than you might wish. You will not regard being tired. You will be perfectly safe, you know, among your friends."

"Oh yes, papa. I have no fears at all for myself; and I should have no scruples of staying as late as Mrs. Weston, but on your account. I am only afraid of your sitting up for me. I am not afraid of your not being exceedingly comfortable with Mrs. Goddard. She loves piquet, you know; but when she is gone home, I am afraid you will be sitting up by yourself, instead of going to bed at your usual time – and the idea of that would entirely destroy my comfort. You must promise me not to sit up."

He did, on the condition of some promises on her side: such as that, if she came home cold, she would be sure to warm herself thoroughly; if hungry, that she would take something to eat; that her own maid should sit up for her; and that Serle and the butler should see that every thing were safe in the house, as usual.

CHAPTER VIII

Frank Churchill came back again; and if he kept his father's dinner waiting, it was not known at Hartfield; for Mrs. Weston was too anxious for his being a favourite with Mr. Woodhouse, to betray any imperfection which could be concealed.

He came back, had had his hair cut, and laughed at himself with a very good grace, but without seeming really at all ashamed of what he had done. He had no reason to wish his hair longer, to conceal any confusion of face; no reason to wish the money unspent, to improve his spirits. He was quite as undaunted and as lively as ever; and, after seeing him, Emma thus moralised to herself:–

"I do not know whether it ought to be so, but certainly silly things do cease to be silly if they are done by sensible people in an impudent way. Wickedness is always wickedness, but folly is not always folly. – It depends upon the character of those who handle it. Mr. Knightley, he is *not* a trifling, silly young man. If he were, he would have done this differently. He would either have gloried in the achievement, or been ashamed of it. There would have been either the ostentation of a cox-comb, or the evasions of a mind too weak to defend its own vanities. – No, I am perfectly sure that he is not trifling or silly."

With Tuesday came the agreeable prospect of seeing him again, and for a longer time than hitherto; of judging of his general manners, and by inference, of the meaning of his manners towards herself; of guessing how soon it might be necessary for her to throw coldness into her air; and of fancying what the observations of all those might be, who were now seeing them together for the first time.

She meant to be very happy, in spite of the scene being laid at Mr. Cole's; and without being able to forget that among the failings of Mr. Elton, even in the days of his favour, none had disturbed her more than his propensity to dine with Mr. Cole.

Her father's comfort was amply secured, Mrs. Bates as well as Mrs. Goddard being able to come; and her last pleasing duty, before she left the house, was to pay her respects to them as they sat together after dinner; and while her father was fondly noticing the beauty of her dress, to make the two ladies all the amends in her power, by helping them to large slices of cake and full glasses of wine, for whatever unwilling self-denial his care of their constitution might have obliged them to practise during the meal. – She had provided a plentiful dinner for them; she wished she could know that they had been allowed to eat it.

She followed another carriage to Mr. Cole's door; and was pleased to see that it was Mr. Knightley's; for Mr. Knightley keeping no horses, having little spare money and a great deal of health, activity, and independence, was too apt, in Emma's opinion, to get about as he could, and not use his carriage so often as became the owner of Donwell Abbey. She had an opportunity now of speaking her approbation while warm from her heart, for he stopped to hand her out.

"This is coming as you should do," said she; "like a gentleman. – I am quite glad to see you."

He thanked her, observing, "How lucky that we should arrive at the same moment! for, if we had met first in the drawing-room, I doubt whether you would have discerned me to be more of a gentleman than usual. – You might not have distinguished how I came, by my look or manner.”

“Yes I should, I am sure I should. There is always a look of consciousness or bustle when people come in a way which they know to be beneath them. You think you carry it off very well, I dare say, but with you it is a sort of bravado, an air of affected unconcern; I always observe it whenever I meet you under those circumstances. *Now* you have nothing to try for. You are not afraid of being supposed ashamed. You are not striving to look taller than any body else. *Now* I shall really be very happy to walk into the same room with you.”

“Nonsensical girl!” was his reply, but not at all in anger.

Emma had as much reason to be satisfied with the rest of the party as with Mr. Knightley. She was received with a cordial respect which could not but please, and given all the consequence she could wish for. When the Westons arrived, the kindest looks of love, the strongest of admiration were for her, from both husband and wife; the son approached her with a cheerful eagerness which marked her as his peculiar object, and at dinner she found him seated by her – and, as she firmly believed, not without some dexterity on his side.

The party was rather large, as it included one other family, a proper unobjectionable country family, whom the Coles had the advantage of naming among their acquaintance, and the male part of Mr. Cox's family, the lawyer of Highbury. The less worthy females were to come in the evening, with Miss Bates, Miss Fairfax, and Miss Smith; but already, at dinner, they were too numerous for any subject of conversation to be general; and, while politics and Mr. Elton were talked over, Emma could fairly surrender all her attention to the pleasantness of her neighbour. The first remote sound to which she felt herself obliged to attend, was the name of Jane Fairfax. Mrs. Cole seemed to be relating something of her that was expected to be very interesting. She listened, and found it well worth listening to. That very dear part of Emma, her fancy, received an amusing supply. Mrs. Cole was telling that she had been calling on Miss Bates, and as soon as she entered the room had been struck by the sight of a pi-anoforte – a very elegant looking instrument – not a grand, but a large-sized square pianoforte; and the substance of the story, the end of all the dialogue which ensued of surprize, and inquiry, and congratulations on her side, and explanations on Miss Bates's, was, that this pianoforte had arrived from Broadwood's the day before, to the great astonishment of both aunt and niece – entirely unexpected; that at first, by Miss Bates's account, Jane herself was quite at a loss, quite bewildered to think who could possibly have ordered it – but now, they were both perfectly satisfied that it could be from only one quarter; – of course it must be from Colonel Campbell.

"One can suppose nothing else," added Mrs. Cole, "and I was only surprized that there could ever have been a doubt. But Jane, it seems, had a letter from them very lately, and not a word was said about it. She knows their ways best; but I should not consider their silence as any reason for their not meaning to make the present. They might chuse to surprize her."

Mrs. Cole had many to agree with her; every body who spoke on the subject was equally convinced that it must come from Colonel Campbell, and equally rejoiced that such a present had been made; and there were enough ready to speak to allow Emma to think her own way, and still listen to Mrs. Cole.

"I declare, I do not know when I have heard any thing that has given me more satisfaction! – It always has quite hurt me that Jane Fairfax, who plays so delightfully, should not have an instrument. It seemed quite a shame, especially considering how many houses there are where fine instruments are absolutely thrown away. This is like giving ourselves a slap, to be sure! and it was but yesterday I was telling Mr. Cole, I really was ashamed to look at our new grand pianoforte in the drawing-room, while I do not know one note from another, and our little girls, who are but just beginning, perhaps may never make any thing of it; and there is poor Jane Fairfax, who is mistress of music, has not any thing of the nature of an instrument, not even the pitifullest old spinet in the world, to amuse herself with. – I was saying this to Mr. Cole but yesterday, and he quite agreed with me; only he is so particularly fond of music that he could not help indulging himself in the purchase, hoping that some of our good neighbours might be so obliging occasionally to put it to a better use than we can; and that really is the reason why the instrument was bought – or else I am sure we ought to be ashamed of it. – We are in great hopes that Miss Woodhouse may be prevailed with to try it this evening."

Miss Woodhouse made the proper acquiescence; and finding that nothing more was to be en-trapped from any communication of Mrs. Cole's, turned to Frank Churchill.

"Why do you smile?" said she.

"Nay, why do you?"

"Me! – I suppose I smile for pleasure at Colonel Campbell's being so rich and so liberal. – It is a handsome present."

"Very."

"I rather wonder that it was never made before."

"Perhaps Miss Fairfax has never been staying here so long before."

"Or that he did not give her the use of their own instrument – which must now be shut up in London, untouched by any body."

"That is a grand pianoforte, and he might think it too large for Mrs. Bates's house."

"You may *say* what you chuse – but your countenance testifies that your *thoughts* on this subject are very much like mine."

"I do not know. I rather believe you are giving me more credit for acuteness than I deserve. I smile because you smile, and shall probably suspect whatever I find you suspect; but at present I do not see what there is to question. If Colonel Campbell is not the person, who can be?"

"What do you say to Mrs. Dixon?"

"Mrs. Dixon! very true indeed. I had not thought of Mrs. Dixon. She must know as well as her father, how acceptable an instrument would be; and perhaps the mode of it, the mystery, the surprize, is more like a young woman's scheme than an elderly man's. It is Mrs. Dixon, I dare say. I told you that your suspicions would guide mine."

"If so, you must extend your suspicions and comprehend *Mr.* Dixon in them."

"Mr. Dixon. – Very well. Yes, I immediately perceive that it must be the joint present of Mr. and Mrs. Dixon. We were speaking the other day, you know, of his being so warm an admirer of her performance."

"Yes, and what you told me on that head, confirmed an idea which I had entertained before. – I do not mean to reflect upon the good intentions of either Mr. Dixon or Miss Fairfax, but I cannot help suspecting either that, after making his proposals to her friend, he had the misfortune to fall in love with *her*, or that he became conscious of a little attachment on her side. One might guess twenty things without guessing exactly the right; but I am sure there must be a particular cause for her chusing to come to Highbury instead of going with the Campbells to Ireland. Here, she must be leading a life of privation and penance; there it would have been all enjoyment. As to the pretence of trying her native air, I look upon that as a mere excuse. – In the summer it might have passed; but what can any body's native air do for them in the months of January, February, and March? Good fires and carriages would be much more to the purpose in most cases of delicate health, and I dare say in her's. I do not require you to adopt all my suspicions, though you make so noble a profession of doing it, but I honestly tell you what they are."

"And, upon my word, they have an air of great probability. Mr. Dixon's preference of her music to her friend's, I can answer for being very decided."

"And then, he saved her life. Did you ever hear of that? – A water party; and by some accident she was falling overboard. He caught her."

"He did. I was there – one of the party."

"Were you really? – Well! – But you observed nothing of course, for it seems to be a new idea to you. – If I had been there, I think I should have made some discoveries."

"I dare say you would; but I, simple I, saw nothing but the fact, that Miss Fairfax was nearly dashed from the vessel and that Mr. Dixon caught her. – It was the work of a moment. And though the consequent shock and alarm was very great and much more durable – indeed I believe it was half an hour before any of us were comfortable again – yet that was too general a sensation for any thing of peculiar anxiety to be observable. I do not mean to say, however, that you might not have made discoveries."

The conversation was here interrupted. They were called on to share in the awkwardness of a rather long interval between the courses, and obliged to be as formal and as orderly as the others; but when the table was again safely covered, when every corner dish was placed exactly right, and occupation and ease were generally restored, Emma said,

"The arrival of this pianoforte is decisive with me. I wanted to know a little more, and this tells me quite enough. Depend upon it, we shall soon hear that it is a present from Mr. and Mrs. Dixon."

"And if the Dixons should absolutely deny all knowledge of it we must conclude it to come from the Campbells."

"No, I am sure it is not from the Campbells. Miss Fairfax knows it is not from the Campbells, or they would have been guessed at first. She would not have been puzzled, had she dared fix on them. I may not have convinced you perhaps, but I am perfectly convinced myself that Mr. Dixon is a principal in the business."

"Indeed you injure me if you suppose me unconvinced. Your reasonings carry my judgment along with them entirely. At first, while I supposed you satisfied that Colonel Campbell was the giver, I saw it only as paternal kindness, and thought it the most natural thing in the world. But when you mentioned Mrs. Dixon, I felt how much more probable that it should be the tribute of warm female friendship. And now I can see it in no other light than as an offering of love."

There was no occasion to press the matter farther. The conviction seemed real; he looked as if he felt it. She said no more, other subjects took their turn; and the rest of the dinner passed away; the dessert succeeded, the children came in, and were talked to and admired amid the usual rate of conversation; a few clever things said, a few downright silly, but by much the larger proportion neither the one nor the other – nothing worse than everyday remarks, dull repetitions, old news, and heavy jokes.

The ladies had not been long in the drawing-room, before the other ladies, in their different divisions, arrived. Emma watched the entree of her own particular little friend; and if she could not exult in her dignity and grace, she could not only love the blooming sweetness and the artless manner, but could most heartily rejoice in that light, cheerful, unsentimental disposition which allowed her so many alleviations of pleasure, in the midst of the pangs of disappointed affection. There she sat – and who would have guessed how many tears she had been lately shedding? To be in company, nicely dressed herself and seeing others nicely dressed, to sit and smile and look pretty, and say nothing, was enough for the happiness of the present hour. Jane Fairfax did look and move superior; but Emma suspected she might have been glad to change feelings with Harriet, very glad to have purchased the mortification of having loved

– yes, of having loved even Mr. Elton in vain – by the surrender of all the dangerous pleasure of knowing herself beloved by the husband of her friend.

In so large a party it was not necessary that Emma should approach her. She did not wish to speak of the pianoforte, she felt too much in the secret herself, to think the appearance of curiosity or interest fair, and therefore purposely kept at a distance; but by the others, the subject was almost immediately introduced, and she saw the blush of consciousness with which congratulations were received, the blush of guilt which accompanied the name of "my excellent friend Colonel Campbell."

Mrs. Weston, kind-hearted and musical, was par-ticularly interested by the circumstance, and Emma could not help being amused at her perseverance in dwelling on the subject; and having so much to ask and to say as to tone, touch, and pedal, totally unsuspicious of that wish of saying as little about it as possible, which she plainly read in the fair heroine's countenance.

They were soon joined by some of the gentlemen; and the very first of the early was Frank Churchill.

In he walked, the first and the handsomest; and after paying his compliments en passant to Miss Bates and her niece, made his way directly to the opposite side of the circle, where sat Miss Woodhouse; and till he could find a seat by her, would not sit at all. Emma divined what every body present must be thinking. She was his object, and every body must perceive it. She introduced him to her friend, Miss Smith, and, at convenient moments afterwards, heard what each thought of the other. "He had never seen so lovely a face, and was delighted with her naivete." And she, "Only to be sure it was paying him too great a compliment, but she did think there were some looks a little like Mr. Elton." Emma restrained her indignation, and only turned from her in silence.

Smiles of intelligence passed between her and the gentleman on first glancing towards Miss Fairfax; but it was most prudent to avoid speech. He told her that he had been impatient to leave the dining-room – hated sitting long – was always the first to move when he could – that his father, Mr. Knightley, Mr. Cox, and Mr. Cole, were left very busy over parish business – that as long as he had staid, however, it had been pleasant enough, as he had found them in general a set of gentlemanlike, sensible men; and spoke so handsomely of Highbury altogether – thought it so abundant in agreeable families – that Emma began to feel she had been used to despise the place rather too much. She questioned him as to the society in Yorkshire – the extent of the neighbourhood about Enscombe, and the sort; and could make out from his answers that, as far as Enscombe was concerned, there was very little going on, that their visitings were among a range of great families, none very near; and that even when days were fixed, and invitations accepted, it was an even chance that Mrs. Churchill were not in health and spirits for going; that they made a point of visiting no fresh person; and that, though he had his separate engagements, it was not without difficulty, without considerable address *at times*, that he could get away, or introduce an acquaintance for a night.

She saw that Enscombe could not satisfy, and that Highbury, taken at its best, might reasonably please a young man who had more retirement at home than he liked. His importance at Enscombe was very evident. He did not boast, but it naturally betrayed itself, that he had persuaded his aunt where his uncle could do nothing, and on her laughing and noticing it, he owned that he believed (excepting one or two points) he could *with time* persuade her to any thing. One of those points on which his influence failed, he then mentioned. He had wanted very much to go abroad – had been very eager indeed to be allowed to travel – but she would not hear of it. This had happened the year before. *Now*, he said, he was beginning to have no longer the same wish.

The unpersuadable point, which he did not mention, Emma guessed to be good behaviour to his father.

"I have made a most wretched discovery," said he, after a short pause. – "I have been here a week to-morrow – half my time. I never knew days fly so fast. A week to-morrow! – And I have hardly begun to enjoy myself. But just got acquainted with Mrs. Weston, and others! – I hate the recollection."

"Perhaps you may now begin to regret that you spent one whole day, out of so few, in having your hair cut."

"No," said he, smiling, "that is no subject of regret at all. I have no pleasure in seeing my friends, unless I can believe myself fit to be seen."

The rest of the gentlemen being now in the room, Emma found herself obliged to turn from him for a few minutes, and listen to Mr. Cole. When Mr. Cole had moved away, and her attention could be restored as before, she saw Frank Churchill looking intently across the room at Miss Fairfax, who was sitting exactly opposite.

"What is the matter?" said she.

He started. "Thank you for rousing me," he replied. "I believe I have been very rude; but really Miss Fairfax has done her hair in so odd a way – so very odd a way – that I cannot keep my eyes from her. I never saw any thing so outree! – Those curls! – This must be a fancy of her own. I see nobody else looking like her! – I must go and ask her whether it is an Irish fashion. Shall I? – Yes, I will – I declare I will – and you shall see how she takes it; – whether she colours."

He was gone immediately; and Emma soon saw him standing before Miss Fairfax, and talking to her; but as to its effect on the young lady, as he had improvidently placed himself exactly between them, exactly in front of Miss Fairfax, she could absolutely distinguish nothing.

Before he could return to his chair, it was taken by Mrs. Weston.

"This is the luxury of a large party," said she:– "one can get near every body, and say every thing. My dear Emma, I am longing to talk to you. I have been making discoveries and forming plans, just like yourself, and I must tell them while the idea is fresh. Do you know how Miss Bates and her niece came here?"

"How? – They were invited, were not they?"

"Oh! yes – but how they were conveyed hither? – the manner of their coming?"

"They walked, I conclude. How else could they come?"

"Very true. – Well, a little while ago it occurred to me how very sad it would be to have Jane Fairfax walking home again, late at night, and cold as the nights are now. And as I looked at her, though I never saw her appear to more advantage, it struck me that she was heated, and would therefore be particularly liable to take cold. Poor girl! I could not bear the idea of it; so, as soon as Mr. Weston came into the room, and I could get at him, I spoke to him about the carriage. You may guess how readily he came into my wishes; and having his approbation, I made my way directly to Miss Bates, to assure her that the carriage would be at her service before it took us home; for I thought it would be making her comfortable at once. Good soul! she was as grateful as possible, you may be sure. 'Nobody was ever so fortunate as herself!' – but with many, many thanks – 'there was no occasion to trouble us, for Mr. Knightley's carriage had brought, and was to take them home again.' I was quite surprized; – very glad, I am sure; but really quite surprized. Such a very kind attention – and so thoughtful an attention! – the sort of thing that so few men would think of. And, in short, from knowing his usual ways, I am very much inclined to think that it was for their accommodation the carriage was used at all. I do suspect he would not have had a pair of horses for himself, and that it was only as an excuse for assisting them."

"Very likely," said Emma – "nothing more likely. I know no man more likely than Mr. Knightley to do the sort of thing – to do any thing really good-natured, useful, considerate, or benevolent. He is not a gallant man, but he is a very humane one; and this, considering Jane Fairfax's ill-health, would appear a case of humanity to him; – and for an act of unostentatious kindness, there is nobody whom I would fix on more than on Mr. Knightley. I know he had horses to-day – for we arrived together; and I laughed at him about it, but he said not a word that could betray."

"Well," said Mrs. Weston, smiling, "you give him credit for more simple, disinterested benevolence in this instance than I do; for while Miss Bates was speaking, a suspicion darted into my head, and I have never been able to get it out again. The more I think of it, the more probable it appears. In short, I have made a match between Mr. Knightley and Jane Fairfax. See the conse-quence of keeping you company! – What do you say to it?"

"Mr. Knightley and Jane Fairfax!" exclaimed Emma. "Dear Mrs. Weston, how could you think of such a thing? – Mr. Knightley! – Mr. Knightley must not marry! – You would not have little Henry cut out from Donwell? – Oh! no, no, Henry must have Donwell. I cannot at all consent to Mr. Knightley's marrying; and I am sure it is not at all likely. I am amazed that you should think of such a thing."

"My dear Emma, I have told you what led me to think of it. I do not want the match – I do not want to injure dear little Henry – but the idea has been given me by circumstances; and if Mr. Knightley really wished to marry, you would not have him refrain on Henry's account, a boy of six years old, who knows nothing of the matter?"

"Yes, I would. I could not bear to have Henry supplanted. – Mr. Knightley marry! – No, I have never had such an idea, and I cannot adopt it now. And Jane Fairfax, too, of all women!"

"Nay, she has always been a first favourite with him, as you very well know."

"But the imprudence of such a match!"

"I am not speaking of its prudence; merely its probability."

"I see no probability in it, unless you have any better foundation than what you mention. His good-nature, his humanity, as I tell you, would be quite enough to account for the horses. He has a great regard for the Bateses, you know, independent of Jane Fairfax – and is always glad to shew them attention. My dear Mrs. Weston, do not take to match-making. You do it very ill. Jane Fairfax mistress of the Abbey! – Oh! no, no; – every feeling revolts. For his own sake, I would not have him do so mad a thing."

"Imprudent, if you please – but not mad. Excepting inequality of fortune, and perhaps a little disparity of age, I can see nothing unsuitable."

"But Mr. Knightley does not want to marry. I am sure he has not the least idea of it. Do not put it into his head. Why should he marry? – He is as happy as possible by himself; with his farm, and his sheep, and his library, and all the parish to manage; and he is extremely fond of his brother's children. He has no occasion to marry, either to fill up his time or his heart."

"My dear Emma, as long as he thinks so, it is so; but if he really loves Jane Fairfax–"

"Nonsense! He does not care about Jane Fairfax. In the way of love, I am sure he does not. He would do any good to her, or her family; but–"

"Well," said Mrs. Weston, laughing, "perhaps the greatest good he could do them, would be to give Jane such a respectable home."

"If it would be good to her, I am sure it would be evil to himself; a very shameful and degrading connexion. How would he bear to have Miss Bates belonging to him? – To have her haunting the Abbey, and thanking him all day long for his great kindness in marrying Jane? – 'So very kind and obliging! – But he always had been such a very kind neighbour!' And then fly off, through half a sentence, to her mother's old petticoat. 'Not that it was such a very old petticoat either – for still it would last a great while – and, indeed, she must thankfully say that their petticoats were all very strong.'"

"For shame, Emma! Do not mimic her. You divert me against my conscience. And, upon my word, I do not think Mr. Knightley would be much disturbed by Miss Bates. Little things do not irritate him. She might talk on; and if he wanted to say any thing himself, he would only talk louder, and drown her voice. But the question is not, whether it would be a bad connexion for him, but whether he wishes it; and I think he does. I have heard him speak, and so must you, so very highly of Jane Fairfax! The interest he takes in her – his anxiety about her health – his concern that she should have no happier prospect! I have heard him express himself so warmly on those points! – Such an admirer of her performance on the pianoforte, and of her voice! I have heard him say that he could listen to her for ever. Oh! and I had almost forgotten one idea that occurred to me – this pianoforte that has been sent here by somebody – though we have all been so well satisfied to consider it a present from the Campbells, may it not be from Mr. Knightley? I cannot help suspecting him. I think he is just the person to do it, even without being in love."

"Then it can be no argument to prove that he is in love. But I do not think it is at all a likely thing for him to do. Mr. Knightley does nothing mysteriously."

"I have heard him lamenting her having no instrument repeatedly; oftener than I should suppose such a circumstance would, in the common course of things, occur to him."

"Very well; and if he had intended to give her one, he would have told her so."

"There might be scruples of delicacy, my dear Emma. I have a very strong notion that it comes from him. I am sure he was particularly silent when Mrs. Cole told us of it at dinner."

"You take up an idea, Mrs. Weston, and run away with it; as you have many a time reproached me with doing. I see no sign of attachment – I believe nothing of the pianoforte – and proof only shall convince me that Mr. Knightley has any thought of marrying Jane Fairfax."

They combated the point some time longer in the same way; Emma rather gaining ground over the mind of her friend; for Mrs. Weston was the most used of the two to yield; till a little bustle in the room shewed them that tea was over, and the instrument in preparation; – and at the same moment Mr. Cole approaching to entreat Miss Woodhouse would do them the honour of trying it. Frank Churchill, of whom, in the eagerness of her conversation with Mrs. Weston, she had been seeing nothing, except that he had found a seat by Miss Fairfax, followed Mr. Cole, to add his very pressing entreaties; and as, in every respect, it suited Emma best to lead, she gave a very proper compliance.

She knew the limitations of her own powers too well to attempt more than she could perform with credit; she wanted neither taste nor spirit in the little things which are generally acceptable, and could accompany her own voice well. One accompaniment to her song took her agreeably by surprize – a second, slightly but correctly taken by Frank Churchill. Her pardon was duly begged at the close of the song, and every thing usual followed. He was accused of having a delightful voice, and a perfect knowledge of music; which was properly denied; and that he knew nothing of the matter, and had no voice at all, roundly asserted. They sang together once more; and Emma would then resign her place to Miss Fairfax, whose performance, both vocal and instrumental, she never could attempt to conceal from herself, was infinitely superior to her own.

With mixed feelings, she seated herself at a little distance from the numbers round the instrument, to listen. Frank Churchill sang again. They had sung together once or twice, it appeared, at Weymouth. But the sight of Mr. Knightley among the most attentive, soon drew away half Emma's mind; and she fell into a train of thinking on the subject of Mrs. Weston's suspicions, to which the sweet sounds of the united voices gave only momentary interruptions. Her objections to Mr. Knightley's marrying did not in the least subside. She could see nothing but evil in it. It would be a great disappointment to Mr. John Knightley; consequently to Isabella. A real injury to the children – a most mortifying change, and material loss to them all; – a very great deduction from her father's daily comfort – and, as to herself, she could not at all endure the idea of Jane Fairfax at Donwell Abbey. A Mrs. Knightley for them all to give way to! – No – Mr. Knightley must never marry. Little Henry must remain the heir of Donwell.

Presently Mr. Knightley looked back, and came and sat down by her. They talked at first only of the performance. His admiration was certainly very warm; yet she thought, but for Mrs. Weston, it would not have struck her. As a sort of touchstone, however, she began to speak of his kindness in conveying the aunt and niece; and though his answer was in the spirit of cutting the matter short, she believed it to indicate only his disinclination to dwell on any kindness of his own.

"I often feel concern," said she, "that I dare not make our carriage more useful on such occasions. It is not that I am without the wish; but you know how impossible my father would deem it that James should put-to for such a purpose."

"Quite out of the question, quite out of the question," he replied; – "but you must often wish it, I am sure." And he smiled with such seeming pleasure at the conviction, that she must proceed another step.

"This present from the Campbells," said she – "this pianoforte is very kindly given."

"Yes," he replied, and without the smallest apparent embarrassment. – "But they would have done better had they given her notice of it. Surprizes are foolish things. The pleasure is not enhanced, and the inconvenience is often considerable. I should have expected better judgment in Colonel Campbell."

From that moment, Emma could have taken her oath that Mr. Knightley had had no concern in giving the instrument. But whether he were entirely free from peculiar attachment – whether there were no actual preference – remained a little longer doubtful. Towards the end of Jane's second song, her voice grew thick.

"That will do," said he, when it was finished, thinking aloud – "you have sung quite enough for one evening – now be quiet."

Another song, however, was soon begged for. "One more; – they would not fatigue Miss Fairfax on any account, and would only ask for one more." And Frank Churchill was heard to say, "I think you could manage this without effort; the first part is so very trifling. The strength of the song falls on the second."

Mr. Knightley grew angry.

"That fellow," said he, indignantly, "thinks of nothing but shewing off his own voice. This must not be." And touching Miss Bates, who at that moment passed near – "Miss Bates, are you mad, to let your niece sing herself hoarse in this manner? Go, and interfere. They have no mercy on her."

Miss Bates, in her real anxiety for Jane, could hardly stay even to be grateful, before she stept forward and put an end to all farther singing. Here ceased the concert part of the evening, for Miss Woodhouse and Miss Fairfax were the only young lady performers; but soon (within five minutes) the proposal of dancing – originating nobody exactly knew where – was so effectually promoted by Mr. and Mrs. Cole, that every thing was rapidly clearing away, to give proper space. Mrs. Weston, capital in her country-dances, was seated, and beginning an irresistible waltz; and Frank Churchill, coming up with most becoming gallantry to Emma, had secured her hand, and led her up to the top.

While waiting till the other young people could pair themselves off, Emma found time, in spite of the compliments she was receiving on her voice and her taste, to look about, and see what became of Mr. Knightley. This would be a trial. He was no dancer in general. If he were to be very alert in engaging Jane Fairfax now, it might augur something. There was no immediate appearance. No; he was talking to Mrs. Cole – he was looking on unconcerned; Jane was asked by somebody else, and he was still talking to Mrs. Cole.

Emma had no longer an alarm for Henry; his interest was yet safe; and she led off the dance with genuine spirit and enjoyment. Not more than five couple could be mustered; but the rarity and the suddenness of it made it very delightful, and she found herself well matched in a partner. They were a couple worth looking at.

Two dances, unfortunately, were all that could be allowed. It was growing late, and Miss Bates became anxious to get home, on her mother's account. After some attempts, therefore, to be permitted to begin again, they were obliged to thank Mrs. Weston, look sorrowful, and have done.

"Perhaps it is as well," said Frank Churchill, as he attended Emma to her carriage. "I must have asked Miss Fairfax, and her languid dancing would not have agreed with me, after your's."

CHAPTER IX

Emma did not repent her condescension in going to the Coles. The visit afforded her many pleasant recollections the next day; and all that she might be supposed to have lost on the side of dignified seclusion, must be amply repaid in the splendour of popularity. She must have delighted the Coles – worthy people, who deserved to be made happy! – And left a name behind her that would not soon die away.

Perfect happiness, even in memory, is not common; and there were two points on which she was not quite easy. She doubted whether she had not transgressed the duty of woman by woman, in betraying her suspicions of Jane Fairfax's feelings to Frank Churchill. It was hardly right; but it had been so strong an idea, that it would escape her, and his submission to all that she told, was a compliment to her penetration, which made it difficult for her to be quite certain that she ought to have held her tongue.

The other circumstance of regret related also to Jane Fairfax; and there she had no doubt. She did unfeignedly and unequivocally regret the inferiority of her own playing and singing. She did most heartily grieve over the idleness of her childhood – and sat down and practised vigorously an hour and a half.

She was then interrupted by Harriet's coming in; and if Harriet's praise could have satisfied her, she might soon have been comforted.

"Oh! if I could but play as well as you and Miss Fairfax!"

"Don't class us together, Harriet. My playing is no more like her's, than a lamp is like sunshine."

"Oh! dear – I think you play the best of the two. I think you play quite as well as she does. I am sure I had much rather hear you. Every body last night said how well you played."

"Those who knew any thing about it, must have felt the difference. The truth is, Harriet, that my playing is just good enough to be praised, but Jane Fairfax's is much beyond it."

"Well, I always shall think that you play quite as well as she does, or that if there is any difference nobody would ever find it out. Mr. Cole said how much taste you had; and Mr. Frank Churchill talked a great deal about your taste, and that he valued taste much more than execution."

"Ah! but Jane Fairfax has them both, Harriet."

"Are you sure? I saw she had execution, but I did not know she had any taste. Nobody talked about it. And I hate Italian singing. – There is no understanding a word of it. Besides, if she does play so very well, you know, it is no more than she is obliged to do, because she will have to teach. The Coxes were wondering last night whether she would get into any great family. How did you think the Coxes looked?"

"Just as they always do – very vulgar."

"They told me something," said Harriet rather hesitatingly; "but it is nothing of any consequence."

Emma was obliged to ask what they had told her, though fearful of its producing Mr. Elton.

"They told me – that Mr. Martin dined with them last Saturday."

"Oh!"

"He came to their father upon some business, and he asked him to stay to dinner."

"Oh!"

"They talked a great deal about him, especially Anne Cox. I do not know what she meant, but she asked me if I thought I should go and stay there again next summer."

"She meant to be impertinently curious, just as such an Anne Cox should be."

"She said he was very agreeable the day he dined there. He sat by her at dinner. Miss Nash thinks either of the Coxes would be very glad to marry him."

"Very likely. – I think they are, without exception, the most vulgar girls in Highbury."

Harriet had business at Ford's. – Emma thought it most prudent to go with her. Another accidental meeting with the Martins was possible, and in her present state, would be dangerous.

Harriet, tempted by every thing and swayed by half a word, was always very long at a purchase; and while she was still hanging over muslins and changing her mind, Emma went to the door for amusement. – Much could not be hoped from the traffic of even the busiest part of Highbury; – Mr. Perry walking hastily by, Mr. William Cox letting himself in at the office-door, Mr. Cole's carriage-horses returning from exercise, or a stray letter-boy on an obstinate mule, were the liveliest objects she could presume to expect; and when her eyes fell only on the butcher with his tray, a tidy old woman travelling homewards from shop with her full basket, two curs quarrelling over a dirty bone, and a string of dawdling children round the baker's little bow-window eyeing the ginger-bread, she knew she had no reason to complain, and was amused enough; quite enough still to stand at the door. A mind lively and at ease, can do with seeing nothing, and can see nothing that does not answer.

She looked down the Randalls road. The scene enlarged; two persons appeared; Mrs. Weston and her son-in-law; they were walking into Highbury; – to Hartfield of course. They were stopping, however, in the first place at Mrs. Bates's; whose house was a little nearer Randalls than Ford's; and had all but knocked, when Emma caught their eye. – Immediately they crossed the road and came forward to her; and the agreeableness of yesterday's engagement seemed to give fresh pleasure to the present meeting. Mrs. Weston informed her that she was going to call on the Bateses, in order to hear the new instrument.

"For my companion tells me," said she, "that I absolutely promised Miss Bates last night, that I would come this morning. I was not aware of it myself. I did not know that I had fixed a day, but as he says I did, I am going now."

"And while Mrs. Weston pays her visit, I may be allowed, I hope," said Frank Churchill, "to join your party and wait for her at Hartfield – if you are going home."

Mrs. Weston was disappointed.

"I thought you meant to go with me. They would be very much pleased."

"Me! I should be quite in the way. But, perhaps – I may be equally in the way here. Miss Woodhouse looks as if she did not want me. My aunt always sends me off when she is shopping. She says I fidget her to death; and Miss Woodhouse looks as if she could almost say the same. What am I to do?"

"I am here on no business of my own," said Emma; "I am only waiting for my friend. She will probably have soon done, and then we shall go home. But you had better go with Mrs. Weston and hear the instrument."

"Well – if you advise it. – But (with a smile) if Colonel Campbell should have employed a careless friend, and if it should prove to have an indifferent tone – what shall I say? I shall be no support to Mrs. Weston. She might do very well by herself. A disagreeable truth would be palatable through her lips, but I am the wretchedest being in the world at a civil falsehood."

"I do not believe any such thing," replied Emma. – "I am persuaded that you can be as insincere as your neighbours, when it is necessary; but there is no reason to suppose the instrument is indifferent. Quite otherwise indeed, if I understood Miss Fairfax's opinion last night."

"Do come with me," said Mrs. Weston, "if it be not very disagreeable to you. It need not detain us long. We will go to Hartfield afterwards. We will follow them to Hartfield. I really wish you to call with me. It will be felt so great an attention! and I always thought you meant it."

He could say no more; and with the hope of Hartfield to reward him, returned with Mrs. Weston to Mrs. Bates's door. Emma watched them in, and then joined Harriet at the interesting counter, – trying, with all the force of her own mind, to convince her that if she wanted plain muslin it was of no use to look at figured; and that a blue ribbon, be it ever so beautiful, would still never match her yellow pattern. At last it was all settled, even to the destination of the parcel.

"Should I send it to Mrs. Goddard's, ma'am?" asked Mrs. Ford. – "Yes – no – yes, to Mrs. Goddard's.

Only my pattern gown is at Hartfield. No, you shall send it to Hartfield, if you please. But then, Mrs. Goddard will want to see it. – And I could take the pattern gown home any day. But I shall want the ribbon directly – so it had better go to Hartfield – at least the ribbon. You could make it into two parcels, Mrs. Ford, could not you?"

"It is not worth while, Harriet, to give Mrs. Ford the trouble of two parcels."

"No more it is."

"No trouble in the world, ma'am," said the obliging Mrs. Ford.

"Oh! but indeed I would much rather have it only in one. Then, if you please, you shall send it all to Mrs. Goddard's – I do not know – No, I think, Miss Woodhouse, I may just as well have it sent to Hartfield, and take it home with me at night. What do you advise?"

"That you do not give another half-second to the subject. To Hartfield, if you please, Mrs. Ford."

"Aye, that will be much best," said Harriet, quite satisfied, "I should not at all like to have it sent to Mrs. Goddard's."

Voices approached the shop – or rather one voice and two ladies: Mrs. Weston and Miss Bates met them at the door.

"My dear Miss Woodhouse," said the latter, "I am just run across to entreat the favour of you to come and sit down with us a little while, and give us your opinion of our new instrument; you and Miss Smith. How do you do, Miss Smith? – Very well I thank you. – And I begged Mrs. Weston to come with me, that I might be sure of succeeding."

"I hope Mrs. Bates and Miss Fairfax are–"

"Very well, I am much obliged to you. My mother is delightfully well; and Jane caught no cold last night. How is Mr. Woodhouse? – I am so glad to hear such a good account. Mrs. Weston told me you were here. – Oh! then, said I, I must run across, I am sure Miss Woodhouse will allow me just to run across and entreat her to come in; my mother will be so very happy to see her – and now we are such a nice party, she cannot refuse. – 'Aye, pray do,' said Mr. Frank Churchill, 'Miss Woodhouse's opinion of the instrument will be worth having.' – But, said I, I shall be more sure of succeeding if one of you will go with me. – 'Oh,' said he, 'wait half a minute, till I have finished my job;' – For, would you believe it, Miss Woodhouse, there he is, in the most obliging manner in the world, fastening in the rivet of my mother's spectacles. – The rivet came out, you know, this morning. – So very obliging! – For my mother had no use of her spectacles – could not put them on. And, by the bye, every body ought to have two pair of spectacles; they should indeed. Jane said so. I meant to take them over to John Saunders the first thing I did, but something or other hindered me all the morning; first one thing, then another, there is no saying what, you know. At one time Patty came to say she thought the kitchen chimney wanted sweeping. Oh, said I, Patty do not come with your bad news to me. Here is the rivet of your mistress's spectacles out. Then the baked apples came home, Mrs. Wallis sent them by her boy; they are extremely civil and obliging to us, the Wallises, always – I have heard some people say that Mrs. Wallis can be uncivil and give a very rude answer, but we have never known any thing but the greatest attention from them. And it cannot be for the value of our custom now, for what is our consumption of bread, you know? Only three of us. – besides dear Jane at present – and she really eats nothing – makes such a shocking breakfast, you would be quite frightened if you saw it. I dare not let my mother know how little she eats – so I say one thing and then I say another, and it passes off. But about the middle of the day she gets hungry, and there is nothing she likes so well as these baked apples, and they are extremely wholesome, for I took the opportunity the other day of asking Mr. Perry; I happened to meet him in the street. Not that I had any doubt before – I have so often heard Mr. Woodhouse recommend a baked apple. I believe it is the only way that Mr. Woodhouse thinks the fruit thoroughly wholesome. We have apple-dumplings, however, very often. Patty makes an excellent apple-dumpling. Well, Mrs. Weston, you have prevailed, I hope, and these ladies will oblige us."

Emma would be "very happy to wait on Mrs. Bates, &c.," and they did at last move out of the shop, with no farther delay from Miss Bates than,

"How do you do, Mrs. Ford? I beg your pardon. I did not see you before. I hear you have a charming collection of new ribbons from town. Jane came back delighted yesterday. Thank ye, the gloves do very well – only a little too large about the wrist; but Jane is taking them in."

"What was I talking of?" said she, beginning again when they were all in the street.

Emma wondered on what, of all the medley, she would fix.

"I declare I cannot recollect what I was talking of. – Oh! my mother's spectacles. So very obliging of Mr. Frank Churchill! 'Oh!' said he, 'I do think I can fasten the rivet; I like a job of this kind excessively.' – Which you know shewed him to be so very... Indeed I must say that, much as I had heard of him before and much as I had expected, he very far exceeds any thing ... I do congratulate you, Mrs. Weston, most warmly. He seems every thing the fondest parent could ... 'Oh!' said he, 'I can fasten the rivet. I like a job of that sort excessively.' I never shall forget his manner. And when I brought out the baked apples from the closet, and hoped our friends would be so very obliging as to take some, 'Oh!' said he directly, 'there is nothing in the way of fruit half so good, and these are the finest-looking home-baked apples I ever saw in my life.' That, you know, was so very.... And I am sure, by his manner, it was no compliment. Indeed they are very delightful apples, and Mrs. Wallis does them full justice – only we do not have them baked more than twice, and Mr. Woodhouse made us promise to have them done three times – but Miss Woodhouse will be so good as not to mention it. The apples themselves are the very finest sort for baking, beyond a doubt; all from Donwell – some of Mr. Knightley's most liberal supply. He sends us a sack every year; and certainly there never was such a keeping apple anywhere as one of his trees – I believe there is two of them. My mother says the orchard was always famous in her younger days. But I was really quite shocked the other day – for Mr. Knightley called one morning, and Jane was eating these apples, and we talked about them and said how much she enjoyed them, and he asked whether we were not got to the end of our stock. 'I am sure you must be,' said he, 'and I will send you another supply; for I have a great many more than I can ever use. William Larkins let me keep a larger quantity than usual this year. I will send you some more, before they get good for nothing.' So I begged he would not – for really as to ours being gone, I could not absolutely say that we had a great many left – it was but half a dozen indeed; but they should be all kept for Jane; and I could not at all bear that he should be sending us more, so liberal as he had been already; and Jane said the same. And when he was gone, she almost quarrelled with me – No, I should not say quarrelled, for we never had a quarrel in our lives; but she was quite distressed that I had owned the apples were so nearly gone; she wished I had made him believe we had a great many left. Oh, said I, my dear, I did say as much as I could. However, the very same evening William Larkins came over with a large basket of apples, the same sort of apples, a bushel at least, and I was very much obliged, and went down and spoke to William Larkins and said every thing, as you may suppose. William Larkins is such an old acquaintance! I am always glad to see him. But, however, I found afterwards from Patty, that William said it was all the apples of *that* sort his master had; he had brought them all – and now his master had not one left to bake or boil. William did not seem to mind it himself, he was so pleased to think his master had sold so many; for William, you know, thinks more of his master's profit than any thing;

but Mrs. Hodges, he said, was quite displeased at their being all sent away. She could not bear that her master should not be able to have another apple-tart this spring. He told Patty this, but bid her not mind it, and be sure not to say any thing to us about it, for Mrs. Hodges *would* be cross sometimes, and as long as so many sacks were sold, it did not signify who ate the remainder. And so Patty told me, and I was excessively shocked indeed! I would not have Mr. Knightley know any thing about it for the world! He would be so very ... I wanted to keep it from Jane's knowledge; but, unluckily, I had mentioned it before I was aware."

Miss Bates had just done as Patty opened the door; and her visitors walked upstairs without having any regular narration to attend to, pursued only by the sounds of her desultory good-will.

"Pray take care, Mrs. Weston, there is a step at the turning. Pray take care, Miss Woodhouse, ours is rather a dark staircase – rather darker and narrower than one could wish. Miss Smith, pray take care. Miss Woodhouse, I am quite concerned, I am sure you hit your foot. Miss Smith, the step at the turning."

CHAPTER X

The appearance of the little sitting-room as they entered, was tranquillity itself; Mrs. Bates, deprived of her usual employment, slumbering on one side of the fire, Frank Churchill, at a table near her, most deedily occupied about her spectacles, and Jane Fairfax, standing with her back to them, intent on her pianoforte.

Busy as he was, however, the young man was yet able to shew a most happy countenance on seeing Emma again.

"This is a pleasure," said he, in rather a low voice, "coming at least ten minutes earlier than I had calculated. You find me trying to be useful; tell me if you think I shall succeed."

"What!" said Mrs. Weston, "have not you finished it yet? you would not earn a very good livelihood as a working silversmith at this rate."

"I have not been working uninterruptedly," he replied, "I have been assisting Miss Fairfax in trying to make her instrument stand steadily, it was not quite firm; an unevenness in the floor, I believe. You see we have been wedging one leg with paper. This was very kind of you to be persuaded to come. I was almost afraid you would be hurrying home."

He contrived that she should be seated by him; and was sufficiently employed in looking out the best baked apple for her, and trying to make her help or advise him in his work, till Jane Fairfax was quite ready to sit down to the pianoforte again. That she was not immediately ready, Emma did suspect to arise from the state of her nerves; she had not yet possessed the instrument long enough to touch it without emotion; she must reason herself into the power of performance; and Emma could not but pity such feelings, whatever their origin, and could not but resolve never to expose them to her neighbour again.

At last Jane began, and though the first bars were feebly given, the powers of the instrument were gradually done full justice to. Mrs. Weston had been delighted before, and was delighted again; Emma joined her in all her praise; and the pianoforte, with every proper discrimination, was pronounced to be altogether of the highest promise.

"Whoever Colonel Campbell might employ," said Frank Churchill, with a smile at Emma, "the person has not chosen ill. I heard a good deal of Colonel Campbell's taste at Weymouth; and the softness of the upper notes I am sure is exactly what he and *all that party* would particularly prize. I dare say, Miss Fairfax, that he either gave his friend very minute directions, or wrote to Broadwood himself. Do not you think so?"

Jane did not look round. She was not obliged to hear. Mrs. Weston had been speaking to her at the same moment.

"It is not fair," said Emma, in a whisper; "mine was a random guess. Do not distress her."

He shook his head with a smile, and looked as if he had very little doubt and very little mercy. Soon afterwards he began again,

"How much your friends in Ireland must be enjoying your pleasure on this occasion, Miss Fairfax. I dare say they often think of you, and wonder which will be the day, the precise day of the instrument's coming to hand. Do you imagine Colonel Campbell knows the business to be going forward just at this time? – Do you imagine it to be the consequence of an immediate commission from him, or that he may have sent only a general direction, an order indefinite as to time, to depend upon contingencies and conveniences?"

He paused. She could not but hear; she could not avoid answering,

"Till I have a letter from Colonel Campbell," said she, in a voice of forced calmness, "I can imagine nothing with any confidence. It must be all conjecture."

"Conjecture – aye, sometimes one conjectures right, and sometimes one conjectures wrong. I wish I could conjecture how soon I shall make this rivet quite firm. What nonsense one talks, Miss Woodhouse, when hard at work, if one talks at all; – your real workmen, I suppose, hold their tongues; but we gentlemen labourers if we get hold of a word – Miss Fairfax said something about conjecturing. There, it is done. I have the pleasure, madam, (to Mrs. Bates,) of restoring your spectacles, healed for the present."

He was very warmly thanked both by mother and daughter; to escape a little from the latter, he went to the pianoforte, and begged Miss Fairfax, who was still sitting at it, to play something more.

"If you are very kind," said he, "it will be one of the waltzes we danced last night; – let me live them over again. You did not enjoy them as I did; you appeared tired the whole time. I believe you were glad we danced no longer; but I would have given worlds – all the worlds one ever has to give – for another half-hour."

She played.

"What felicity it is to hear a tune again which *has* made one happy! – If I mistake not that was danced at Weymouth."

She looked up at him for a moment, coloured deeply, and played something else. He took some music from a chair near the pianoforte, and turning to Emma, said,

"Here is something quite new to me. Do you know it? – Cramer. – And here are a new set of Irish melodies. That, from such a quarter, one might expect. This was all sent with the instrument. Very thoughtful of Colonel Campbell, was not it? – He knew Miss Fairfax could have no music here. I honour that part of the attention particularly; it shews it to have been so thoroughly from the heart. Nothing hastily done; nothing incomplete. True affection only could have prompted it."

Emma wished he would be less pointed, yet could not help being amused; and when on glancing her eye towards Jane Fairfax she caught the remains of a smile, when she saw that with all the deep blush of consciousness, there had been a smile of secret delight, she had less scruple in the amusement, and much less compunction with respect to her. – This amiable, upright, perfect Jane Fairfax was apparently cherishing very reprehensible feelings.

He brought all the music to her, and they looked it over together. – Emma took the opportunity of whispering,

"You speak too plain. She must understand you."

"I hope she does. I would have her understand me. I am not in the least ashamed of my meaning."

"But really, I am half ashamed, and wish I had never taken up the idea."

"I am very glad you did, and that you communicated it to me. I have now a key to all her odd looks and ways. Leave shame to her. If she does wrong, she ought to feel it."

"She is not entirely without it, I think."

"I do not see much sign of it. She is playing *Robin Adair* at this moment *his* favourite."

Shortly afterwards Miss Bates, passing near the window, descried Mr. Knightley on horseback not far off.

"Mr. Knightley I declare! – I must speak to him if possible, just to thank him. I will not open the window here; it would give you all cold; but I can go into my mother's room you know. I dare say he will come in when he knows who is here. Quite delightful to have you all meet so! – Our little room so honoured!"

She was in the adjoining chamber while she still spoke, and opening the casement there, immediately called Mr. Knightley's attention, and every syllable of their conversation was as distinctly heard by the others, as if it had passed within the same apartment.

"How d' ye do? – how d'ye do? – Very well, I thank you. So obliged to you for the carriage last night. We were just in time; my mother just ready for us. Pray come in; do come in. You will find some friends here."

So began Miss Bates; and Mr. Knightley seemed determined to be heard in his turn, for most resolutely and commandingly did he say,

"How is your niece, Miss Bates? – I want to inquire after you all, but particularly your niece. How is Miss Fairfax? – I hope she caught no cold last night. How is she to-day? Tell me how Miss Fairfax is."

And Miss Bates was obliged to give a direct answer before he would hear her in any thing else. The listeners were amused; and Mrs. Weston gave Emma a look of particular meaning. But Emma still shook her head in steady scepticism.

"So obliged to you! – so very much obliged to you for the carriage," resumed Miss Bates.

He cut her short with,

"I am going to Kingston. Can I do any thing for you?"

"Oh! dear, Kingston – are you? – Mrs. Cole was saying the other day she wanted something from Kingston."

"Mrs. Cole has servants to send. Can I do any thing for *you*?"

"No, I thank you. But do come in. Who do you think is here? – Miss Woodhouse and Miss Smith; so kind as to call to hear the new pianoforte. Do put up your horse at the Crown, and come in."

"Well," said he, in a deliberating manner, "for five minutes, perhaps."

"And here is Mrs. Weston and Mr. Frank Churchill too! – Quite delightful; so many friends!"

"No, not now, I thank you. I could not stay two minutes. I must get on to Kingston as fast as I can."

"Oh! do come in. They will be so very happy to see you."

"No, no; your room is full enough. I will call another day, and hear the pianoforte."

"Well, I am so sorry! – Oh! Mr. Knightley, what a delightful party last night; how extremely pleasant. – Did you ever see such dancing? – Was not it delightful? – Miss Woodhouse and Mr. Frank Churchill; I never saw any thing equal to it."

"Oh! very delightful indeed; I can say nothing less, for I suppose Miss Woodhouse and Mr. Frank Churchill are hearing every thing that passes. And (raising his voice still more) I do not see why Miss Fairfax should not be mentioned too. I think Miss Fairfax dances very well; and Mrs. Weston is the very best country-dance player, without exception, in England. Now, if your friends have any gratitude, they will say something pretty loud about you and me in return; but I cannot stay to hear it."

"Oh! Mr. Knightley, one moment more; something of consequence – so shocked! – Jane and I are both so shocked about the apples!"

"What is the matter now?"

"To think of your sending us all your store apples. You said you had a great many, and now you have not one left. We really are so shocked! Mrs. Hodges may well be angry. William Larkins mentioned it here. You should not have done it, indeed you should not. Ah! he is off. He never can bear to be thanked. But I thought he would have staid now, and it would have been a pity not to have mentioned ... Well, (returning to the room,) I have not been able to succeed. Mr. Knightley cannot stop. He is going to Kingston. He asked me if he could do any thing..."

"Yes," said Jane, "we heard his kind offers, we heard every thing."

"Oh! yes, my dear, I dare say you might, because you know, the door was open, and the window was open, and Mr. Knightley spoke loud. You must have heard every thing to be sure. 'Can I do any thing for you at Kingston?' said he; so I just mentioned ... Oh! Miss Woodhouse, must you be going? – You seem but just come – so very obliging of you."

Emma found it really time to be at home; the visit had already lasted long; and on examining watches, so much of the morning was perceived to be gone, that Mrs. Weston and her companion taking leave also, could allow themselves only to walk with the two young ladies to Hartfield gates, before they set off for Randalls.

CHAPTER XI

It may be possible to do without dancing entirely. Instances have been known of young people passing many, many months successively, without being at any ball of any description, and no material injury accrue either to body or mind; – but when a beginning is made – when the felicities of rapid motion have once been, though slightly, felt – it must be a very heavy set that does not ask for more.

Frank Churchill had danced once at Highbury, and longed to dance again; and the last half-hour of an evening which Mr. Woodhouse was persuaded to spend with his daughter at Randalls, was passed by the two young people in schemes on the subject. Frank's was the first idea; and his the greatest zeal in pursuing it; for the lady was the best judge of the difficulties, and the most solicitous for accommodation and appearance. But still she had inclination enough for shewing people again how delightfully Mr. Frank Churchill and Miss Woodhouse danced – for doing that in which she need not blush to compare herself with Jane Fairfax – and even for simple dancing itself, without any of the wicked aids of vanity – to assist him first in pacing out the room they were in to see what it could be made to hold – and then in taking the dimensions of the other parlour, in the hope of discovering, in spite of all that Mr. Weston could say of their exactly equal size, that it was a little the largest.

His first proposition and request, that the dance begun at Mr. Cole's should be finished there – that the same party should be collected, and the same musician engaged, met with the readiest acquiescence. Mr. Weston entered into the idea with thorough enjoyment, and Mrs. Weston most willingly undertook to play as long as they could wish to dance; and the interesting employment had followed, of reckoning up exactly who there would be, and portioning out the indispensable division of space to every couple.

"You and Miss Smith, and Miss Fairfax, will be three, and the two Miss Coxes five," had been repeated many times over. "And there will be the two Gilberts, young Cox, my father, and myself, besides Mr. Knightley. Yes, that will be quite enough for pleasure. You and Miss Smith, and Miss Fairfax, will be three, and the two Miss Coxes five; and for five couple there will be plenty of room."

But soon it came to be on one side,

"But will there be good room for five couple? – I really do not think there will."

On another,

"And after all, five couple are not enough to make it worth while to stand up. Five couple are nothing, when one thinks seriously about it. It will not do to *invite* five couple. It can be allowable only as the thought of the moment."

Somebody said that *Miss* Gilbert was expected at her brother's, and must be invited with the rest. Somebody else believed *Mrs.* Gilbert would have danced the other evening, if she had been asked. A word was put in for a second young Cox; and at last, Mr. Weston naming one family of cousins who must be included, and another of very old acquaintance who could not be left out, it became a certainty that the five couple would be at least ten, and a very interesting speculation in what possible manner they could be disposed of.

The doors of the two rooms were just opposite each other. "Might not they use both rooms, and dance across the passage?" It seemed the best scheme; and yet it was not so good but that many of them wanted a better. Emma said it would be awkward; Mrs. Weston was in distress about the supper; and Mr. Woodhouse opposed it earnestly, on the score of health. It made him so very unhappy, indeed, that it could not be persevered in.

"Oh! no," said he; "it would be the extreme of imprudence. I could not bear it for Emma! – Emma is not strong. She would catch a dreadful cold. So would poor little Harriet. So you would all. Mrs. Weston, you would be quite laid up; do not let them talk of such a wild thing. Pray do not let them talk of it. That young man (speaking lower) is very thoughtless. Do not tell his father, but that young man is not quite the thing. He has been opening the doors very often this evening, and keeping them open very inconsiderately. He does not think of the draught. I do not mean to set you against him, but indeed he is not quite the thing!"

Mrs. Weston was sorry for such a charge. She knew the importance of it, and said every thing in her power to do it away. Every door was now closed, the passage plan given up, and the first scheme of dancing only in the room they were in resorted to again; and with such good-will on Frank Churchill's part, that the space which a quarter of an hour before had been deemed barely sufficient for five couple, was now endeavoured to be made out quite enough for ten.

"We were too magnificent," said he. "We allowed unnecessary room. Ten couple may stand here very well."

Emma demurred. "It would be a crowd – a sad crowd; and what could be worse than dancing without space to turn in?"

"Very true," he gravely replied; "it was very bad." But still he went on measuring, and still he ended with,

"I think there will be very tolerable room for ten couple."

"No, no," said she, "you are quite unreasonable. It would be dreadful to be standing so close! Nothing can be farther from pleasure than to be dancing in a crowd – and a crowd in a little room!"

"There is no denying it," he replied. "I agree with you exactly. A crowd in a little room – Miss Woodhouse, you have the art of giving pictures in a few words. Exquisite, quite exquisite! – Still, however, having proceeded so far, one is unwilling to give the matter up. It would be a disappointment to my father – and altogether – I do not know that – I am rather of opinion that ten couple might stand here very well."

Emma perceived that the nature of his gallantry was a little self-willed, and that he would rather oppose than lose the pleasure of dancing with her; but she took the compliment, and forgave the rest. Had she intended ever to *marry* him, it might have been worth while to pause and consider, and try to understand the value of his preference, and the character of his temper; but for all the purposes of their acquaintance, he was quite amiable enough.

Before the middle of the next day, he was at Hartfield; and he entered the room with such an agreeable smile as certified the continuance of the scheme. It soon appeared that he came to announce an improvement.

"Well, Miss Woodhouse," he almost immediately began, "your inclination for dancing has not been quite frightened away, I hope, by the terrors of my father's little rooms. I bring a new proposal on the subject:– a thought of my father's, which waits only your approbation to be acted upon. May I hope for the honour of your hand for the two first dances of this little projected ball, to be given, not at Randalls, but at the Crown Inn?"

"The Crown!"

"Yes; if you and Mr. Woodhouse see no objection, and I trust you cannot, my father hopes his friends will be so kind as to visit him there. Better accommodations, he can promise them, and not a less grateful welcome than at Randalls. It is his own idea. Mrs. Weston sees no objection to it, provided you are satisfied. This is what we all feel. Oh! you were perfectly right! Ten couple, in either of the Randalls rooms, would have been insuffer- able! – Dreadful! – I felt how right you were the whole time, but was too anxious for securing *anything* to like to yield. Is not it a good exchange? – You consent – I hope you consent?"

"It appears to me a plan that nobody can object to, if Mr. and Mrs. Weston do not. I think it admirable; and, as far as I can answer for myself, shall be most happy – It seems the only improvement that could be. Papa, do you not think it an excellent improvement?"

She was obliged to repeat and explain it, before it was fully comprehended; and then, being quite new, farther representations were necessary to make it acceptable.

"No; he thought it very far from an improvement – a very bad plan – much worse than the other. A room at an inn was always damp and dangerous; never properly aired, or fit to be inhabited. If they must dance, they had better dance at Randalls. He had never been in the room at the Crown in his life – did not know the people who kept it by sight. – Oh! no – a very bad plan. They would catch worse colds at the Crown than anywhere."

"I was going to observe, sir," said Frank Churchill, "that one of the great recommendations of this change would be the very little danger of any body's catching cold – so much less danger at the Crown than at Randalls! Mr. Perry might have reason to regret the alteration, but nobody else could."

"Sir," said Mr. Woodhouse, rather warmly, "you are very much mistaken if you suppose Mr. Perry to be that sort of character. Mr. Perry is extremely concerned when any of us are ill. But I do not understand how the room at the Crown can be safer for you than your father's house."

"From the very circumstance of its being larger, sir. We shall have no occasion to open the windows at all – not once the whole evening; and it is that dreadful habit of opening the windows, letting in cold air upon heated bodies, which (as you well know, sir) does the mischief."

"Open the windows! – but surely, Mr. Churchill, nobody would think of opening the windows at Randalls. Nobody could be so imprudent! I never heard of such a thing. Dancing with open windows! – I am sure, neither your father nor Mrs. Weston (poor Miss Taylor that was) would suffer it."

"Ah! sir – but a thoughtless young person will sometimes step behind a window-curtain, and throw up a sash, without its being suspected. I have often known it done myself."

"Have you indeed, sir? – Bless me! I never could have supposed it. But I live out of the world, and am often astonished at what I hear. However, this does make a difference; and, perhaps, when we come to talk it over – but these sort of things require a good deal of consideration. One cannot resolve upon them in a hurry. If Mr. and Mrs. Weston will be so obliging as to call here one morning, we may talk it over, and see what can be done."

"But, unfortunately, sir, my time is so limited–"

"Oh!" interrupted Emma, "there will be plenty of time for talking every thing over. There is no hurry at all. If it can be contrived to be at the Crown, papa, it will be very convenient for the horses. They will be so near their own stable."

"So they will, my dear. That is a great thing. Not that James ever complains; but it is right to spare our horses when we can. If I could be sure of the rooms being thoroughly aired – but is Mrs. Stokes to be trusted? I doubt it. I do not know her, even by sight."

"I can answer for every thing of that nature, sir, because it will be under Mrs. Weston's care. Mrs. Weston undertakes to direct the whole."

"There, papa! – Now you must be satisfied – Our own dear Mrs. Weston, who is carefulness itself. Do not you remember what Mr. Perry said, so many years ago, when I had the measles? 'If *Miss Taylor* undertakes to wrap Miss Emma up, you need not have any fears, sir.' How often have I heard you speak of it as such a compliment to her!"

"Aye, very true. Mr. Perry did say so. I shall never forget it. Poor little Emma! You were very bad with the measles; that is, you would have been very bad, but for Perry's great attention. He came four times a day for a week. He said, from the first, it was a very good sort – which was our great comfort; but the measles are a dreadful complaint. I hope whenever poor Isabella's little ones have the measles, she will send for Perry."

"My father and Mrs. Weston are at the Crown at this moment," said Frank Churchill, "examining the capabilities of the house. I left them there and came on to Hartfield, impatient for your opinion, and hoping you might be persuaded to join them and give your advice on the spot. I was desired to say so from both. It would be the greatest pleasure to them, if you could allow me to attend you there. They can do nothing satisfactorily without you."

Emma was most happy to be called to such a council; and her father, engaging to think it all over while she was gone, the two young people set off together without delay for the Crown. There were Mr. and Mrs. Weston; delighted to see her and receive her approbation, very busy and very happy in their different way; she, in some little distress; and he, finding every thing perfect.

"Emma," said she, "this paper is worse than I expected. Look! in places you see it is dreadfully dirty; and the wainscot is more yellow and forlorn than any thing I could have imagined."

"My dear, you are too particular," said her husband. "What does all that signify? You will see nothing of it by candlelight. It will be as clean as Randalls by candlelight. We never see any thing of it on our club-nights."

The ladies here probably exchanged looks which meant, "Men never know when things are dirty or not;" and the gentlemen perhaps thought each to himself, "Women will have their little nonsenses and needless cares."

One perplexity, however, arose, which the gentlemen did not disdain. It regarded a supper-room. At the time of the ballroom's being built, suppers had not been in question; and a small card-room adjoining, was the only addition. What was to be done? This card-room would be wanted as a card-room now; or, if cards were conveniently voted unnecessary by their four selves, still was it not too small for any comfortable supper? Another room of much better size might be secured for the purpose; but it was at the other end of the house, and a long awkward passage must be gone through to get at it. This made a difficulty. Mrs. Weston was afraid of draughts for the young people in that passage; and neither Emma nor the gentlemen could tolerate the prospect of being miserably crowded at supper.

Mrs. Weston proposed having no regular supper; merely sandwiches, &c., set out in the little room; but that was scouted as a wretched suggestion. A private dance, without sitting down to supper, was pronounced an infamous fraud upon the rights of men and women; and Mrs. Weston must not speak of it again. She then took another line of expediency, and looking into the doubtful room, observed,

"I do not think it *is* so very small. We shall not be many, you know."

And Mr. Weston at the same time, walking briskly with long steps through the passage, was calling out,

"You talk a great deal of the length of this passage, my dear. It is a mere nothing after all; and not the least draught from the stairs."

"I wish," said Mrs. Weston, "one could know which arrangement our guests in general would like best. To do what would be most generally pleasing must be our object — if one could but tell what that would be."

"Yes, very true," cried Frank, "very true. You want your neighbours' opinions. I do not wonder at you. If one could ascertain what the chief of them – the Coles, for instance. They are not far off. Shall I call upon them? Or Miss Bates? She is still nearer. – And I do not know whether Miss Bates is not as likely to understand the inclinations of the rest of the people as any body. I think we do want a larger council. Suppose I go and invite Miss Bates to join us?"

"Well – if you please," said Mrs. Weston rather hesitating, "if you think she will be of any use."

"You will get nothing to the purpose from Miss Bates," said Emma. "She will be all delight and gratitude, but she will tell you nothing. She will not even listen to your questions. I see no advantage in consulting Miss Bates."

"But she is so amusing, so extremely amusing! I am very fond of hearing Miss Bates talk. And I need not bring the whole family, you know."

Here Mr. Weston joined them, and on hearing what was proposed, gave it his decided approbation.

"Aye, do, Frank. – Go and fetch Miss Bates, and let us end the matter at once. She will enjoy the scheme, I am sure; and I do not know a properer person for shewing us how to do away difficulties. Fetch Miss Bates. We are growing a little too nice. She is a standing lesson of how to be happy. But fetch them both. Invite them both."

"Both sir! Can the old lady?"...

"The old lady! No, the young lady, to be sure. I shall think you a great blockhead, Frank, if you bring the aunt without the niece."

"Oh! I beg your pardon, sir. I did not immediately recollect. Undoubtedly if you wish it, I will endeavour to persuade them both." And away he ran.

Long before he reappeared, attending the short, neat, brisk-moving aunt, and her elegant niece, – Mrs. Weston, like a sweet-tempered woman and a good wife, had examined the passage again, and found the evils of it much less than she had supposed before – indeed very trifling; and here ended the difficulties of decision. All the rest, in speculation at least, was perfectly smooth. All the minor arrangements of table and chair, lights and music, tea and supper, made themselves; or were left as mere trifles to be settled at any time between Mrs. Weston and Mrs. Stokes. – Every body invited, was certainly to come; Frank had already written to Enscombe to propose staying a few days beyond his fortnight, which could not possibly be refused. And a delightful dance it was to be.

Most cordially, when Miss Bates arrived, did she agree that it must. As a counsellor she was not wanted; but as an approver, (a much safer character,) she was truly welcome. Her approbation, at once general and minute, warm and incessant, could not but please; and for another half-hour they were all walking to and fro, between the different rooms, some suggesting, some attending, and all in happy enjoyment of the future. The party did not break up without Emma's being positively secured for the two first dances by the hero of the evening, nor without her overhearing Mr. Weston whisper to his wife, "He has asked her, my dear. That's right. I knew he would!"

Books For ALL Kinds of Readers

At ReadHowYouWant we understand that one size does not fit all types of readers. Our innovative, patent pending technology allows us to design new formats to make reading easier and more enjoyable for you. This helps improve your speed of reading and your comprehension. Our EasyRead printed books have been optimized to improve word recognition, ease eye tracking by adjusting word and line spacing as well as minimizing hyphenation. Our EasyRead SuperLarge editions have been developed to make reading easier and more accessible for vision-impaired readers. We offer Braille and DAISY formats of our books and all popular E-Book formats.

We are continually introducing new formats based upon research and reader preferences. Visit our web-site to see all of our formats and learn how you can Personalize our books for yourself or as gifts. Sign up to Become A RHYW Registered Reader.

www.readhowyouwant.com

Printed in Great Britain
by Amazon.co.uk, Ltd.,
Marston Gate.